WICKED HOT
Boston's Eli

Tess Summers

Seasons Press LLC

Published: 2021

Published by Seasons Press LLC.

Copyright © 2021, Tess Summers.

Edited by Susan Soares, SJS Editorial Services.

Cover by OliviaProDesign.

ISBN: 9798486996573

This is a work of fiction. The characters, incidents and dialogues in this book are of the author's imagination and are not to be construed as real. Any resemblance to actual events or persons, living or dead, is completely coincidental.

This book is for mature readers. It contains sexually explicit scenes and graphic language that may be considered offensive by some.

All sexually active characters in this work are eighteen years of age or older.

BLURB

A single doctor and a single lawyer walk into a bar...

Dr. Steven Ericson never thought a parking ticket would change his life, but that's exactly what happened the day he goes downtown to pay his forgotten ticket for an expired meter.

As the head of Boston General's ER, he doesn't have time for relationships, or at least he's never met a woman who made him want to make time.

That all changes when he meets Whitney Hayes. The dynamo attorney in high heels entices him to imagine carving out time for more than his usual one-night stand. Imagine his dismay to find out that she, too, doesn't do relationships—they're not in her 5-year plan.

Yeah, eff that. Her plan needs rewriting, and Steven's more than willing to supply the pen and ink to help with that.

Free Book!

THE PLAYBOY AND THE SWAT PRINCESS

BookHip.com/SNGBXD Sign up here to receive my weekly newsletter, and get your free book, exclusively for newsletter subscribers!

She's a badass SWAT rookie, and he's a playboy SWAT captain... who's taming who?

Maddie Monroe

Three things you should not do when you're a rookie, and the only female on the SDPD SWAT Team... 1) Take your hazing personally, 2) Let them see you sweat, and 3) Fall for your captain.

Especially, when your captain is the biggest playboy on the entire police force.

I've managed to follow rules one and two with no problem, but the third one I'm having a little more trouble with. Every time he smiles that sinful smile or folds his muscular arms when explaining a new technique or walks through the station full of swagger.... All I can think about is how I'd like to give him my V-card, giftwrapped with a big red bow on it, which is such a bad idea because out of Rules One, Two, and Three, breaking the third one is a sure-fire way to get me kicked off the team and writing parking tickets for the rest of my career.

Apparently my heart—and other body parts—didn't get the memo.

Craig Baxter

The first time I noticed Maddie Monroe, she was wet and covered in soapy suds as she washed SWAT's armored truck as part of her hazing ritual. I've been hard for her ever since.

I can't sleep with a subordinate—it would be career suicide, and I've worked too damn hard to get where I am today. Come to think of it, so has she, and she'd probably have a lot more to lose.

So, nope, not messing around with Maddie Monroe. There are plenty of women for me to choose from who don't work for me.

Apparently my heart—and other body parts—didn't get the memo.

Can two hearts—and other body parts—overcome missed memos and find a way to be together without career-ending consequences?

Table of Contents

WICKED HOT DOCTOR

BOSTON'S ELITE

PROLOGUE

Steven

He looked at the parking ticket on his stack of bills and sighed. He'd been planning on fighting it, then missed the deadline. Now, it was due tomorrow, which meant a trip downtown to pay it on time. Good thing he was off tomorrow. His friend, Zach's office was right around the corner from the courthouse, so Steven thought he might as well take his friend to lunch while he was in the neighborhood.

Glancing at the clock, he knew it wasn't too late to fire off a text to his college roommate.

Steven: Hey, I'm going to be downtown tomorrow. Do you want to have lunch?

The dots indicating his friend was replying showed up immediately.

Zach: Depends. How flexible are you? I'm in court all day, so I don't have a set time that we'll break for lunch. All I can tell you is it's normally between 11:30 and 12:30.

Steven: For you? I'll be flexible. I'll get us a table at Rousso's at 11:30 and drink beer until you show up.

Zach: Not on-call, I see.

Steven: I'm off until Saturday. I've been working a shit ton and have to be at the hospital all weekend, so I decided to take a few days off and relax.

Zach: And coming into downtown to buy me lunch is your idea of relaxing?

Steven: Not really. But since I have to be downtown anyway, I thought I'd work off some of my debt.

Zach: Compound interest, my friend. Your debt is only getting bigger.

Steven grinned. He would owe his friend lunch for the rest of his life. Zach had helped him with the contract for his house on the Cape and wouldn't even consider letting Steven pay him.

"Just pick up the tab every time we go to lunch," he'd replied when Steven asked how much he owed him. So, unless Zach somehow needed Steven's services in return, and as the head of the ER at Boston General, Steve preferred that not be the case, he would be indebted to his friend for a while.

Steven: I'll gladly keep paying. I'll be waiting at Rousso's.

CHAPTER ONE

Steven

Zach gave him a big grin when he walked through the restaurant doors at noon and saw him sitting at a high-top table in the bar area.

"That your second or third one?" He smirked as he slid onto his chair, picked up the half-empty frosty mug sitting in front of Steve, and took a drink.

"First, smartass. How much time do you have for lunch?"

Zach glanced at his watch. "I have to be back by one. What are you doing downtown, anyway?"

"I had to pay a parking ticket."

The attorney laughed. "So, you decided to come downtown to pay it? Why didn't you just do it online, dumbass?"

Steven rubbed the back of his neck. "You gotta be kidding me. I could have paid it online?"

"Yeah, it says so right on the ticket." Zach grinned and took a sip of the water Steven had ordered for him.

"I thought I had to pay it in person since I missed the court date. Dammit. And I'd wanted to go to the Cape, but then I saw the ticket sitting there..." He shook his head, disgusted with himself, and muttered under his breath.

Steven was an outstanding doctor, but his attention to detail outside of the emergency room was lacking lately. Let this be a lesson to him.

"Yeah, but you got to see me and buy me lunch, so it's almost as good, right?"

"Hmm, spend time at a house I paid a lot of money for but never get to go to, or buy you lunch… tough call."

"Speaking of, am I ever going to get another invite?"

"Yes. I'm going next weekend to finish the dock and do some other repairs, but I was thinking about having people down for the Fourth."

Zach took another sip of Steve's beer, then set it down abruptly when he looked at the entrance. Hissing, "Shit," he discreetly pushed the mug back at Steven and wiped his mouth.

Steven immediately looked toward the front to see what was causing his friend distress. What he saw was anything but distressing.

In a low voice, Zach murmured, "Make sure you keep that in front of you. The opposing counsel just walked in, and I don't want to give her any ideas."

"What, that you were drinking my beer? Which you were."

"My case is a slam-dunk. Hell, I could argue it drunk and still win. But I think the judge would frown upon that."

Steven's eyes went back to the entrance. The chestnut-haired beauty standing at the hostess stand with her shoulders back and chin up, looked like she owned the restaurant. Her long hair was curled and styled around her shoulders, and her eyes appeared to be the color of his parents' swimming pool back in San Diego, as she surveyed her surroundings. And her body... Hot damn. The tailored business suit she wore hugged her curves just right, and her black open-toed heels with the strap around her ankle drew his attention to where he'd like his tongue to start as it made its way up her body.

"Are you talking about the brown-haired woman in the grey suit waiting at the hostess stand?"

Zach didn't even look over. "Yeah, that's her. Whitney Hayes."

"Holy shit. She's stunning."

"And fucking brilliant. It's a good thing she keeps me on my toes, otherwise I'd have a boner every time she walked in the courtroom."

Steve finally brought his attention back to his friend with a chuckle. "I would imagine that could get in the way of giving an effective argument."

"That would be an understatement."

Just then, the hostess showed Whitney to the table next to theirs.

She acknowledged Zach with a polite nod and smile before sitting down. "Zachary."

"Whitney."

Steven nudged his friend with his foot and widened his eyes, causing Zach to say, "Whitney, this is my friend, Dr. Steven Ericson; Steve, Whitney Hayes, Esquire."

Steve rolled his eyes at the pretentious introduction while offering his hand and grinned when he noticed she'd done the same.

His eyes widened when he touched her soft hand, and he held onto it far longer than socially acceptable. His eyes glued to hers the entire time. Reluctantly, he let go when she finally withdrew from his grasp.

"Are you meeting someone? Would you like to join us?" Steven asked her as he gestured to one of the empty chairs at their table.

She glanced at Zach. "I'm here alone, but I don't think it would be appropriate for opposing counsel to be seen having lunch together. I'm already risking my reputation just talking to him outside the courtroom. Wouldn't want anyone to question if I'd fallen victim to Zachary's Rudolf's notorious charm."

Zach clutched his chest. "You wound and flatter me all at the same time, Counselor."

Whitney cocked her head and pursed her lips. *Her perfect, kissable, red lips.* Steven knew he was staring at her mouth. If she noticed, she graciously didn't acknowledge it.

"It wasn't meant to be flattery," she said dryly, although the hint of a smile told them she was teasing.

She opened her menu, effectively dismissing them. Except Steven couldn't help stealing glances at her all through lunch—barely listening to his friend talk about his latest snorkeling trip to Aruba. The corner of her mouth turned up in an almost flirty grin when she caught him staring too long.

Unashamed at being busted, he winked at her, which turned her grin into a laugh as she glanced down coyly and tucked her hair behind her ear.

Visions of his fingers in her hair as he helped guide her mouth up and down his cock popped in his head, causing a slight bulge in his crotch. Good thing he had his napkin in his lap.

He saw the server hand her the black book that held the check with her credit card sticking out of the end of it, and a sense of panic crept up his chest as he watched her open it and sign her receipt. He needed more time with this woman, even if it was just to watch her from afar.

Whitney stood and slid her satchel over her shoulder, then turned to them. He could tell by her smirk that she was going to say something smart. "Zachary, see you back in court. You probably don't want to have any more beer—you need to be sharp for my cross examination." She then turned to Steven and softened her expression. At least that's how he perceived it. "It was nice meeting you, Steven."

"You too," he murmured. His eyes were glued to her ass as she sashayed out of the restaurant. When she finally walked out the door, he turned to Zach. "I think I'll come watch my famous friend in action this afternoon. See what all the fuss is about."

"Don't even fucking insult me with your *coming to watch my friend* bullshit. I know exactly who you're coming to watch."

He didn't even bother trying to deny it. "Is she single?"

"As far as I know."

Steven nodded his head thoughtfully as Zach studied him.

"I'll give you props; at least your standards are improving. She actually has a brain in addition to a hot body."

"Oh, is that what I've been doing wrong?"

Zach shrugged. "I didn't say it was wrong. It's worked so far for you. But if you're anything like me, lately I've been thinking I'd like some substance with my hot sex."

"How's that working out for ya?"

Zach stood and tightened his tie with a grin. "I'm making plans with *you* for the holiday weekend. What do you think?"

****

Whitney

She was talking to her client, George Tannen, before the judge appeared for the afternoon session when she noticed someone slip in through the courtroom's double wooden doors—a six-foot-tall someone with sandy-blond hair and blue eyes that twinkled with mischief. He hardly looked like a doctor in his faded jeans, black Converse shoes, and untucked black button-down shirt. He was dressed casually, but there was no disguising his toned runner's body.

Butterflies erupted in her stomach as she tried to maintain her focus on what the man sitting next to her was grumbling about. He was a rich, arrogant prick who had no problem wasting his money on longshot lawsuits, and, as always, Whitney had drawn the short straw when he showed up at her firm, wanting to sue over the latest perceived slight.

She was always given the bullshit cases, and her record reflected that. When she was young and naïve, she'd thought it meant her bosses had that much belief in her abilities that they gave her the tough cases. They had, after all, financed her law school tuition through a scholarship. It didn't take long for her to realize they gave her the shit cases so they could continue taking the frivolous suits and charge exorbitant rates, while keeping the other, mostly male, attorneys' wins record high.

"Just do the best you can with what you've got. If he knows you worked hard to represent him, he doesn't complain," Arthur Crane had told her when she voiced her doubts over the case's merits.

So that's what she would do. Crawford, Holden, and Crane paid her well enough, so until Whitney finally had enough saved to finally hang her own shingle, she'd continue working the cases she was given to the best of her ability. Which meant she was going to wipe the floor with the defendant's witness this afternoon, provided a certain doctor didn't distract her.

She wondered if Zach had noticed her attraction to his friend and arranged for Steven to be in court this afternoon to throw her off her game.

Not likely. She'd worked hard to act like she wasn't affected by his stare, but there had been a jolt when their eyes met the first time. That had never happened to her before. She'd read about it in magazines and romance novels, but until today, she had thought it was a myth. The way he kept looking at her through lunch, she felt confident he felt the electricity, too.

There was no more time to analyze it when the bailiff said, "All rise for the Honorable Judge Johnson."

CHAPTER TWO

Steven

Watching Whitney cross-examine witnesses for Zach's client had felt like watching porn. His dick had been hard all afternoon as she hammered away with total confidence in her abilities; he'd never been so turned on without even being touched.

She was in control as she thundered on, and all Steve could think about was what it would be like to dominate her—naked.

He knew he'd have to earn her submission, but the way she'd looked down and tucked her hair behind her ear when she'd caught him staring, made him think it was possible.

Now they were all sitting in the bar across from the courthouse. Closing arguments had been delivered and jury deliberations would begin tomorrow.

Both attorneys had shed their jackets, and Zach was now sans-tie as he raised his glass of amber liquid in a toast.

"To a worthy opponent. You did a helluva job, in spite of having a shitty case."

They clinked glasses, and all took a sip before she responded defensively, "It's not a shitty case."

Steven shook his head as he swallowed his drink. "It's a shitty case."

"You're biased."

"Normally, I'd agree with you. But from what I heard this afternoon... even if my friend wasn't the defending counsel, your client doesn't have a leg to stand on."

Whitney set her drink on the table with a thud and turned to him with her hand on her hip. "Wanna bet?"

She was on her second drink, and their food hadn't arrived yet, so he knew she was tipsy. It wouldn't be very gentlemanly of him to take advantage of her inebriated state. Still, he found himself saying, "Absolutely. Name your terms."

What could he say? She made him want to do very non-gentlemanly things with her.

"*When* my client wins, you have to donate a hundred dollars to the Animal Rescue Foundation of Boston, and you have to get your hospital to buy a table at their charity auction at the end of next month."

He felt the corners of his mouth turn up. She was a fucking adorable powerhouse, even slightly drunk.

"The Animal Rescue Foundation? ARF? That's what you want if you win?"

She shrugged. "It's important to me."

Steven countered with, "I accept. But, when your client *loses*, I'll donate a *thousand* dollars to ARF, personally sponsor a table at their charity auction, *and* get the hospital to as well. And *you* have to spend the weekend with me at my house on the Cape next weekend."

Whitney narrowed her eyes. "A weekend away with you? That's pretty bold. I don't even know you."

She hadn't outright refused him, so he backpedaled, trying to think of more favorable terms she'd agree to. He didn't want to let her get away over a detail he could change. "Okay, dinner then. Tomorrow night, so you can get to know me."

She leaned back with one arm around her middle and bit down on the tip of her manicured thumb as she stared at him while contemplating his wager. It was the first time she looked unsure of herself all day. It made him want to gather her up in his arms and hold her tight against him.

Finally, she sat up straight and offered her hand. "Deal."

He felt himself break into a wide grin as he took her soft hand. Instead of shaking it, though, he brought it to his lips and kissed her knuckles while staring into her baby blues.

And just like before, the moment her skin touched his, it felt like electricity buzzing through him.

She must have felt it too because her eyes grew wider, and she took a noticeable shaky breath, then slid from her stool. "I... this..." She was at a loss for words, which seemed very out of character for her. "I'll be right back," and she walked toward the restrooms.

Zach looked over at him with a grin. "She likes you."

Steven thought she seemed freaked out.

"I had thought so, too. But I think she may have had a change of heart."

His friend shook his head. "She took the bet—and even she knows her case is bullshit."

Steven hopped off his chair. "Be right back." He needed to find her before she talked herself out of their wager.

****

Whitney

She stared at her flushed face in the mirror as she washed her hands in the restroom sink. *What am I doing?*

Dr. Steven Ericson was way out of her league. Yeah, she'd googled him on her walk back to the courthouse from the restaurant. He was handsome, rich, successful, and came from an accomplished—and by all article accounts, supportive family. Every girl's dream—except hers. She preferred to stay in her lane and remain focused.

Then he came in her courtroom and whenever she made the mistake of glancing his way, he was intently focused on her every move—like he thought she was the most fascinating woman in the world.

That was probably what compelled her to accept his invitation to grab a drink and some food with him and Zach after they'd wrapped up court today. And now at the table, he looked at her like he wanted to devour her, and it made her brain short circuit. So much so, that not only had she just agreed to something as unethical as betting on the outcome of her client's trial, but she'd been the one to suggest it.

That was not like her. She never did things like that. She was a rule follower—a planner. Yet, a few butterflies from a sexy ER doctor, and she was throwing caution to the wind. Whitney didn't throw caution to the wind—she'd learned her lesson with that. She didn't come from a wealthy, supportive family that she could rely on if something went bad. She only had herself—and a life plan, and it'd take more than a few drinks and a handsome, sandy-blond man to derail her.

Taking a cleansing breath, she closed her eyes and envisioned armor coming around her body—like a soldier in a sci-fi movie. She was invincible.

I'll go back, apologize for the lapse of judgment, get my food to go, and take a cab home. And never see Steven Ericson again.

That last thought made her sad—even in her armor.

Come on, Whit. Focus. Life plan... remember?

After another deep breath and a reassuring nod to herself in the mirror, she yanked open the restroom door with renewed resolve.

And walked smack dab into Steven Ericson's broad chest.

CHAPTER THREE

Whitney

She felt her armor slipping out of place as his arms came around her waist to help steady her.

What would it be like to just lean against him and have him hold her? Let him protect her?

You know better than that. That fairytale shit is only for other people.

"Are you okay?" his deep voice murmured close to her ear. She could smell his aftershave and soap. It was a clean, woodsy scent.

Trouble, her inner voice whispered. Still, she didn't move from his hold right away. It wouldn't hurt to bask here for a few seconds...

"I'm fine." Her voice was husky, even to her own ears.

"You certainly are," he teased with a chuckle.

That caused her spine to stiffen, and she hastily took a step back.

"About that bet..." She stared at the buttons on his shirt, not trusting herself to look at his handsome face. "It was inappropriate... and, frankly, unethical. I don't know what I was thinking, suggesting such a thing or agreeing to those terms."

Steven lifted her chin with his knuckle, so she had to look at him.

"It was a lighthearted wager between friends. You and Zach had both made your closing arguments—it was already out of your hands when we made the bet. There was nothing unethical about it."

She blinked at him. "We're friends?"

The corner of his mouth lifted, and he swiped at his bottom lip with his thumb as he stared at her reapplied lipstick. He placed his other hand on the wall beside her— semi-boxing her between his body and the cement and leaned down to say softly, "Well, if I'm being honest, I'd like to be more than your friend."

"I think that would be a bad idea," she whispered as she glanced up at him, then quickly looked down and pressed her lips together, trying to quell the desire she had for him to kiss her.

The way her body was responding to him so close to hers—she had no doubt he'd know exactly what he was doing, and it would be done perfectly. It made her want to yield to him.

And that was dangerous.

Being in charge meant being safe. Letting someone else have control equaled giving away her power. And that wasn't happening.

But damn him for moving closer, his mouth inches from hers when he replied, "Or a very, very good one," before capturing her lips with his.

And damn her for melting into the kiss instead of stopping it. But his lips... they felt so soft and perfect against hers.

He took a deep breath when she clutched his shirt, then slowly broke away, but he rested his forehead against hers while tracing the backs of his fingertips against her collarbone.

"You can't renege on the bet now, sweetness. We not only shook on it, but we just sealed it with a kiss."

To her once-again mush brain, that was sound logic, and she found herself mumbling her agreement.

So much for protecting herself. Apparently, Steven Ericson was the chink in her armor.

For the first time in as long as she could remember— Whitney Hayes, the woman who was always prepared for any possible outcome, told herself she'd worry about the consequences later.

****

Steven

Her cheeks were flushed when they returned to their table, and Zach looked at them with a smirk. "I see Steve found you okay."

"What do you mean?" she said as she opened her phone wallet and made a few swipes at her screen before glancing up at him while she closed it. "I just went to the bathroom."

The smirk that hadn't left Zach's face got bigger. "Huh. Interesting. I could have sworn Steve wasn't wearing your shade of lipstick when he left here the same time you did, and yet, now..." He tapped the corner of his own mouth as he looked at his friend, gesturing where the stray makeup was. "He is, and yours seems to have gone missing."

Steven wiped the corner of his mouth with a napkin where Zach had indicated and glanced down to see a shade of plum on the white cotton. He didn't give a shit—it was a badge of honor.

She did the same, although more self-consciously, but her tone was full of bravado when she replied, "Hmm, I'm not sure how that happened." Reaching into her purse, she pulled out a tube of lipstick and reapplied it using her phone as a mirror, like she didn't have a care in the world.

He shook his head subtly and leaned over to mutter in her ear, "I'm just going to kiss it off you again, you know."

She rolled her eyes, but a small smile escaped her lips as she slipped the makeup back in her purse, then closed it with authority. *Yeah, she likes that idea.* So did Steve. A lot.

Sitting up straight, she changed the subject. Pointing between the two men, she asked, "How do you two know each other?"

Zach spoke up first, "We met our freshmen year at Stanford." He clutched Steve's shoulder. "This lucky son of a bitch got matched to be my dormmate, and that was the start of our bromance. We were roommates the whole four years."

"It would have been eight if he would have stayed in Cali for law school," Steven interjected. "But he decided to come back East for that."

Zach looked at Steve with faux longing. "Yet here we are—together again in Boston."

"Not living together this time, thank God."

"Hey! You've been to my place—I'm a lot neater now than I was in my youth."

"That's true," Steven conceded. "But I think that has more to do with being able to afford a cleaning lady than a change in your habits."

Zach grinned. "I do pay her well." He turned toward Whitney. "What about you? Where'd you go to law school?"

She glanced down, as if embarrassed. "Harvard."

Both men broke out into huge grins.

"Wh-at? You went to Harvard?" Zach asked as he sat up straighter—the awe in his voice evident. He'd tried to get into Harvard and was denied. "What the fuck are you doing wasting your talents with bullshit cases at Crawford, Holden, and Crane?"

"Um..."

He didn't let her finish. "I could get you a job at McNamara, Wallace, and Stone tomorrow. Come to the dark side."

She laughed. "The dark side seems to be working out well for you."

"I can't complain. But seriously, Whitney. You're a fucking great attorney, but some of your cases..." He winced. "They're pulling your record down. Whatever you're making with your firm, McNamara would double it—easily. A Harvard grad who looks like you? He'd be salivating."

"Thanks," she said with a dismissive smile. "I'll definitely keep it in my mind. It's nice to have options."

Steve wondered what that was about. Her case today wasn't exactly like she was doing the Lord's work. If it wasn't about the caliber of the cases she was getting, why wouldn't she be interested in at least entertaining the idea of doubling her salary?

He doubted it was because of Zach. If she didn't like him, she would never have agreed to coming out for drinks and dinner after court.

She slid off her seat with a sly smile. "How about a game of darts? Loser buys the next round?"

He was quickly learning she was a master at changing the subject.

"You're on," Steven replied as he stood.

"Count me in. There's a hottie over by the dartboard that I've had my eye on since she walked in. Thanks, Whit—you're a better wingman than my wingman."

"Glad to be of service."

****

Whitney

Oh my god, these two are fun.

They were the perfect foil for one another, and they had her laughing all night as they ribbed each other mercilessly while they played darts, then shuffleboard, followed by pool. She could tell all the teasing was with love though.

Steve took every opportunity he could to wrap his hand around her waist or touch the small of her back and whisper semi-inappropriate things in her ear—or out loud if he thought it would fluster her.

"Your ass looks amazing when you're bent over like that," he called as she lined up the cue ball with the eight ball for the winning shot.

She knocked the ball in with authority, then turned around and looked at him with a victorious grin. "I know. And your ass looks amazing at the bar, buying the winner her drink."

"Oh, damn!" Zach roared, his knuckles going to his mouth with a laugh. "You need some aloe for that burn?"

He ignored his friend and bowed at the waist. "What can I get you, pool goddess?"

She lifted her glass. "Another one of these, please. Last one, though. I have to get home pretty soon."

Steven looked at Zach's half-full glass. "You good?"

"Yeah, I'm good. I gotta get going soon, too." Zach winked at Whitney. "I've got to be bright eyed and bushy tailed for the verdict tomorrow."

As Steven headed to the bar, Zach turned to her with a genuine smile. "I'm glad you came out tonight. You and Steven are perfect for each other. Promise you won't break his heart."

"Oh, we're not..."

He held up his hand. "Save it, Counselor. Anyone with eyes can see you are."

"Please. We just met."

He shook his head with a knowing grin. "It doesn't matter. He feels it, you feel it—"

Whitney interrupted him, "How do you know what he feels?"

"I've known the guy twenty years, and I've never—not once—seen him look at a woman the way he's been looking at you all night."

She couldn't even hide her smile at his revelation.

"Is he as genuine as he seems?" Not like she could take his best friend's word for it.

"You won't meet a better guy, Whitney. He's who I want to be when I grow up."

"You're going to grow up? When the fuck is that finally going to happen?" Steven laughed as he clasped his friend's shoulder in one hand and set Whitney's drink in front of her with the other.

She wondered how much Steven had heard, but the way he was acting, he'd only caught the tail end about Zach growing up.

"Someday I will. Maybe."

Steven shook his head. "Unless you see a shiny object or a beautiful woman first."

Zach shrugged, unapologetic. "Sounds about right."

"At least you're a good attorney," Whitney interjected, trying to be helpful. It had sounded good in her six-drinks-in head.

The other lawyer slowly turned to her with an incredulous look. "You think I'm a good attorney?"

"Oh, shut up, Zach," she said as she took a drink, now embarrassed that she'd voiced her observation out loud. "You know you are."

"Well, yeah. But it's nice to hear—especially from opposing counsel. For the record, I think you are, too. I like going up against you—you give me a run for my money."

"Your client's money," she corrected.

He finished the last of his beer and set the empty mug on the table. "Speaking of... I need to get home." He turned toward Steven. "Make sure she gets home okay."

"Already planning on it."

Zach grinned at Whitney. "See you tomorrow," then at Steven. "Thanks for dinner and drinks. I'll note it on your tab."

She wondered what that was all about and was going to ask, when she felt a strong hand at her waist and a deep voice in her ear. "We should probably go, too."

Steven

Part of him wanted to push her to go home with him, but he knew that had the strong possibility of landing him in the *regretted one-night stand* category. And he was going to be neither her regret nor a one-time thing—he'd make sure of it.

It took everything he had in him, but he left her at her front door, after kissing the hell out of her for five minutes before finally tapping out and saying goodnight.

Then she whispered, "Do you want to come in?" and he bit back a groan.

"More than anything. But if I do, I promise you won't sleep a wink—and I know you have to work in the morning. Let's wait and have dinner tomorrow night, sweetness—get to know each other. I promise I'll make the wait worth it."

A soft groan escaped her lips, and she kissed his jaw. "What happens if my client wins?"

Steven wrapped a strand of her hair around his finger. He didn't fucking care who won at this point.

"The offer to have dinner with me isn't contingent on you losing the bet, you know. And since my terms were more favorable anyway, maybe you should just concede to me now."

"Never."

He smirked—he wasn't surprised that was the little spitfire's response.

Pulling his finger from her strands to leave a perfectly formed ringlet on her shoulder, he leaned in to murmur in her ear, "Sweetness, I promise you—there will come a time when you'll happily concede to me."

****

Whitney

That's what she was afraid of.

CHAPTER FOUR

Whitney

The tiny headache when she woke up was an unpleasant reminder of her extracurricular activities after work yesterday. But she couldn't help but smile when she touched her lips as the night's events came back to her.

Steven Ericson was Trouble—with a capital T, just like the song said. And she'd invited him in last night. So much for her armor.

Yet, he'd turned her down, saying something about knowing she had to work in the morning. She'd been disappointed and was sure the pout on her face conveyed that. But then he'd ran his hands along her hips and winked when he told her he'd make it worth her wait.

Who *was* this guy? She'd offered him a one-night stand, and he'd *declined*. They were obviously not on the same page.

As if on cue, her phone dinged with a text. She glanced down at the name on the screen. Funny, she didn't remember giving him her phone number. And she knew she didn't plug his name and number in her directory—yet there it was, staring at her. She couldn't help but laugh out loud when she saw it.

Steve 'Boyfriend Material' Ericson: Make sure you drink plenty of water, in addition to your morning coffee. I'll pick you up after work around 6.

Was it arrogance or confidence that he thought he was boyfriend material, or that he felt it was a foregone conclusion she would be having dinner with him? Although, even she had to admit, George's case was a longshot at best. If he won, it'd only be because she was that good of an attorney.

But she *was* fucking good—not that the partners had noticed, so there was a possibility.

As far as the boyfriend thing... nope. Not happening.

Her phone dinged again with another message.

Steve 'Boyfriend Material' Ericson: Oh, and make sure you answer your door this morning. PS— the driver has already been tipped.

What had he done? Normally, she didn't consider herself the flowers type. But maybe that was because she'd never had someone send them to her before.

She wasn't sure how to respond, and she had to pee, so she set the phone on her nightstand without replying.

The *thump thump* of her beagle/Labrador mix's tail on the hardwood floor when he saw her sit up in bed made her smile. She loved that dog. She'd forever be grateful to the Animal Rescue Foundation for rescuing him and keeping him comfortable and safe until she found him.

"Good morning, Ralph. I'll let you out in just a sec," she told him as she patted his head on her way to the bathroom.

She knew he'd be waiting by the door for her to let him outside in her little fenced yard—it was their morning routine. Some mornings, they even managed to get a quick run in, but not today.

"I'll make it up to you this weekend, Buddy. We'll go for a walk twice a day, every day. I promise. And you might get to go home with Claire after your walk today," she told him when she opened the screen door to let him back inside.

Claire, her dog walker, sometimes came to her rescue when she had to work late, or on the rare occasion had a date or some other social function. It wasn't free, but Whitney didn't care. She'd spend her last dollar on Ralph.

As the door slammed shut, it occurred to her that maybe Steven hated dogs, and she'd have nothing to worry about. No complications—just how she liked it.

The thought made her stop short before setting Ralph's food bowl down. Is that what she was doing? Living an uncomplicated life?

No. She had a plan, and she was sticking to it, that's all. Planning kept her in control and not having to rely on anyone else. She liked having a plan.

I wasn't very worried about my plan last night when I invited him in. She shook her head at the inner voice chastising her. There had been nothing wrong with wanting to have sex with him—she was a modern, single girl and perfectly entitled. A night of fun would have no bearing on her long-term goals.

At Ralph's hungry whine, she set the bowl down, her brows still furrowed.

A boyfriend on the other hand... That was a complication she needed to avoid.

The doorbell rang, and she smiled when she opened the door, expecting a delivery person to be standing there with a pretty floral arrangement like she'd seen delivered to her assistant's desk. But instead of flowers, the man on her doorstep had a big brown paper bag in one hand and a cup of coffee in the other.

"Whitney Hayes?"

"Yes."

He handed her the waxed paper cup with black lid along with the bag, then pulled a piece of paper from his pocket and read from it.

"Steve wants to make sure you eat breakfast. It's the most important meal of the day. And to remind you to drink plenty of water. Also, he'll pick you up at six and to dress casually."

With that, he turned and ran down the steps to his waiting little white car while she stood in the doorway, dumbfounded, and watched him drive off.

Glancing at her front door, she remembered how she'd had her back pressed against it last night while being kissed goodnight. And how she had wanted more.

The smell of the food emanating from the bag brought her back to the present. She shook her head with a smile as she closed the door. How thoughtful do you have to be to have breakfast delivered to someone? She had to admit—that was some boyfriend material shit.

She fired off a text before opening her delivered breakfast at her little kitchenette table.

Whitney: Thank you for breakfast. That was really thoughtful of you. However, we'll wait to see about a ruling before I worry about dinner or what to wear.

He responded right away.

Steve 'Boyfriend Material' Ericson: It's my pleasure; I would have rather had breakfast in bed together, but who knows what tomorrow morning will bring. Drink your water.

This could be very bad.

She remembered his voice last night when he'd responded to that sentiment, "Or very, very good."

She still had hope that he hated dogs. Considering he'd agreed to donate a thousand dollars to ARF if he *won* their bet, she wasn't optimistic.

****

Steven

He'd just gotten back from a run when his phone rang. Zach's name popped up on the screen, so he answered it with, "What's up?"

"We've got a ruling."

A ruling. He was glad he'd made that dinner reservation this morning.

Part of him hoped Whitney had won. Both for the sake of her career, but also to see if she'd choose to have dinner with him if she wasn't obligated by a bet. Not that she didn't always have the option to say no, regardless of whether she lost. But it would make him feel better if she did so on her own accord.

"Well? Has it been announced?"

"Yeah, just left the courthouse. The judge ruled in our favor."

He was glad his friend couldn't see him frown over the phone when he replied, "That's great, man. Congratulations."

"So, it looks like you have a date tonight."

Steve couldn't help but grin at the idea of taking Whitney out to dinner and spending time alone with her. Still, he wasn't counting his chickens just yet.

"We'll see. She might decide to back out."

"I don't think so. That's not her style. She wouldn't have taken the bet if she wasn't prepared to lose."

"Yeah, but she'd been drinking. She'd pretty much told me she wanted to call it off, but I kind of pressed her."

Why had he done that?

Oh yeah, because he'd been fucking gaga over the woman and desperate to spend time with her.

"Well, let me know if you end up wanting company."

"If she bails, the only thing I'll want to do is get drunk."

Zach laughed. "No shit, why do you think I offered to join you? It's not for your sparkling personality, dumbass—more like your extensive bourbon selection. And it'd be lame to let my friend drink alone."

"I'll keep you posted. No offense, but I hope I don't see you."

"None taken. And I really don't want to see you either, but it seemed like the polite thing to offer."

"You're a dick," Steven said with a smile. "Congratulations on the victory. I'll call you Monday."

"I hope you have a great weekend. Call me if you need me."

He glanced at his watch. He still had a few reports to dictate before showering, but he had plenty of time before having to pick Whitney up at six. That is, if she didn't back out.

No time like the present to find out.

Steven: Pick you up at 6? I made a reservation at Michelangelo's, but I can cancel that if there's somewhere else you'd rather go.

She responded a few minutes later.

Whitney: Good news travels fast, I see.

He was writing his response that included giving her an out if she didn't want to go when another message from her popped up on his phone.

Whitney: I love Italian. But I'll just meet you at the restaurant; I won't have time to go home after work.

Relieved that she wasn't hesitating about their date, he deleted the paragraph he'd written and started over.

Steven: I can see if I can push back the reservation. If I can't, I'll just cancel it, and we'll go somewhere else. I don't want you to feel rushed.

He couldn't wait to see her, but he understood about having to work late. It happened to him all the time, not to mention being called in on his days off.

It was part of the reason he hadn't had a serious relationship since college. Well, that and he hadn't met anyone who made him think he could have what his parents had, and he decided a long time ago he wouldn't settle for anything less—not after what Marie did to him.

"You'll know," his dad had told him when he'd voiced his doubts about ever finding the right woman.

"How?"

"I can't explain it, but you will. And then you'll move heaven and earth to be with her."

No one had even come close to making Steven think he'd found *the one*, until now, and that made zero sense to his analytical brain. He'd just met her yesterday. But his father was the most sensible, level-headed man Steven knew, and from the stories his mother told, Richard Ericson had been completely irrational when it came to his future wife from the day he met her.

Steven felt a connection with Whitney he'd never felt before, and he suddenly understood what his dad had been talking about.

Whitney: No, 6 will be okay. I just won't be dressed 'casual.'

Steven: Then neither will I. See you then, sweetness.

CHAPTER FIVE

Whitney

She had a smile on her face after reading his text. He really did seem like a great guy. Handsome, successful, and not a rich asshole.

"In other words, he doesn't stand a chance," her BFF, Gwen stated when Whitney had called to tell her about the bet, and about Steven in general, while she walked to the restaurant from her office. She'd wanted to call her friend all day but couldn't get away from eavesdropping co-workers until then.

"What do you mean?"

"After Derek?"

"I'm over that."

Whitney could practically see Gwen's nose scrunching when she replied, "Mmm, are ya though?"

"Yes. Why would you say that?"

She knew damn well why. Because it was true.

"Because you refuse to date anyone. Either they make too much money, or not enough."

She'd had one rich boyfriend in her life, and that had blown up in her face. And no matter how much money she now made or where she'd earned her degrees, when she was around rich people, she felt like that poor girl who didn't eat when school wasn't in session and wore the same dirty clothes every day.

It was just easier not to date—period. It helped her stay on track and not rock the boat with the universe.

"Except, here I am—on my way to dinner with a gorgeous doctor."

"So, what's wrong with him?"

"What the hell? If he's dating me, there has to be something wrong with him?"

Gwen let out an exasperated sigh. "Hardly. I just mean, if he's so handsome and successful…at his age, why isn't he already married, or at least with someone? What's wrong with him. Is he a player?"

Whitney thought about it. She would be okay if he was a player; she'd probably prefer it, actually. Players weren't complicated once you recognized that's what they were. And the beauty of that was once they realized you knew their game, they were no longer interested and moved along.

She could usually spot a player from a mile away. Her law firm was crawling with them. But Steven hadn't given her that vibe.

"I don't think so. At least, he hasn't come across as one. I guess it's still early, though."

Maybe she was losing her touch.

"Well, try to keep an open mind and have fun. Let him spoil you, for Chrissake. And let yourself like it."

"Come on. You know better than that." Whitney glanced at the sign on the door. "I'm here."

"Have fun tonight. Not every rich guy is a Derek Farnsworth, you know."

Maybe not, but there was a younger version of herself still inside her who wasn't willing to risk it.

She opened the door to Michelangelo's and froze when she saw him. Dressed in a navy-blue suit and white shirt open at the collar, he looked like a model. He was so damn handsome, it took her breath away. And he was waiting to have dinner with *her*.

At that moment, Whitney didn't care what was wrong with him, or how much money he had. She'd worry about that later.

He noticed her standing at the door and stood to greet her—a slow smile spread across his face as he did. His warm gaze on her made her feel like the only woman in the room.

Crossing the crowded lobby to meet her where she still stood staring, he leaned down to kiss her cheek while his fingertips skimmed her hip. "Hi, you look beautiful."

Whitney might not have had time to change her clothes, but she did refresh her hair and makeup before leaving her office. She appreciated that he noticed.

"Thanks." But still. It was no comparison to what he looked like. "So do you."

The corner of his mouth turned up at her attempt at a compliment.

Tess Summers

"I mean... You look..." She ran her gaze over him again. "Wow." Then blurted out, "You are definitely rocking that suit."

Whitney was flustered—and she never got flustered. Still, he didn't make her feel embarrassed. Taking her hand, he led her toward the hostess and murmured in her ear, "I couldn't let you be *not casual* by yourself."

"I appreciate that."

Judging by the double takes and sneaky, long glances— and some overt ones—of the women in the lobby, Whitney wasn't alone in that sentiment.

He didn't seem to notice anyone but her.

She continued with a smile, "Although you didn't have to."

"Like I was going to show up looking like a slouch when my date is a total professional." The corner of his mouth turned up. "People would wonder what in the world you were doing with me and think you were just using me for sex."

The image of him naked, between her legs, popped into her head, and her brain seemed to stop working. Her mouth gaped open as she tried to think of a witty comeback, but all she could think of was using him for sex. Fortunately, it was their turn to be seated.

The warmth of Steven's hand possessively on her back as the hostess showed them to their table made her feel safe. As if he'd somehow keep her out of harm's way should some mysterious restaurant ninjas appear while her brain was in a sex daydream fog.

They sat down, and the hostess asked to take their drink order. Steven cocked his head and looked at Whitney. "Do you want to get a bottle of wine, or do you feel like a cocktail? Or both?"

"I'd like a gin and tonic now, but maybe wine with dinner?"

He turned to the server as if she hadn't just heard Whitney's order. "She'll have a gin and tonic—" He paused and looked at Whitney. "Lime?"

"Please."

"With a lime, and I'll have a Maker's Mark on the rocks. Thanks."

He smiled dismissively at the young woman who'd been practically swooning at him, then focused on Whitney. "How was work today?"

She snorted. "Other than I lost a case?"

"Come on, you had to have been expecting that."

"I don't want to discuss my client—that would be unethical." She leaned forward and dropped her voice, "And I'm already skating that line with this bet."

A new person—a man this time—arrived to deliver their drinks and water and asked if they were ready to order.

"We haven't even looked at the menu. Give us a few minutes—we're not in a rush. Although—" He looked at Whitney, "Do you want an appetizer?"

She flipped open her menu to peruse the starter selections. "I'm starving, so that would be great."

"What looks good?"

"How about the antipasto?"

He gave a curt nod. "Perfect."

When they were alone again, he picked up his drink and looked at her over the rim. "I think we already established it was a lighthearted bet. It didn't matter who won, you were going to go out with me anyway, and I was going to make the donation and buy the tables for the benefit."

Was that true?

Yeah, probably. She knew the likelihood of her winning George's case was low, and yet she still took the bet. Because even though she wouldn't have admitted it at the time, she wanted to go out with him.

With a wink, she teased, "I might have even agreed to the weekend on the Cape if you'd have held firm. Well, and if Zach hadn't been there to witness the whole thing."

She wasn't sure if the other attorney was a gossip, but most lawyers were in some shape or form. She'd had enough of her wits about her to recognize what going away with a man she'd just met could do to her ice queen reputation.

"Fucking Zach," Steven muttered with a grin. "Ruins everything." He sat back and stared thoughtfully at her from across the table. "I guess we'll have to make a new bet then, since he's not around."

She returned his stare and stirred her gin and tonic with the little blue straw. "That sounds intriguing."

****

Steven

Intriguing. Yeah, that was one way to describe it.

When she walked in the restaurant in her business suit with her hair down and flowing, and a fresh application of lipstick on her lips that was just begging to be messed up, his dick stood up and took notice. She was the perfect combination of tough and tender.

He had to will himself not to devour her mouth the second he reached her, then whisk her off to the nearest hotel and have his way with her. All night long. Fuck dinner, they could get room service.

Somewhere between where he'd been sitting while he waited for her and when he reached her at the entrance, he'd regained some control of his senses.

When she fumbled and told him he looked beautiful, too, he knew she was nervous. It was so fucking endearing. This woman who handed men their balls for breakfast in the courtroom on a regular basis was nervous about having dinner with *him*.

After a cocktail and some conversation, she relaxed and flirted with him a little, which reduced him to wanting to kiss her again.

Hoping to distract himself and his chubby dick from wanting to make out with her right there in the restaurant booth, he made small talk about local politics. Nothing too charged—he knew better than that, especially on a first date. And goddamn, she was as fucking brilliant as she'd been in the courtroom yesterday—when he'd been hard all afternoon watching her. Not much had changed.

"I heard Zach call you Steve at lunch and again at the bar last night—and noticed that's how you put your name in my phone; we'll talk about that later. Do you prefer to be called Steven or Steve?"

He chuckled. "Oh, you saw that?" He'd wondered what she'd have to say about that. He guessed he'd find out later. "Both, I suppose. I view Steve as a nickname that people who know me use, so it's comfortable. But I usually introduce myself as Steven."

She nodded in understanding.

"And did you always want to be a doctor?"

"No, up until the middle of my freshman year in college, I wanted to be a marine biologist and work at SeaWorld as a dolphin trainer."

"SeaWorld?"

"Yeah—there's one in San Diego where I grew up. They had some summer programs that I went to as a kid that I loved."

"What made you change your mind?"

That was a long story—and not one for a first date. Easier to go with the version he told everyone.

"I found out how much they made. We did a life simulation in one of my classes, and I quickly realized I would have to adjust my career goals or tame down my tastes—and *that* wasn't going to happen."

That made her laugh out loud. "Lucky they did that for you early on then and not after you already had your degree."

He felt his smile fall when he thought back to that time. "Yeah, lucky me. What about you? Did you always want to be a lawyer?"

She traced the condensation on the side of her highball glass. "No. I wasn't sure I would even be able to go to college until my senior year in high school—after everyone else's applications were already in."

That surprised him. "Really? You seem like the type of girl who knew what college she wanted to go to back in second grade and would have had her application in the day she could send it."

Her laugh was mirthless. "I wish that's what I was worrying about back then." They were quiet for a beat, then she looked up at him with a polite smile. "Fortunately, things fell into place, and I was able to go."

Steven knew there was more to her story, but it felt like she'd closed that part of their conversation down, so he didn't push further. They were both entitled to their secrets—for now. That was a discussion for maybe Date Five. And they were having a Date Five, as well as a Date Fifty—at least if he had anything to say about it.

"Did you decide what you want for dinner?" he asked as he perused his menu.

"I was thinking the chicken marsala, but I wanted to have red wine with dinner, and I know you're supposed to have white wine with chicken."

"Not necessarily. You wouldn't want a bolder red like a Cabernet or Zinfandel that you'd have with a tomato-based sauce, but you could easily do a light-bodied red like a Pinot Noir or a Gamay with the marsala sauce."

She stared at him like he'd grown an extra head. "That's—Wow. I'm impressed. I'm afraid to ask, but how do you know all that?"

He chuckled and took another sip of his whiskey. "Well, my mother made me take cotillion classes when I was in seventh grade. She wanted to make sure if I was going to grow up to be a heathen, at least I'd be a refined one. When I became an adult, I realized that I had actually used a lot of what I learned in the classes, so I took a grown-up version the summer before starting med school."

She narrowed her eyes at him. "Please tell me you were never a debutante's date to her coming-out ball."

He laughed out loud. "I plead the fifth, Counselor. But if it means anything, my sisters all refused to have a coming-out party."

"I think I'd like your sisters."

"I think they'd like you, too." He reached for her hand across the table. "We can find out next week—well, at least with one of the three. I'll introduce you to my sister, Hope when she gets into town. She's moving in with me— temporarily."

She cocked her head in a questioning manner, silently spurring him to go on.

"She just got hired by Boston General and is moving from San Diego. We thought it'd be easier if she stayed at my condo with me until she got her bearings. I've got plenty of room. Besides, she can help me out with things there."

"Win—win."

He shrugged. "Maybe. Until she wants to bring somebody home with her. Then she might not be so hip on the idea of living with her big brother and want her own place."

"What if you do? Want to bring someone home, I mean. While she's there."

He felt the corners of his mouth turn up in a devilish grin. "You offering, sweetness?"

She rolled her eyes like she was unaffected, but her nipples poking through her silk blouse suggested otherwise.

"Hypothetically speaking. I'm just curious if you have a double standard."

"Hell yeah, I do," he groused. "One, she's my *baby* sister. Two, it's *my* house. If anyone's getting lucky in it, it's going to be me."

"Maybe you both just need to be celibate while you're living together."

Fuck that. Not after meeting Whitney. He had plans to break his unintentional six-month sex hiatus. Not tonight, but very soon.

"Or just go home with someone who doesn't have a roommate." He stared at her deliberately, knowing she lived alone.

At least, he'd thought she did.

"That counts me out. I guess I'm safe, then."

Well, shit.

"You have a roommate?"

"Mmm hmm." She flipped the menu's page. "His name's Ralph. He's very protective of me."

"Are you two..." He nodded, not wanting to finish his thought, but then she looked at him over the menu with a confused expression, like she didn't understand what he was getting at. "You know... an item?"

Her eyebrows relaxed, and she turned the menu page. "Oh, no. Nothing like that."

That was a relief.

Except, now how would he be alone with her in Boston? Unless it was before Hope got here, but he didn't want to rush things.

Well, he *did*. God, he did. But he liked this woman—a lot. Yet he couldn't help but get the feeling he needed to go slow, or he would spook her.

He'd need to convince her to go to the Cape next weekend with him. They'd be alone for two nights. Maybe they wouldn't even get out of bed the whole time. He could hire someone to work on the dock.

He guessed if all else failed, there was always the Marriott in their future.

CHAPTER SIX

Whitney

After an argument about the check, which she lost and tried to be gracious about, they walked along the street, hand in hand. She'd stop to look at a store window, then they'd walk a little, and he'd stop. Their conversation never lagged, and they talked about everything from the recent movies they'd seen, to the Boston news, to work stories... laughing the entire time.

It was a fantastic first date. He even bought them ice cream from one of the food trucks on their path.

Whitney popped the last bite of her vanilla single serve in her mouth and looked up at him with a smile as she pulled the red spoon from her mouth. She tossed her trash in the nearby can, then he slid an arm around her waist to draw her to him.

"You are so beautiful," he murmured as he stared into her eyes, then slowly lowered his mouth to hers.

His kiss was as intoxicating as it had been last night. He tasted like the mint chocolate chip flavor he'd just finished, and his soft lips were tender, but firm. He used the perfect amount of tongue to make her belly warm. She could feel her pussy getting wet.

"Do you want to have a nightcap at my place?" she murmured against his lips.

She hoped he understood that was code for, "Let's go have sex."

Steven pulled away and looked down at her. "Isn't Ralph home?"

"He's spending the night with a friend."

He stared at her for a beat, then reached for her hand. "Yeah, let's go have a drink."

There was something about the way he'd spelled out *have a drink* that made her think he was taking her offer literally.

She stopped walking, and he turned to look at her with raised eyebrows.

"Um, you know I'm not actually inviting you for a drink, right?"

He cocked his head. "Then why did you ask me over for a nightcap?"

"Because asking you in for a nightcap still lets me sound like a lady, when what I really mean is something very unladylike altogether."

He chuckled. "I see. And here I thought that was your way of slowing things down."

"No. Quite the opposite. I don't even think I have any alcohol in the house, other than maybe a half a bottle of wine in the fridge."

The corner of his mouth went home. "Well, we can stop and pick up a bottle of something."

"It's okay, I have plenty of lube."

That made him burst out laughing, then he tugged on her hand. "Come on."

They better be picking up a box of condoms along with their bottle of *something*, or she would be very disappointed.

****

Steven

Ain't this a kick in the head.

Instead of figuring out how to get in a woman's pants, he was trying to figure out how to keep her out of his.

What the fuck was wrong with him?

Nothing was *wrong* with him. His dick worked just fine—as evidenced by how many times it'd gotten hard just looking at her tonight. But, just like last night, he didn't want to fall into the one-night stand category. He was getting the vibe that was exactly what she was angling for.

Sorry, sweetness. I want multiple nights with you.

As he perused the candy aisle at the drug store they'd walked into, Whitney set a box of condoms next to the Kahlua and vodka in the grocery basket he was carrying on his arm and looked at him with a wicked smile.

Damn, she was adorable. He couldn't help but grin back at her.

Maybe they could just do some heavy petting tonight. Although, he seriously doubted his ability to restrain himself if they did.

He fished the purple box out and turned it over to examine it closer.

"Sweetheart, when I fuck you, we're going to need more than three. Go get the party pack."

She plucked the package from his hands and rolled her eyes as she turned on the ball of her foot. "I don't think that's what it's called."

"Well, it should be!" he called after her.

Steven grabbed a bag of chocolate-covered almonds—his weakness—from the shelf. There was always a bag in his desk drawer at work and another in his kitchen at home. Whitney appeared with the bigger box and put it in the green basket.

"Here's your party pack. I thought you had to work tomorrow?"

"I do. But we can take them when we go to the Cape next weekend."

"I didn't agree to go to your house with you."

He shrugged, undeterred. "You will."

On the other side of the candy aisle were games and puzzles. She picked up a blue box and waved it at him with a sinister smile. "Wanna bet?"

The only word he caught on the front of the box was *trivia. Oh, baby girl... it's on.*

"Hell yes, I do. Name your terms."

****

Whitney

Well, damn. She hadn't been expecting him to be so eager.

"Okay, so you win—I go to the Cape with you." He nodded his agreement. "I win..." she thought about it. What did she want? "We have sex tonight and call it good."

But was that what she wanted? Yes, to the sex, but she wasn't so sure about not seeing him again—even if that was the smart play.

She got her answer when he uttered, "Nope," and she was secretly relieved.

"What do you mean, *nope*? Not so confident in your trivia abilities after all?"

"Oh, I'm going to win. But there's no way I'd even risk not seeing you again."

That made her toes curl, and she tried to disguise her smile.

He leaned closer and lowered his voice. "How about, you win—I'll lick your pussy tonight until you come all over my tongue?"

Whitney couldn't help but let out a little gasp. "Oh..."

His grin was cocky when he asked, "Do we have a deal?"

She swallowed hard and nodded her head—not quite trusting herself to speak yet.

Steven bent his head and captured her lips with his. It was hardly appropriate for aisle A5 of the local pharmacy, but it felt so good, she didn't care.

Breaking the kiss, he rested his forehead against hers, just like he had at the bar last night and said pretty much the same thing he'd said at the time.

"You can't renege on me now, sweetness. We sealed it with a kiss."

Like she even wanted to.

CHAPTER SEVEN

Steven

He shouldn't have been so cocky. His little lawyer was a damn worthy opponent, and she had him sweating his win.

His only consolation was that, although the blow to his pride would hurt, paying his debt would not. He looked over to where she sat cross legged on her living room rug, in her yoga pants and tank top that she'd changed into once they got to her house. *No, it wouldn't hurt in the least.*

As a matter of fact, even if he won... no, when he won, he was a believer in positive thinking... he was still licking her pussy tonight until she screamed his name.

"Do you want another?" she gestured to his empty glass as she stood up.

"Getting me drunk won't help you win. I'm only better when I'm sloshed."

"No," she called over her shoulder. "But it might help me take advantage of you."

He watched her ass as she sashayed out of the room.

Yeah, even though technically, he was winning, it was time to pay up.

Following her into the kitchen, Steven wrapped his arms around her middle from behind and nuzzled her neck.

"No alcohol necessary, sweetness."

She melted into his embrace, and he slowly moved his hands under her shirt. His touch was firm as he roved up her stomach until he tugged her sports bra down so her tits were free. He kneaded her flesh, then rolled her stiff nipples between his fingers.

"God, that feels good," she moaned with her head thrown back against his chest.

Steven pulled her tank top over her head, along with her sports bra, and spun her around to face him. Wasting no time, he cupped one breast and pushed it into his hungry mouth.

Whitney let out a gasp as his lips came around her nipple, and he sucked gently while his tongue swirled around the hard peak. He gently bit down before releasing and tending to her other tit.

He felt her hands in his hair as she cooed, "Oh, Steve..."

"That's it, baby. Say my name."

Cupping her ass in both hands, he lifted her onto the counter, then pressed on her shoulders, so she was leaning on her elbows. He ran his fingertips under her waistband, then tugged the fabric down. She lifted her ass to help him.

He groaned out loud when he found she wasn't wearing any panties. And she was fucking waxed.

Steve pulled her lips apart to find her pink middle glistening under the kitchen lights.

"Fuuuuuck, your pussy is so pretty," he growled before dipping his tongue down her seam and back up again.

She bucked off the counter at the first touch of his tongue and pressed her hips up into his mouth while moaning, "Ohhhhh, yes."

"And it tastes so good, too."

He slid a finger inside her heat, then another—finger fucking her as his tongue explored her folds.

With her hands buried in his hair, she tried steering his mouth to her clit, and he lifted his head with a smile.

"I know where your magic button is, sweetness. And trust me, I'm going to get there and press it until you're quivering. Just relax right now and let me enjoy you for a while, first."

She let out an audible sigh as she spread her legs wider and relaxed all the way onto the counter.

"That's it, baby. Get comfortable. We're going to be here a while."

****

Whitney

As her legs quivered around his head for a second time, she thought, *Oh my god. What has he done to me?* She'd never achieved more than one orgasm in a night before, and Steven had just pulled two from her with ease.

It was like he'd read the owner's manual on her body and knew how to do things to it she'd never thought possible.

"Damn, you must have paid close attention in anatomy class," she quipped with her hand on her stomach as she tried to regain her breathing. "Because you certainly know your way around a woman's body."

"I have a sweet tooth, and you taste like candy."

She lifted her body halfway off the counter and gaped at him. "Oh my god. That's the cheesiest thing I've ever heard."

He broke out into a grin and offered his hand to help her up. "That was pretty cheesy." He pecked her softly on the lips once she sat up straight. "But it's true, so, I'm not even sorry I said it."

Whitney hopped off the counter and rubbed the outline of his hard cock over his suit pants.

"Can I reciprocate?" she purred.

"Fuck, sweetness, I want to say yes, but I need to go home and get to bed. I have to be at the hospital early tomorrow."

"Oh." She tried to hide her disappointment by pulling on her yoga pants, then tugging the tank top over her head—but she left her bra off. He looked down at her nipples showing through the fabric and reached out to fondle them over her shirt.

"Raincheck? Like next weekend at my place on the Cape?"

Whitney found herself relieved he wanted to continue what they'd started. "You are technically winning."

He grinned and pinched her nipple. "I'll take that as a yes."

"Not so fast. I want to finish our game. I'm not losing by much."

Not that it mattered, she'd already made up her mind she would go with him—especially if it meant more of what he'd just done to her. Still, she didn't want to appear to be a pushover.

"Fair enough. Are you available on Sunday night?"

Whitney shook her head. "No. I have a meeting for the silent auction committee for the animal rescue gala."

"Skip it and have dinner with me."

"Since I'm the chair, and I'm the one who scheduled it, that would probably be frowned upon."

She wanted to suggest tomorrow night, but since he'd skipped over Saturday and went straight to Sunday with his suggestion, she guessed he probably already had plans. Maybe even a date?

As if reading her mind, he said, "I'd say tomorrow but A) I don't want to be presumptuous and assume you're not busy on a Saturday night, and B) I'm on call tomorrow night, and weekend nights are notoriously busy, so I don't want to make plans with you only to have to cancel them."

"You assumed I wasn't doing anything on a Friday," she reminded him.

"That was just wishful thinking. Plus, I wasn't on call. I thought it couldn't hurt to try."

She smiled. "Proof that it never hurts to ask."

He planted his hands on her hips and pulled her closer. "Man, I'm glad I did. I had a great time with you tonight."

Whoa there, Nicholas Sparks. Pump your brakes. It was one thing to feel it, it was entirely different to say it out loud.

Standing on her tiptoes, she murmured, "Me too," as she pecked his lips dismissively, then pulled away before things got too touchy-feely. Whitney didn't do feelings very well.

He took the hint and walked toward the front door. "I'll text you this weekend, and maybe we can figure out a time to go to dinner this week, then finish the game."

"Sounds good—I'll look for your text. Thank you for dinner. You're right—it was a nice night."

I'm just being polite. That's what civilized people do.

Except, when he kissed her at the door, she realized she didn't want him to go. Asking him to stay would send the wrong message.

But man, she wanted to.

CHAPTER EIGHT

Whitney
Their schedules didn't line up that week. He had to work late on Monday, and she had to prepare for court Tuesday night. Maybe that was a good thing.

They exchanged flirty texts during the day though, starting on Saturday, and he'd called her each night after she'd gotten in bed to wish her sweet dreams. Whitney wouldn't admit it out loud, but she liked knowing that he was thinking about her.

Tuesday night, she answered the phone and smiled when his deep voice greeted her with his usual, "Hey, sweetness."

"Hi. How was work today?"

"The usual—saving lives and limbs," he jested. "How about you? Are you ready for court tomorrow?"

"I think so. It's a pretty solid case." *For once*—she kept that part to herself.

"Do you want to have lunch with me on your break?"

That surprised her. People usually avoided downtown unless they had no choice.

"Are you coming downtown?"

"Yeah. To have lunch with you. I want to see you, and if this is the only way I get to, then so be it."

That made her toes tingle.

"Okay. I'll probably only have an hour, and I'm not sure what time we'll break for lunch."

"I understand. I've had lunch enough times with Zach to know the drill. I'll be at Rousso's at eleven thirty, and we'll have lunch whenever you get there."

"That sounds great. I'll see you tomorrow."

"Sweet dreams."

She fell asleep with a smile on her face.

The next morning, it took her longer than normal to pick out her outfit and how to do her hair.

"No walk this morning, Ralph, but I promise an extra-long walk when I get home tonight," she said as she patted her pup's head.

Her daily dog walker's fees were well worth her guilt being alleviated on the mornings she didn't have time to walk her dog. Knowing he would be walked in the afternoon was worth any price Claire wanted to charge.

The morning session in court seemed to take forever. Whitney had to focus her attention on the case and not daydream about lunch. What was up with that? Shouldn't that concern her?

Like she'd been doing a lot when it came to Steven Ericson, she decided she'd worry about it later.

The judge finally excused them for lunch, giving them an hour and a half before the afternoon session. After quickly conferring with her client and declining his offer for lunch, she rushed to the bathroom to check her hair and makeup, then power walked to Rousso's.

Steven was as handsome as ever in his faded jeans and untucked sky-blue oxford while he waited for her at the same table he'd been at on the day she met him. Today, instead of Converse, he wore loafers. He looked like he worked at a tech company instead of saving lives for a living.

He stood and greeted her with a kiss on the cheek while he tenderly rubbed his hand up and down her back.

"Hi, you look beautiful."

"You look very handsome. I wasn't sure if you'd be in jeans or a suit today."

He winked as he sat down. "I'm versatile. I thought this would be okay for lunch."

"Looks good from where I'm sitting."

The waitress came and took her drink order, then Steven asked, "How'd court go this morning?"

"Great. Right on schedule and everything according to plan with no surprises so far—knock on wood." She rapped the wooden edge of the table with her knuckles. "How about you? Work seems to be keeping you busy."

"We're down an ER doc, so until we get the new hire finalized, it'll be this way for a while. But since I'm taking a three-day weekend, I've been putting a lot of hours in this week. My sister gets here tomorrow afternoon, and I'm going to help her unload the moving truck when it arrives on Friday. Then after I pick you up when you get off work, and we're safely at the Cape, I'm shutting my phone off until Sunday afternoon."

"I never agreed to go. You haven't officially won the game."

"There's a three-day rule—you have to finish within that time, or the game is called. Whoever is ahead is declared the winner. It's in the rule book—look it up."

That made her laugh as the waitress set her iced tea in front of her and took their lunch order.

"I'll go on one condition—my roommate can come, too."

His eyebrows went up. "Ralph? Your roommate? The one you said is protective of you? How's he going to feel about you sleeping in my room? I mean, you know, if you want to sleep in my room."

After what he'd done to her on her kitchen counter? Hell yes, she did. She could only imagine what he could do in a bed. "I think he'll be okay as long as he has a comfy bed."

Steven shrugged and fumbled over his words. "I mean— um, sure. If you want him to come, he's welcome. What does he like to do?"

"Honestly? He'll probably want to run on the beach, eat, and then fall asleep. He's protective, but he's also easily won over with the right bribes."

"If that's the only way I can get you to come, bring him along."

Whitney wasn't sure why she was testing him. Maybe she hoped that including 'her roommate' would be a dealbreaker. The fact that he was willing to let her bring who he thought was a man just so he could spend the weekend with her only made him that much more endearing.

Dammit.

Maybe he hated dogs.

"I can leave as soon as we have a verdict, which should be Friday in the early afternoon at the latest."

"What about Ralph? Does he work? Will we need to wait for him?"

"He doesn't work. I think he's independently wealthy—although he doesn't spend a lot."

"And how do you know him?"

"We met at a social event and immediately hit it off. He was looking for a place to live, and I was happy to help. And before you ask—he had excellent references."

"But you're still strictly platonic?"

"I love him, but we have no interest in each other *that* way."

An evil grin crossed his lips. "I'm very interested in you *that* way."

"Well, you're in luck—I'm free this weekend for lots of *that* way time."

"And it won't be weird with Ralph there?"

Whitney could tell he didn't like the idea of her 'roommate' tagging along and was trying to talk her out of bringing him. She wasn't sure how long she would keep him on the hook, but at least a little while longer.

"It'll be fine."

"If you say it will be, then I won't worry about it. We'll have a great time."

They spent the rest of lunch discussing their week so far and what there was to do at his place, besides sit on the beach and the unspoken obvious.

"What should I pack?"

"Most of the weekend should be casual, but we can go out to dinner and dress up if you want. Don't forget your swimsuit." He paused, then looked at her with a wicked smile. "Actually, I'm okay if you forget your suit. I like skinny dipping."

"I'm not really an exhibitionist. Going nude on the beach doesn't appeal to me. And after seeing *Jaws* when I was a kid, I will never swim in the ocean at night. No, thank you, not happenin'. I like my limbs intact, thank you."

Steven laughed. "Well, how about in my hot tub on my patio?"

She gave him a flirty smile. "Maybe."

"I can work with *maybe*."

Whitney glanced at her watch and was surprised it was already time to head back to the courthouse.

"Do you need to go?" he asked when he noticed her looking around for their waitress.

"I do. Have you seen our server? I need the check."

He almost looked offended. "I'm buying you lunch."

Sliding off her chair, she leaned over and kissed his cheek. "Thank you. I'll buy next time."

He scoffed. "The fuck you will."

She looked at him with one eyebrow raised and said flatly, "Yeah. I will."

Taking her hand between his, he brought her closer. "Sorry, sweetness. I know you're a modern, self-sufficient woman, and I respect that. But, there's just some things I'm old fashioned about. Like, opening your door, driving, picking up the check." He leaned in to whisper in her ear, "Being in charge when I take your clothes off..."

A small whimper escaped her lips as she envisioned it, and he pulled back with a grin. "Just to name a few." Then he kissed her cheek.

Normally, she'd protest and put her foot down. When a man paid, he thought she was then somehow indebted to him—or in some cases, that he was superior. She didn't know whether she didn't believe Steven would ever view it that way, or she liked his idea of chivalry, but she didn't voice any objection. Instead, she whispered back, "That's an interesting list, Dr. Ericson."

"Like I told you, Counselor, I only named a few. I'll fill you in on the rest this weekend."

She needed to go, so she reluctantly withdrew her hand from his grasp and put her bag over her shoulder.

"Do I get any say about this list?"

"I'm flexible—about some things."

"I'm flexible, too," she said with a wink, hoping to convey her double meaning.

He looked at her like he wanted to devour her for dessert. She guessed he got her innuendo.

"You better leave right now, sweetness, or you're going to be in contempt of court when you don't show up this afternoon."

"I'm not scared. I know you have to go to work soon."

"Damn this *having a job* bullshit."

She rolled her eyes. "Yeah, I hate being able to pay my bills."

He laughed. "I guess there is an upside. I'll text you tonight. Maybe we can have lunch again tomorrow?"

"You know where to find me."

"Good luck in court, baby."

She found herself smiling all the way back to the courthouse, and that was so not like her. Normally, she was hyper-focused on her case. Instead, she was daydreaming about frolicking in the sand this weekend with the handsome doctor and her dog.

"You need to get your shit together, Whit," she chided herself when the courthouse came in view. This was a rare slam dunk case she'd been given—if she fucked it up, she'd have to answer to the partners. And that was something she had no interest in doing. Steven was proving to be a distraction. She preferred to keep her head down and nose to the grindstone.

Maybe someday she'd branch out on her own. Then she could stop and smell the roses. Even have a real boyfriend—

someone in her social status, and that ruled Steven Ericson out.

Fortunately, that was a worry for the future.

But probably even not then, because then she'd have a whole different set of concerns, not in the least was having to market herself to get new clients. Right now, she was just handed her cases—shitty as they were—without having to do any self-promotion on her part. She'd tried that, and the client she'd finessed at an ARF luncheon was given to one of the partners.

Ugh. One more thing to add to her list of worries about opening her own practice. It was getting longer every time she considered hanging her shingle. Good thing it was going to be a while until she was ready.

Maybe she could take on a partner.

But that would mean giving up control and trusting someone. Things she was notoriously bad at.

Which reminded her. She needed to cool things off with the sexy doctor. Well, starting Monday. After their weekend away.

****

Steven

Work was kicking his ass, and he was looking forward to the long weekend away from the hospital. Not to mention Hope arriving.

He ended up not getting home until early Thursday morning, and he stayed awake long enough to shoot Whitney a text explaining why he wouldn't be able to make lunch.

She responded immediately, thank goodness, so he could go straight to bed.

Whitney: No worries, whatsoever. Get some rest. We'll talk later.

Steven: Thanks for understanding. I'll text you when I wake up. Good luck in court today.

Whitney: Sweet dreams.

Steven: If they're about you, sweetness, they will be. Goodnight.

With that, he closed his blackout curtains tight, put his phone on silent, and set an alarm for three p.m. Hope's plane was scheduled to arrive at four and even though his cleaning lady had just come on Tuesday, he wanted time to run the robot vacuum and the dishwasher before she got to his condo.

He'd offered to pick her up once he found out his schedule, but she insisted on getting an Uber.

"You have better things to do than fight rush-hour traffic to pick me up when I'm perfectly capable of getting a rideshare," his practical little sister had told him on the phone.

"Don't say I didn't offer."

"Besides, I'm going to use up all your goodwill when you help me unload the moving truck on Friday."

"They're still on schedule?"

"According to the website, they're slated to arrive at eight a.m."

"I'll be up and eager to help. That is, if we don't drink too much wine and stay up all night catching up. You're going to be on California time for a while."

"Actually, I've been slowly trying to adjust my sleep schedule this last week to East Coast time."

"That's very pragmatic and clever at the same time."

"Well, I don't want to be jet lagged when I start work on Monday. Although, I don't know how successful I've been. It's hard to get out of bed when the sun is barely up, not to mention you know how I like my sleep."

Steven chuckled. That was something he remembered vividly. Both Hope and Grace were notorious for sleeping late and were grumpy as hell if awoken before they were ready.

"Well, I have blackout curtains in the guest room; the sun comes up a little earlier here in the summer than it does in Cali."

"That's good. Fortunately, I'm not scheduled to meet with Dr. Parker until ten on Monday morning. We already had a discussion at my interview about my hours and working remotely."

"Ah, it's good to be the queen in high demand."

"It definitely doesn't suck. My bank account appreciates it, but the flexibility is almost as important, if not more. I want to be able to go home to San Diego regularly and see everyone. Ava's kids are growing up so fast, and it won't be long before Gracie gets married and has kids, too. I don't want to miss any of that."

"You won't."

"You have," she pointed out.

"My job is a lot different from yours, kiddo. I can't exactly work from home a few days a week. They kind of need me in the ER tending to people with emergencies."

"That's true. But I won't be able to work from home until everything is up and running. Still, Parker knows not to expect me before ten and not to schedule any meeting before then, either."

"Like I said, it's good to be the queen in high demand. But remember, you're still just a princess when you're living with me."

"You can't see me, but I'm rolling my eyes so hard at you right now."

"I know. I can hear it through the phone."

She giggled. "I'll see you tomorrow, big brother."

"See you tomorrow, roomie."

Now, tomorrow had arrived, and Steve had worked a sixteen-hour shift in the meantime. Time for some sleep and hopefully dreams of doing dirty things to a chestnut-haired attorney.

Dreams he knew would pale in comparison to the real thing. He couldn't wait for their weekend away. Even if it included her roommate.

CHAPTER NINE

Steven

He woke up before his alarm went off, something he tended to do, especially when he was trying to sleep in the middle of the day. The blackout curtains helped, as did cranking the air conditioning down, but he still could only sleep six hours. He'd take it—especially being on call again tonight. With any luck, it'd be a slow night, and he'd get some rest when the sun was down.

He'd told Hope that they'd have a bottle of wine and catch up. There'd be no wine on his part, but hopefully lots of catching up. He missed his family. When Hope settled on Boston General, he couldn't have been happier—even if Frannie Ericson was not.

"Just another reason for you to come visit, Mom."

She'd scoffed, but Ava told him later that she'd pointed out to their mother that Hope had had a lot of offers around the world, and at least she was going somewhere close to family. That seemed to cool Frannie's jets a little.

As excited as he was for his little sister's arrival, he was even more excited to be spending the weekend away with Whitney.

The feisty attorney had captivated him.

The ringing of his doorbell had him hurrying to the door, but not before Lola, his terrier/poodle mix, beat him to it. His pup hopped up and down, barking excitedly at the prospect of someone new to pet her.

"Lola!" Hope exclaimed when his dog burst through the threshold once Steve opened the door. She bent down to pet behind her ears and accept the pooch's kisses in return. She then stood with a big smile, holding her arms out like she'd just had when she greeted Lola.

"Big brother!"

"Hey, sis. How was your flight?" He pulled her in for a long hug, not releasing her until she let go of him first. Then he reached for her biggest piece of luggage, and she waited for him to pull it through the door before tugging two more matching pieces inside.

"It was nice—Parker sprang for first-class again. A girl could get used to that."

He chuckled. The chief of staff had wanted Hope on his team, *badly*, and had been willing to pull out all the stops including paying for her travel across the country and a moving company to bring her things.

They rolled the luggage toward the guest bedroom.

"It's worth the cost when you're flying across the country."

"Do *not* tell me you pay for first class when you fly home."

"Guilty. What else do I have to spend my money on?"

"I don't know. Your sisters' birthday presents. A place in San Diego. Your retirement fund. Just about anything else."

"Do I get you bad gifts?" His tone implied he was offended at the suggestion.

"Well, no..."

"And *you* just said you could get used to flying first class."

"Yeah, when it's on someone else's dime. Paying for it myself is something entirely different."

"We'll see the next time you fly coach. You'll change your tune. Do you give Ava a hard time about flying first class? Because you know damn well that's the only way Travis travels."

"Come on, even *I* know better than that."

Their sister had married the named partner of the best law firm in San Diego County. Travis Sterling did not skimp on anything—especially when it came to making his wife happy.

They deposited her luggage in her room, but not before Lola sniffed every inch of each of the suitcases.

"Oh, Lola, Grandma Frannie didn't forget about you. She sent you treats," Hope said as she hauled her carryon onto the bed and unzipped it. Lola's nose was working overtime when Hope pulled out a Ziploc bag with homemade dog biscuits. She looked at Steven. "Can she have one?"

"I'd kind of be a dick if I said *no* now, wouldn't I? You don't ask while waving the bag in front of her."

"You sound like Ava. She says the same thing about sweets and her kids."

"And yet, I get the feeling you don't care what Ava says either."

Opening the bag, she pulled out a treat and handed it to Lola, who had been waiting patiently. His dog took it gently, then ran off to eat it undisturbed. Hope looked at him with a grin. "Nope. I like being the favorite aunt."

Steven shook his head and returned her smile while rolling his eyes only slightly.

"You hungry?" he asked as he turned toward the kitchen.

"Starving."

"I'll make dinner."

"I think you promised me wine, too."

"I'm on call so none for me, but there's a bottle of your favorite red on the counter waiting for you."

"You are my favorite brother for a reason."

Steven could argue the other obvious reason but knew it was pointless.

She used the wine opener and poured herself a glass while he got to work pulling ingredients from the refrigerator and freezer.

His phone buzzed with an incoming text, and he stopped what he was doing to look at who it was from.

He felt his mouth curve into a smile when he saw it was from Whitney. Something his little sister didn't miss.

"Uh oh."

Steven looked up from his screen before replying. "Uh oh?"

"Who's got you all smiley about a text message?"

"Nunya."

"Aw, come on, Steve. Spill. We're living together now—I'm going to find out sooner or later. It's your choice on how many embarrassing stories I tell once I finally do meet her."

He sighed like it was a hardship to share with Hope, but he was happy to talk about Whitney with someone.

"She's an attorney, and we're going to the Cape this weekend. And no, you aren't invited. But I am hoping you can watch Lola."

Although, maybe Hope could run interference with Ralph if he brought her...

"I don't want to go anyway; moving truck tomorrow, remember? But I do want to meet her—soon. And, of course I'll watch Lola."

"Thanks, I appreciate that."

"But I don't think I'll unpack anything this weekend other than clothes since," she gestured to their surroundings, "you seem to have everything we need and then some."

"Mom did come out for a week when I first bought this place, so of course I have everything I could ever need and even some things I never knew I needed."

"Say no more—she did the same with all of us. Anyway—back to the attorney." In a singsong voice, Hope asked, "What's her name?"

"Whitney."

Still with the singsong. "Where'd you meet her?"

"She was opposing counsel against my friend, Zach."

"Zach, your roommate from college?" A slow smile formed on her lips. "He was hot. Is he still single?"

"Yes, but that doesn't matter because as far as you're concerned, he is unavailable."

"Aw, you're no fun." Undeterred, she continued, "So, she was opposing counsel... what did that have to do with you?"

"I met him for lunch while he was in the middle of the trial, and she showed up at the same restaurant. He introduced me and, well, as Mom would say, I was smitten."

"Wow, my brother—a smitten kitten. I never thought I'd see the day. So, I'm assuming she's pretty..."

"She's beautiful."

"And smart."

"Fucking brilliant."

"A dangerous combination."

Steven snorted. "You could say that. You, of all people, should know all about what that's like."

"Aw, thanks for the compliment. A little advice, from a smart and, I'd argue beautiful but will accept cute, woman?"

"Sure, I'm all ears."

Hope gestured to the phone still in his hands. "You shouldn't keep her waiting for your reply."

"Oh, good point."

He opened his message app.

Whitney: Were you able to get some rest?

Steven: I did, thanks. Sorry again that I couldn't make lunch, but I promise I'll make it up to you this weekend. Do you still think we can leave by tomorrow afternoon?

Whitney: The jury got the case a few hours ago, and they decided to keep deliberating instead of going home at five, so I'm still hanging around the courthouse, hoping for a verdict tonight.

Steven: I wish I wasn't on call tonight; we could take off as soon as you're done.

Before he could hit send, he heard, "No, you couldn't. You have to help me unload the moving truck tomorrow morning, remember?"

He looked to find Hope reading his message over his shoulder and quickly angled his body so she could no longer see his phone.

"Do you mind?"

"I'm just saying, you promised you'd help."

"Well, I'm on call, so I couldn't leave tonight even if I wanted to."

Still, he deleted that message and started again.

Steven: So, we can leave as soon as I'm done helping my sister unload her moving truck?

Whitney: Fingers crossed that we get a verdict tonight. I'll be ready to go whenever you are. What time are you thinking?

Steven: Just depends on if the truck gets here on time, but hopefully no later than noon.

Whitney: Ralph and I will be ready.

Oh yeah, Ralph. Greeeat.

Steven: See you tomorrow, sweetness. Text me when you get a verdict.

Whitney: Will do. Have a nice night with your sister.

He tossed his phone on the counter and went about making dinner. Hope caught him up on what he'd missed in San Diego since Mother's Day, and he tried to fill her in on some of the hospital politics.

"Evan Lacroix is an asshole doc in the ER, so avoid him if you can. His sister is an OB/GYN there, but she's much more levelheaded."

"Why do you say he's an asshole?"

"He wanted the ER director job, and I got it. He doesn't even try to hide his sour grapes. His mother didn't teach him the art of losing gracefully."

"Neither did our mother," Hope pointed out.

Steve grinned at her. "Good thing we don't lose very often, then."

"Oh my god, I never realized how cocky you are."

"Seriously? Never?"

She pushed the food around on her plate and furrowed her brows. "Okay, that's not true. I know exactly how cocky you are. To be honest, I always kind of admired that about you."

"Really? Why? I've been told it's very unbecoming."

"I just love how sure you are of yourself. Me, I spend half my life second guessing every decision I make."

"I don't believe that. I've seen you working. You know exactly what you're doing, and you don't seem to second guess your abilities."

"I guess I try to emulate you when I'm doing my job. People want the person in charge to be confident. Don't let this go to your head, big brother, but, you're kind of my hero."

He felt like puffing his chest out.

"That's the nicest thing anyone has ever said to me."

"Like I said, don't let it go to your head."

He took a bite of food with a smirk. "Too late."

Hope wadded up her napkin and threw it at him. "I knew I shouldn't have told you."

They laughed and joked throughout dinner, just like they always did at their parents' and were in the middle of cleaning up when his phone dinged again.

He quickly reached for it, and Hope teased, "You really like this girl."

"It could be the hospital."

"Uh huh, sure."

It wasn't the hospital.

Whitney: Judgement in my client's favor. I'm headed home. Let me know what time tomorrow when you know.

Hope's voice came from behind him. "You should invite her over to celebrate."

He spun around and stared at her. "We are seriously going to have to establish some boundaries here. Stop reading my texts over my shoulder."

She shrugged unapologetically. "I'm just saying, inviting her over is the right move here."

"I'm on call."

She shrugged again. "I'd still invite her."

Steven scowled at his little sister and walked into the living room, away from her prying eyes, as he typed his reply.

Steven: Congratulations! Want to come over and celebrate? I'm on call, so I can't join you in a toast, but I can give you a nice foot massage.

Whitney: As heavenly as a foot massage sounds, I can't. I need to get home to Ralph.

It was probably for the best. It was a little too soon to be to be allowing Hope anywhere near her. But he was still disappointed, and now more curious than ever to meet this Ralph. Why would she need to get home to him?

Steven: Okay. Maybe this weekend. Congratulations again. I'll call you tomorrow when I have a better idea of a time.

Her next text made him laugh out loud. Sneaky girl.

Whitney: I hope you have something bigger than your Porsche, since I don't think Ralph will fit in the back.

Attached was a photo of a black lab with longer than usual ears. He was adorable.

It looked like his plans to leave Lola with Hope had just changed.

CHAPTER TEN

Whitney

She stared at the picture of the grey and white dog that looked like it belonged in a Disney movie. Steven's caption read: **Well, aren't you tricky. Lola is going to love Ralph. We'll see you tomorrow.**

He not only liked dogs, but he had one himself.

Whitney was so screwed.

No, I'm not. I don't have to get involved with him. She could keep things light between them.

Steven sent another text around noon the next day, telling her he could pick her up in an hour, if that worked for her.

Whitney: We'll be ready.

The doorbell rang almost exactly an hour later, causing Ralph to bark excitedly and race her to the entrance.

"Ralph, sit," she said and waited for him to comply before she opened the door. The sight of Steven took her breath away. He was ready for the beach or boat in his tan cargo shorts, white t-shirt, and teal short-sleeved button down, open all the way to the bottom. A brown pair of boat shoes rounded out his look.

"Hi," he said with a smile as he surveyed Ralph with his tail thumping against her upright carryon. Her fur baby's travel bag was right next to it.

"You must be Ralph." Steven reached his hand down to let the dog sniff it before kneeling and rubbing the pup's face between his hands.

He stood back up—his eyes twinkling when they met hers.

"Are you ready?"

"Almost," she said, putting her hand on the telescopic luggage handle to prevent him from taking it. "We need to discuss some ground rules for this weekend."

He cocked his head. "Ground rules?"

"Expectations."

"Ah," he said, nodding in understanding. A small grin escaped his lips as he leaned against her doorjamb. "Well, *my* expectations are we'll go to my house on the ocean, soak up some sun and sand, and have some great food and conversation in the meantime. I also expect we'll relax, enjoy each other's company, and it's up to you whether you sleep in the guest room or my room."

He reached for her bag, but she didn't relinquish it as she mulled over what he said. She liked his answer but hadn't expected him to be so accommodating. With a smirk, he tapped her nose. "Is that okay, or should we talk about safe words, too?"

She replied flatly, "Ha ha," but still didn't move.

"For the record, beautiful, I promise you won't need a safe word. I'll take care of you."

Whitney tried to suppress the shiver down her spine and ignore his sexy banter as she pressed on. "I just think we should be clear about things, so there's no hard feelings later."

He looked down at her patiently. "What do we need to be clear about? I like you; you like me. There's obviously a physical attraction between us—but if you've changed your mind about that... well, I won't love it, but I'll respect it."

"No, quite the opposite, actually."

He grinned. "Then what's the problem?"

"I just want to make sure you know I'm not looking for a relationship right now."

He stared at her, his face unreadable when he finally nodded. "Understood."

A tinge of disappointment settled in her stomach when he didn't argue. But that's what she wanted, right?

She locked the front door with Ralph's leash wrapped around her wrist, and he growled in her ear, "I can still do dirty things to you though, right? Even if we're not in a relationship."

She turned to him with a smug smile. "I'm counting on it."

They approached his SUV, and she noticed his dog in the backseat. "We should introduce Ralph and Lola before we expect them to go on a car ride together."

Of course, the pups got along great.

They got Lola and Ralph situated, then he opened her car door and murmured as she got in. "We're going to have a great time, baby girl. Just try to let go and enjoy yourself. Let me worry about everything. I've got you."

Whitney rolled her eyes and got in. He simply grinned as he closed the door and came around to the driver's side.

Visions of what it would be like to do just that as she lay naked underneath him danced in her head, and she pressed her thighs together. Could she relinquish control and let him worry about everything?

A quick glance at his strong profile when he got in the car, and she knew it would be easy—against her better judgment. Still, she grumbled, "I'm not very good at giving up control," as he shut the door.

He replied with an unworried, "We'll work on that," and started the engine.

What did that mean?

He looked almost regal as he drove the Land Rover through Friday traffic with ease. A thought struck her as she stared at his sexy forearms while he turned the steering wheel—she never got to sit back and enjoy the ride. But being in the passenger seat with him driving felt comfortable.

This better not be a fucking life metaphor.

The loud crash from behind as she was jolted forward told her that's exactly what it was.

****

Steven

"Are you okay?" he asked, then glanced back to see the Volkswagen Jetta that had smashed into his rear bumper.

Whitney looked at the dogs who were still safely strapped into their harnesses and uttered, "I think so."

With a sigh, he pulled to the side to inspect the damage. Fucking weekender traffic. He'd thought they'd get a jump start on the other mainlanders headed down the Cape for the weekend, but apparently he wasn't the only one who considered leaving before rush hour.

As he suspected, there was no damage to the Land Rover's bumper; the Jetta's grill, however, didn't fare as well.

"Good thing we didn't take the Porsche," Whitney teased when they got back in the SUV ten minutes later. "That would have been wicked expensive."

He grinned at her Boston slang. "Your accent's showing."

"How long have you been here?"

"Six years."

"And how many Red Sox, Patriots, or Celtics games have you gone to?"

"A few Celtics games, one Patriots. But I have season tickets to the Sox."

"And you don't use *wicked* as a modifier?"

"I'd feel like an imposter if I did."

Whitney patted his hand. "Oh, Steve, you've been here long enough—you've earned the right."

He turned his palm to capture her hand in his and drew it to his mouth, kissing the pulse of her wrist. "I'll keep that in mind."

She let out a small gasp that made his cock move, and he reluctantly let go when she pulled away and changed the subject.

"So, a house on the Cape, huh?"

"I grew up surfing in San Diego. I missed the ocean."

"But you have a condo in Boston?"

He nodded.

"Did you get your sister moved in?"

"Well, we got her boxes moved in. She said she's not going to unpack anything but the clothes she needs for work, but I'll believe it when I see it when I get back Sunday. She'll get bored and want something to do."

"Does she have friends she can hang out with?"

"Not yet."

"Tell me again, why did she move here?"

"She starts her new job at Boston General on Monday. She's an engineer savant who has a patent on cutting-edge prosthetics technology. Every hospital in the world was courting her."

"But her big brother only works at one of them."

"Something like that."

"I imagine your bosses were grateful for your influence."

"Yeah, I'm not going to lie... I scored some major brownie points bringing Hope on board. But I'm pretty fucking good at what I do, so I don't need them. I'm just tucking them away for a rainy day," he glanced at her with a wink. "Although I'll spend a couple to get the hospital to sponsor a table at the Animal Rescue Foundation's fundraiser."

"And I appreciate that. How come your sister's living with you? Doesn't she want her own place? Aren't you two trust fund kids?"

He couldn't help but snort.

"My parents are comfortable, but they made sure their children understood the value of money. They gave us a real gift by paying our college tuition that wasn't covered by scholarships—but, no trust fund. We all know and appreciate hard work and have made our own way."

She gave him a small smile. "A self-made man who likes dogs *and* can kiss? I think I might be in trouble."

He flashed her a cocky grin. "Your panties are definitely in trouble, but the rest of you, I promise is safe with me."

And he meant it—both the part about her panties being toast, because let's face it, he wasn't above laying on the charm to get her out of them. But also the part where he said he wouldn't hurt her. Steven had a sense that underneath her tough exterior, lie a vulnerable woman he had a desire to protect.

And if he were being honest, to conquer, too. Her submission was something he craved.

CHAPTER ELEVEN

Whitney

She could smell the ocean the second they pulled through a set of gates that led to a classic Cape Cod-style house. The backdrop was the Atlantic Ocean.

"Are you kidding me?"

He looked over at her as he put the Land Rover in park. "What?"

"I obviously chose the wrong profession."

Whitney made a decent living and could afford a modest place in the city, along with designer-label clothes she usually bought from the sales rack, a newer-used mid-level BMW, and a retirement account, but this was way out of her league. Just like he was.

"I've seen you in action, you're doing exactly what you're supposed to. As far as this place, I got a great deal. The previous owners were in the middle of a messy divorce."

"Great deal or not, there's no way I'd ever be able to afford something like this. Not unless..." She didn't continue her thought.

"I do okay for myself. I'm a single guy with not a lot of expenses." He got out and went around to open her door. "Not unless what? Are you considering what Zach suggested?"

"No. I need to stick with my firm."

She owed the partners. They were the ones who'd put her in touch with the Harvard recruiter when she'd been interning with them and then wrote her a stellar letter of recommendation to include with her application. They even created a scholarship for her when she'd been accepted.

"Do you want to make partner?"

She took his offered hand and slid out of her seat. "Honestly, no. I want to hang my own shingle rather than jump through all the hoops it will take to make partner."

"Zach is killing himself right now trying to make partner, not to mention all the ass he has to kiss."

She frowned skeptically. "Every time I see him, he's coming back from a vacation at some exotic locale. I have a hard time believing he's suffering."

That elicited a deep laugh from him as they helped the dogs out. Whitney liked the sound of it.

"He plays as hard as he works."

"Oh, I'm not begrudging him. If I'm being honest, I'm envious."

The dogs were sniffing along the lawn when he asked, "Why are you envious? You could do the same. You're successful and single, too."

"I'm too practical to take off on a whim to exotic places for a long weekend. I have to plan my vacations well in advance."

"Don't tell me. You have a daily itinerary for every day you're on vacation."

Ralph galloped toward her, and she knelt as she replied defensively, "There's nothing wrong with a schedule."

He was grinning when she glanced up at him. "Schedules when you're on vacation keep you from being spontaneous. What if I want to spend an afternoon pleasuring you, but it's not on the calendar?"

She felt her tummy dip, remembering what he'd done to her after their dinner on Friday night. A whole afternoon of that? She couldn't even imagine it.

And that wicked, self-assured grin of his left her no doubt that he'd be true to his word.

Standing to her full height, with her shoulders back, Whitney replied, "Are you saying you don't have an agenda this weekend?" while Ralph took off again in search of his new friend.

His grin morphed into a broad smile, and he stepped forward to wrap his arm around her waist and utter in her ear, "Oh, I definitely have an agenda."

"The first rule of scheduling is to allow for flexibility."

Steven ran his hand over her backside before squeezing subtly. "Flexibility is very important for what I have in mind."

It was a good thing she tried to make yoga class four days a week.

She felt her nipples stiffen at the same time Lola and Ralph bounded up, and Steven pulled away with a sigh. Which was a good thing, because she wanted to grind all over his stiff cock right there in the driveway. That was probably frowned upon in this neighborhood.

He reached for her hand, "Come on, let's go inside."

She took a step, then hesitated, looking back at the SUV. "Should we grab our bags?"

"I'll get them after I've given you a tour."

"I'm capable of bringing my own bag in."

He stopped short and turned to her, his tone stern. "Let's get one thing straight. I have no doubt about your abilities. I'm a gentleman because I was raised that way, and because I happen to think you're *worth* it—it has nothing to do with what I think you're capable of."

Whitney swallowed hard, unable to form a coherent sentence.

"And don't look at me like that unless you want to get kissed," he added gruffly.

That might be the hottest thing anyone had ever said to her.

****

Steven

He'd been annoyed at being interrupted by Ralph and Lola but then realized it'd be better if he took things slower tonight anyway. Yeah, he wanted to do obscene things to and with her, but he also wanted to get to know everything about

94

her. Screwing her in the driveway before they even got inside the house wouldn't exactly set the right tone for the weekend.

She could take that bullshit of not wanting a relationship and stick it.

But he knew better than to tell her that, so he'd play along—for now.

She was staring back at him with wide eyes and her mouth slightly agape, her nipples stiff under her mint-green sundress.

"And don't look at me like that unless you want to get kissed."

Her tongue darted out to her bottom lip as if she were imagining it, causing his self-control to crumble. He put his hand behind her neck and pulled her into him, crushing her mouth with his.

A whimper escaped her as she melted into him.

They were never going to make it inside.

And Steven had a hard time caring.

Chapter Twelve

Whitney

The nudge of dog noses followed by a whine brought them back to reality.

"I've been wanting to do that since you opened your front door," he confessed as he rested his forehead against hers.

"So, why didn't you?"

"You were creating safe words before you'd even walk out the door with me. I didn't think it was the right time."

Whitney stepped out of his embrace. "I did *not* create a safe word."

His devilish grin was back when he grabbed her hand and pulled her toward the front porch. "Good, baby doll, because I told you, you won't need one with me. I'll take care of you."

"You're insufferable."

He kissed her hand, not missing a step. "I know. But, my mother calls it endearing."

Goddammit, it *was* endearing.

She wasn't going to fall for this guy. No way would she let someone take care of her. Her own parents couldn't even do that. She learned long ago not to rely on anyone but herself. And the gorgeous playboy doctor wasn't about to change that.

But maybe, just for this weekend, she'd let herself see what it would be like.

But it was only for the weekend.

****

Steven

"Your home is beautiful. I think it might even be worth the commute to live here every day."

Whitney swirled the cabernet around in her glass as she sat at the kitchen island and watched him pull pots and pans from the cabinets while he searched for his favorite one.

"Maybe if I get a bigger boat, I'd consider commuting a few days a week. At least in the summer."

"That would be cool. You'd really impress the ladies bringing them here by boat."

Steve set the pan he'd been looking for on the granite counter with a thud and didn't bother putting the others away before he came around to where she was sitting. Spinning her stool so she was facing him, he wedged his thigh between hers and lifted her chin with his knuckle.

"Despite what you may think, I don't give a damn about impressing anyone but you. And for the record, I've never brought a woman here before."

She snorted. Actually *snorted*.

"Yeah, okay. Sure, you haven't."

He wasn't sure how to respond. He'd never had anyone not take him at his word. At least not to his face.

"Are you calling me a liar?"

"I'm calling you a playboy who knows what to say to a woman to make her weak in the knees. Unfortunately, weak in the knees, or *anywhere,* isn't my style. For the record, you don't have to bullshit me. I'm okay with what this weekend is."

He felt himself frowning. "And what is that?"

"Intellectual conversation, great sex, maybe some manufactured romance with a few walks on the beach holding hands while our dogs run around. A good time with no strings attached." She narrowed her eyes and wagged her finger at him, lowering her voice, like he'd seen her do in the courtroom. "So, don't bullshit me."

Steven grabbed her finger and caressed her palm, his face inches from hers.

"No bullshit, Counselor. I have never brought a woman here." He kissed her wrist, then inside her elbow—working up to her shoulder, "I've never had sex in this house," then below her ear. "And while I like your plans for our weekend, and now want to christen every room in this place with you..." He ran his hands down her side to rest on her hips as he whispered, "I also like the idea of strings with you. A lot."

Whitney groaned and moved her head to allow him better access to her neck.

"If that's a euphemism for being tied up, I *might* be on board. Otherwise—I'm not interested, Dr. Ericson."

Women always said they were okay with no commitment when he warned them that he didn't do relationships, when they truly weren't but thought they could change his mind. Now, he was telling a woman that he was interested in more than a fling, and she was turning him down?

Was there a new dating book out that he didn't know about? Rejection made him want her even more now.

Except when he looked in her eyes, he knew—she was dead serious.

"Let's just see what happens this weekend without labeling it."

Whitney shook her head. "I think it's better if we go into things with a clear understanding of our expectations."

"And what are your expectations?"

"I already told you. Conversation, sex, just a nice time away, and—"

He put his fingertips to her lips before she could add the part about no strings. "I can deliver all of that—and more. All I'm asking is that you remain open about what happens Monday."

Her eyes were on his mouth, and he noticed that she swallowed hard before whispering, "I think that might be a bad idea."

Steve tucked her hair behind her ear. "Or a very, very good one."

"I don't see how."

"Have a little faith in me, Whitney. I promise, it'll be worth it."

Her smile was weak. "I'm not at a place in my life where I can give you anything past Sunday, Steven. Please understand that."

He neither liked nor understood it. But she was there with him now—for the entire weekend, and he would focus on that. He'd show her such a good time—in and out of bed, she'd be begging to see him again.

Steven rubbed her shoulders, refusing to concede to not seeing her once they were back in Boston. She let out a little moan that made his cock spring up.

"Let's have dinner, then we'll sit in the hot tub, and I'll rub your back. I'm worried you're going to be sore from our little accident earlier."

"Mmm, sounds heavenly."

That was the idea. Well, and have her screaming his name as she came all over his tongue.

But first things first—dazzle her with his culinary skills. His cunnilingus talents would have to wait until she was fed and relaxed.

****

Whitney

Goddammit, the man could cook.

"No man who looks like you should be able to cook like this," she observed as she took another bite of dinner. "How would a woman even stand a chance?"

He laughed but didn't deny it. "So, what are you saying? That you don't stand a chance, or that you can't cook?"

She ignored the first part of his question. "I can cook, I just don't see the point. Cooking for one is too time consuming. It's just easier to pick up takeout or have something delivered."

"I agree. Although I enjoy it and find it relaxing, I don't cook a lot when it's just me." He gave her a pointed look. "I'm happy to have someone to cook for."

"Well, I'm glad to reap the benefits."

"You'll be reaping all weekend long. In more ways than one, baby."

They stared at each other for a long moment, then Whitney broke their gaze and looked around the kitchen.

"You cooked—I'll clean."

He accepted her offer but then worked alongside her— never missing an opportunity to run his hand along her backside or kiss her neck as they passed each other.

When the dishwasher started, he threw a dish towel on the counter. "Hot tub?"

"Yes!"

Steven grabbed the bottle of wine they'd been drinking at dinner, along with their glasses and started toward the French door leading to his back deck.

"Don't you need to change into your suit?"

The corner of his mouth turned up in his signature mischievous grin. "Nope."

"Well, I'm going to change."

He opened the door with a wink. "I'll be out here waiting."

Oh lord. Images of him naked under the swirling bubbles filled her head as she found her suitcase.

Just for the weekend. But she was going to enjoy every second of it.

CHAPTER THIRTEEN

Steven

His dick was already hard as he sat in the warm, bubbling water, but when she walked out onto the back patio in her black bikini, he could have hammered nails with the thing.

"Holy fuck," he muttered as he stood and offered her his hand to help her in—careful to stay in the deepest part to keep the water waist high. "You are stunning."

The way she nervously tucked her hair behind her ear as she dropped into the water seemed to indicate she wasn't nearly as confident as she had every right to be.

He put her in front of him—out of dick's reach and rubbed her neck and shoulders. "I don't want you sore in the morning," he leaned over and murmured against her ear. "Well, not your neck and back anyway. No guarantees about other places."

Her moan as he pressed his thumbs at the base of her neck had his cock on high alert. He couldn't wait to hear her make those sounds again as she lay in his bed, being pleasured in an entirely different way.

He could feel the tension leave her body as he massaged her for the next forty minutes, until she finally turned to face him with a relaxed smile. "Thank you. That felt amazing."

"We'll do it again tomorrow."

Steve topped her wine glass off and handed it to her before refilling his own and offering it up as he proposed a toast.

"To a weekend of possibility."

She looked at him skeptically—his not-so-subtle push for more obviously not lost on her, but she still clinked her glass against his. Then added, "And to expectations being met."

He paused, poised to re-clink their glasses after correcting her. "Expectations *exceeded*. With more to follow."

He hit her glass with his and took a sip, but instead of drinking, she cocked her head and asked, "Why are you so determined? Do you have a bet going with Zach? For all you know, you might be sick of me by Sunday. Or maybe the sex will be bad."

"Of course I don't have a bet with Zach—I'm thirty-eight, not sixteen." He put his hand around her waist and pulled her against him. "As for the other gibberish—that's doubtful on all counts, doll. I'm already addicted to your taste."

She immediately wrapped her legs around his middle and bobbed her bathing-suit-clad pussy up and down on his rock-hard cock.

"Only one way to find out," she purred before catching his lips with hers.

Oh, fuck yes.

He held back and let her control the kiss—at first. Then he wove his hands in her hair and took over without even realizing it. His hard cock was notched between her legs at just the right angle, and he deepened the kiss.

Only when he felt her sigh as she relaxed into his body did he become cognizant that the power had shifted.

Steven could tell she was used to being the one in control. *Not with me, baby girl.* The heat emanating from her pussy told him she was okay with their current arrangement.

So, he wasn't prepared when he felt the sharp tug of his hair, drawing his eyes up to meet hers, as she growled, "Fuck me," while grinding against his cock.

It wasn't a submissive request.

Unlike his dealings with Evan Lacroix at the hospital, this was one power struggle he could get on board with.

****

Whitney

He stood and stepped out of the hot tub while her legs were still wrapped around his waist and his lips still planted on hers.

"Be careful. Don't slip," she giggled against his mouth as he strode toward the French door.

"Don't worry, baby. I've got you."

"So you keep saying."

"Maybe if I say it enough, you'll start to believe it."

The dogs had been sacked out together on a big round dog bed in a corner of the kitchen but got up to investigate just what exactly their owners were doing.

Whitney felt a cold nose goose her, and the way Steven jumped, he'd gotten the same treatment.

"Ralph's not going to bite my bare ass, is he?"

"I don't think so."

Then again, she'd never had her legs wrapped around a naked man in front of him before.

"Let's take this into the bedroom," he suggested.

"Good idea," she giggled again.

What was with all the giggling? She wasn't a giggly kind of a woman. She was a badass, boss lady who knew what the fuck she wanted.

Except, right now, she wanted to be giggly and taken care of. Maybe even bossed around a little.

And the man she had in mind to take charge was strutting naked up the stairs of his house with her in his arms.

He kicked the bedroom door closed with his heel, shutting it with a loud thud. The room was dark, and Whitney had a hard time seeing when he set her on the floor.

The carpet felt soft and plush under her feet. Expensive.

That was the last coherent thought she had before she was pressed against the wall, her arms pinned over her head as his mouth came down on hers.

It wasn't a gentle kiss. It was possessive and passionate. His tongue explored her mouth with authority, like he owned it. Her brain told her to push back—never relinquish control. But then his mouth found her neck as he rocked his naked dick between her legs—her arms still trapped against the wall by his strength, and all she wanted to do was surrender to him.

He pulled the strings of her bikini top, and it easily dropped to the floor. She arched her back to press her breasts against his mouth as he hungrily suckled her left boob, then her right. Moaning, "So fucking beautiful," when he mashed them together and alternated sucking and biting each stiff nipple.

She could feel how wet her pussy was and shamelessly rubbed against his stiff cock that was nestled between her legs. The bikini bottoms provided just enough barrier to be a tease to them both.

"I have condoms in my suitcase," he whispered when he finally let her arms down.

She smirked. "I brought the party pack, too. We can use them... if you want. I'm on the pill, and I'm clean."

He'd been directing her toward his king-size bed but stopped short. "You'd trust me to go bareback?"

She felt the scowl form on her lips. *Way to kill the mood, Romeo.*

"Should I not? I guess I just assumed you were smart about safe sex and probably got tested regularly—given where you work."

"Oh, I always wrap my little general."

"Oh my god. Did you just call your dick *your little general?*"

"I did." He seemed not the least embarrassed about that. "And I was clean the last time I was tested about six months ago." He quickly added, "I mean, I've always been clean—but the last time, I was also clean."

"Six months, though?" *A condom it is.*

He grinned when he reached between her legs and pulled her swimsuit to the side to run his fingers through her wet folds. "The last time I had sex was seven months ago."

"You have me beat by a month."

"So, you're okay not using a condom?"

"You know, all this talk about sex with other people, STD tests, generals, and condoms is going to make whether to wear one moot."

"Point taken."

He picked her up at the waist and tossed her onto the bed, then stalked toward her on the mattress on his hands and knees. Tugging her swimsuit off in one movement, he spread her legs wide and nestled his broad shoulders between them.

"Where were we?" he asked, his hot breath teasing her wet center that was on full display for him.

"You asked about a condom."

He swiped his tongue down her slit, then up again. "Oh yeah. Well, we're not going to need to worry about that for a while. Get comfortable, beautiful; you're not going anywhere until you've screamed my name more than once. I don't care if it takes all night."

He'd told her that before, then had her seeing stars.

Trouble...

****

Steven

He felt her legs tighten as he swirled his tongue around her clit. His fingers continued fucking her, and she panted, "Oh, god, Steven."

"That's it, baby. Say my name when you come again."

Her first orgasm was with his tongue inside her while he polished her clit with his fingers. He'd simply switched positions for Round Two.

Witnessing her come undone was the sexiest thing he'd ever seen, and he wanted nothing more than to sink himself deep inside her. But he was on a mission—he'd told her she was going to come more than once from his tongue before he was through, and he meant it.

"Fuck, you taste good," he moaned.

Her spasming body as she called out his name fed his ego. *Mission accomplished.* He didn't relent until she squeezed her legs tight around his head and cried out, "No more!"

With a satisfied grin, he slid up the side of her body and kissed her shoulder while her chest heaved up and down as she gulped for air.

"You're pretty damn good at that."

"I aim to please."

Rolling to her side to face him with a siren's smile, she then leaned over and put her lips on his chest, murmuring, "What a coincidence. So do I," before kissing down his stomach.

She took her time moving down his body while his cock throbbed in anticipation—something he was sure was her intention. It'd already been leaking the entire time he was between her legs, and he was worried the minute her lips touched his dick, he would explode.

His stomach clenched when he felt her tongue swirl around his helmet, then down his shaft and back up. When she took him deep in her throat, he started going through the Padres baseball stats—he did have his pride; coming like a schoolboy only a minute after she touched him would *not* be cool.

Her mouth bobbed up and down on his cock, while one hand stroked from the base and the other cupped his balls.

"Fuuuuuck," he groaned loudly.

Then she moaned—the vibrations hitting his dick meant game over.

"Baby, I'm going to come."

It was just good manners not to erupt in a woman's mouth without warning.

She kept sucking and stroking, and he worried she hadn't heard him, so he tugged on her hair. "Whitney…"

Their eyes locked, and she smiled as she took him deeper in her throat.

"You are so fucking hot."

She continued bobbing her head up and down as if to say, "I know."

Steve felt his balls tighten, and he grunted loudly, until he let out a long, "Fuuuuck yesss," as he shot his load into her mouth.

Whitney was fucking amazing and kept going until he'd spilled every drop and his sensitive cock made him jumpy.

Hopping off the bed, she returned a minute later with a towel and cleaned him up. Apparently, she was a spitter—he'd had no idea.

"That was… damn," he crooned as he stared down at her tending to his cock. He liked how that looked.

"I told you, I also aim to please."

Steven took the towel from her and tossed it toward the hamper in his closet, then tugged her hand until she was nestled next to him.

"Get your rest, baby. You're going to need it."

CHAPTER FOURTEEN

Whitney

The morning alarm on her Fitbit went off, and she groaned out loud as she turned over. Steven had woken her up in the middle of the night to have sex—no condom, and he was as good with his cock as he was with his tongue. Which had been totally worth the sleep interruption, but now, the dogs needed to be let out.

"I've got them," he said with a peck to her temple. "Go back to sleep."

"Thank you," she murmured and dozed off again.

The smell of coffee woke her the second time. A quick glance at her wrist told her she'd slept for another hour and a half.

She ran a brush through her hair and brushed her teeth before slipping on the button-up he'd worn yesterday and going down to the kitchen.

"Good morning," she said with a shy smile when she saw him sitting at the breakfast nook looking at his phone.

He looked up with a wide grin. "Good morning, beautiful. There's coffee. Are you hungry?"

"I can just make toast or something," she replied as she opened the cabinet nearest the coffee maker and pulled out a mug.

The chair made a scraping noise as he stood up. "Nonsense. Breakfast is the most important meal of the day."

He skimmed his arm around her waist as he walked by her pouring coffee and murmured in her ear, "Especially after all the calories we burned last night."

She couldn't help but smile as she sat on the barstool at the island and scooped sugar into her mug. "Can I help?"

"Nope."

"Oh, come on, let me do something."

He whisked eggs in a bowl. "There's not much for you to do. I guess you could make toast."

"On it."

They danced around each other in the kitchen, laughing and talking while the dogs lay side by side on the fluffy dog bed, intently watching their owners.

"I think Ralph's in love," she quipped.

Steven looked over at the pups from where he was flipping an omelet and smiled. "Lola, too."

He set a plate with the piping-hot breakfast in front of her. "Want to take them for a walk on the beach after breakfast for some of that manufactured romance you were talking about?"

She had a feeling romance with the sexy doctor—manufactured or not—was dangerous.

Still, she heard herself saying, "That sounds like fun."

****

Steven

He wasn't sure who had more fun that day—the dogs or him. He and Whitney walked along the beach, holding hands, as Ralph and Lola frolicked in the surf, and then they all walked to MacMillan Wharf and had lunch on the dog friendly patio.

There hadn't been a lull in their conversation the entire day. She was a few years younger than him and had three half-siblings: two brothers from her dad's side and a sister on her mom's.

"I have three younger sisters. Two are doctors, and Hope, the one who just moved in with me, is an engineer by trade."

"Wow, your parents must be proud. Three physicians and an engineer."

"Well, sort of. Ava, my partner-in-crime growing up, has her PhD in chemistry and used to work in a research lab—although right now she's a successful real estate agent, and Grace, the baby of the family, just graduated with her degree in psychiatry and will be starting her residency in the fall."

"Wow... that's quite an accomplishment. I think one of my brothers is in jail, and the other was working landscaping last time I checked. My sister just started high school this year."

He nodded in understanding. "I was eleven when Grace was born. My mom had a hard time getting pregnant after Ava."

"Amber was my mom's second-chance baby. My parents were junkies when I was growing up, but my senior year in high school, my mom met a man, got clean, and got pregnant my sophomore year in college."

What the fuck?

"So, who took care of you? Did you have grandparents to help raise you?"

Her smile was polite.

"Sort of. They didn't know I even existed until Family Services contacted them when I was thirteen. My mom's parents agreed to take me to keep me out of foster care, and my dad's parents had me visit during the summers, but again, I didn't meet them until I was already a teenager." She gave a little laugh. "And teenagers aren't exactly known for their sparkling personalities. To say I had a big chip on my shoulder would be an understatement."

"Who could blame you?" He could only imagine what her childhood was like but didn't want to pry. He had a feeling she didn't share that part of her life with just anyone—and he was honored that she trusted him with it. The fact that she was so successful seemed to say a lot about her fortitude. "What about now? Are you close with them?"

"I visit on holidays."

He didn't get to see his family as much as he'd like, only getting away two or three times a year to travel across the country to visit. But he talked to someone from his family—be it his mom, dad, or sisters a few times a week. They were his support, even from three thousand miles away. Who did Whitney have in her corner?

"Stop it." Her tone was sharp.

He furrowed his brows. "Stop what?"

"Feeling sorry for me. No, my childhood wasn't ideal like yours was, but I survived. And it made me who I am—a kickass lawyer who doesn't need to rely on anyone. So, save your pity."

"It's not pity. If anything, it's admiration. But there's nothing wrong with people being in your corner, Whit. Someone having your back doesn't make you weak."

"I agree. But relying on them does."

He wasn't sure how, but he was going to prove to her that she could count on him, and it wouldn't make her weak. If anything, she'd be stronger for it.

CHAPTER FIFTEEN

Whitney

"I can't remember the last time I was this relaxed," she murmured with her head resting against the lounger on his patio, a glass of red wine in her hand, as she looked out at the sun low on the ocean. He'd just finished giving her another massage. The man had magic hands.

Steven was stretched out in the matching lounger next to hers, while the dogs lay together not far away on the brick pavers. They'd had a great day together—the best she'd had in a long time. And they didn't do much, just walked on the beach, then around the little shops, had lunch, talked, and laughed—a lot. Dr. Ericson was witty as hell, with charm to boot, and Whitney found her cheeks hurting by mid-afternoon from smiling and laughing so much.

"The ocean tends to have that effect on you."

"I think it was the massage," she teased. "But the water is nice, too."

"I'm glad you enjoyed it. There's more where that came from. All you have to do is say when."

"I'll keep that in mind." They lay quiet for a minute, listening to the waves crashing onto the beach.

"Even growing up surfing the Pacific almost every day, I'll never get tired of this. I was going crazy in the city being away from it. To be honest, I don't know what I would have done if I hadn't been able to find a place close to the water. I probably would have moved."

"Would you have gone back to San Diego?"

"I think so. Leaving my family to go away for my residency was tough, and I'd always planned on returning to Cali. But my fellowships fell in place, and then the position at Boston General became available, and it felt like I was supposed to be on the East Coast rather than the Pacific. Finding this house seemed to confirm that—much to my mother's dismay and disagreement. I'm on her shitlist again for bringing Hope here, although I made a surprise trip to see her on Mother's Day weekend, so that bought me some forgiveness."

"I'm sure it wasn't hard for her to forgive you—I bet she adores you."

He flashed her his toothpaste-commercial smile. "Of course she does. Have you met me?"

"Yeah, exactly."

He slid off his lounger and onto hers, wrapped his hand around her waist, and brushed his nose against her neck.

"Are you succumbing to my charms, Counselor?"

"Obviously—you got me here, didn't you? You weren't supposed to like dogs, too."

That made him laugh out loud. "Who doesn't like dogs?"

"Lots of people."

"Well, I guess fortunately for me then, I happen to love dogs. Are you going to be my date to the Animal Rescue Foundation fundraiser? I'm buying a table, you know."

His cockiness made her smile.

"I wish I could, but I have my own table."

That caused his face to fall.

"Seriously? That was supposed to be part of my attempt to court you."

"Did you just use the word *court* as a verb? What are you—ninety?"

"I happen to think it's an excellent word—especially given your profession, and it perfectly describes what I'm going to do to you." He massaged her breasts over her t-shirt, "Among other things."

The sex she could handle. The relationship thing? *Courting...* as he called it, *that* was a bad idea.

She traced her finger along the outline of the bulge in his shorts. "I like what you've been doing so far."

"You don't say..."

He tasted like the expensive red they'd been drinking as his tongue plundered her mouth in search of hers until they happily tangled together.

A small groan escaped his throat when he turned in the lounger to envelop her body under his. Normally, this would have made her feel claustrophobic, and she would have quickly switched positions. Instead, she felt safe. Protected.

Why did he have to be so dang *likeable* in addition to being sexy as hell? She'd been looking for a reason all day to write him off, and he'd only gotten more endearing. There was no doubt, he was used to being in charge, but he did so in a way that almost made her feel like a princess—not just with his gentlemanly ways, but how he'd doted on her. She'd felt special.

And he was so flipping hot. His surfer-boy good looks got him more than one doubletake from the opposite sex while they were on the wharf that day. She couldn't even blame the women. He was tall, blonde, and tan, with a great body—not too bulky and not too skinny.

Yet, he'd only had eyes for her. Making her feel even more special.

And he was a successful doctor, who loved dogs.

Dammit.

Then there was the matter of his magic tongue and yummy cock.

She didn't stand a chance.

As his fingers skimmed her thigh under her dress, she wondered, maybe that wasn't such a bad thing?

****

Steven

She'd been driving him crazy all day in that little aqua-blue sundress that slid up her thigh when she'd readjust her ponytail. She caught him staring in one of the shops and gave him a little laugh while muttering, "Weirdo."

"Honey, I'd be weird if I *didn't* stare."

That garnered him a shy smile.

He liked when she was unsure and vulnerable. He got the feeling few got to see that side of her.

Now she was underneath him on the patio lounger, arching her body up to meet his and mewling as his fingers inched up her thighs toward the promised land.

Something the dogs didn't approve of because they had gotten up from the rug they had been lying on and were now barking at them.

"Ralph! It's okay!" Whitney assured her pup while Steven did the same with Lola.

"I think they're confused," she said with a laugh.

He rolled to the side of her, grumbling, "Cockblocked by my own dog," while the dogs nudged their noses between their bodies, as if to separate them.

She rubbed the bulge over his shorts and kissed his cheek. "Not blocked—just delayed a little."

He stood up and offered his hand. "Let's give them a treat to keep them busy while I take you to the bedroom and do dirty things to you."

She took his offered hand. "How dirty are we talking here, doctor?"

"Filthy."

"I like a man who can talk dirty..."

She said it like a challenge. And Steven was more than up for the task.

"I'd smack your ass right now, but I'm pretty sure Ralph would bite my hand off, so I'm going to wait until we're behind closed doors."

Whitney chuckled in response. "That's probably a good idea. I think the hospital would frown on you practicing medicine with a mangled hand."

"Ralph would not like what I'm going to do to his owner." He leaned down to murmur in her ear, "But I think you will."

Her nipples were points when she turned to face him. "Mmm, I bet I will."

"Wait for me in the bedroom, dirty girl. I'll get the dogs situated, then be back in a minute."

She was on the bed, naked with her legs spread wide when Steven walked in the room. "Fuuuuuck," he groaned, dispatching his shirt as he stalked toward her. "You look good enough to eat, baby." His shorts and underwear fell in a heap, and he crawled onto the bed, between her legs.

He could see her center glistening in the moonlight.

"Such a good girl—you're already wet for me."

Her body stiffened when he called her a *good girl*, but she didn't argue or sass him, like he knew she was dying to.

Steven stroked her inner thighs and murmured, "Just relax, Whitney. Let me take care of you, baby."

There was a double entendre in his meaning, and he was certain she knew it. Still, she did as he instructed and relaxed her body, and he dipped his tongue along her slit as she did.

"Fuck, you taste as good as you look."

She bowed off the bed when his tongue found her clit, and he screwed one finger inside her pussy.

"Such a tight, pretty pussy," he hummed against her folds, and she let out a long moan. His little attorney really did like dirty talk.

Increasing the tempo with his fingers, he used his other hand on her clit. "You're a naughty girl. Lying here with your legs spread, waiting for me to fuck you."

Her breathing quickened, and her body tensed, and he knew she was close.

"Come for me, dirty girl. I want to taste you, baby."

Her moans turned into chants of, "Oh god," as her body coiled like a spring. When her entire body shuddered, and she cried out Steven's name while she came undone, he felt like he could conquer the world.

Not giving her any time to recover, he slid his cock inside her quivering pussy and fucked her with the machismo coursing through his veins. He didn't relent until he grunted his release deep inside her, while she raked her nails down his back.

He collapsed on his forearms with his head on the pillow next to hers. His dick was still inside her, while he encased her body under him like he had on the lounger before the dogs so rudely interrupted them.

She strummed the tips of her fingers along his spine and whispered, "We are definitely doing *that* again."

Sign him up. Every damn day.

CHAPTER SIXTEEN

Whitney

Sunday afternoon brought a sense of dread that their time together was coming to an end. Maybe seeing each other occasionally wouldn't be so bad. At least for a booty call.

And a dinner every now and then.

Possibly a few lunches here and there.

And perhaps a few happy hours sporadically.

Ralph and Lola worked together to carry a big stick on the sand while they took one last walk on the beach before getting ready to go back to Boston.

"Look how much they like being together," he laughed as he sat in the sand next to Whitney. "We can't break them up, now."

"Better now than before they get too attached."

He tossed a stone into the ocean and said softly, "What if it's too late?"

What was he saying? That he was already attached to her after only a few dates and a weekend away? That seemed highly unlikely. Still, she heard herself suggesting, "Maybe we could get them together for playdates."

He eagerly pushed closer to her. "Please tell me we can have playdates, too. And in case I'm not making it painfully obvious— when it comes to ours, *playdate* is code for sex."

That made her laugh out loud. "We could probably squeeze in some recreation time."

"How about dinner and a playdate tomorrow night? There's this little restaurant not far from your brownstone that has a dog friendly patio."

"Franco's?"

"Oh, you know it? I like to take Lola there when the weather's nice. I'd invite you to my condo, but I think Hope will be there."

"I love Franco's. We've probably crossed paths there and never even known it."

He took her hand and kissed her knuckles. "Doll, I would have definitely known if I'd crossed your path *anywhere*. So, dinner tomorrow? Does seven thirty work?"

Before she could think twice, she found herself agreeing that the time worked. Then she shook her head, as if snapping herself out of a trance.

"Wait. This..." She gestured between the two of them with her index finger. "It was supposed to be for the weekend only."

He shrugged. "You changed your mind. You're entitled, you know. You're a grown woman who gets to decide who she sees and when."

Steven was right. She *was* a grown woman in charge of her own life. Seeing him again didn't mean her plans changed. She could do what she wanted. And right now, she wanted to have dinner with him tomorrow, so that's what she would do.

CHAPTER SEVENTEEN

Steven

He groaned out loud when he heard the ringtone for the hospital. They were all packed up, but he'd been hoping for one last romp before leaving and had just pulled her onto his lap.

He answered with, "This is Dr. Ericson."

His brows must have furrowed as he listened to the voice on the other end because Whitney shot him a look of concern and stood up.

"I'm at the Cape, but I'll leave now and get there as soon as I can." He ended the call and answered her unspoken question. "There's been a train accident. Casualties are unknown."

She gasped and put her hand to her lips. "Oh, no."

"I'm sorry I have to cut things short."

"Oh my god, don't be sorry. I completely understand. I'm ready if you are."

They were on the road five minutes later. Even the dogs seemed to understand something somber happened; they were the most subdued they'd been all weekend. Either that, or they were just worn out from the nonstop playing they'd done.

The hospital called him with updates, and he did his best to give instructions from the car. If he hurried, he'd arrive just after the first victims.

"I have to drop off my friend, then take my dog home, but I'll get there as soon as I can," he told Dr. Preston through the speakerphone in the Land Rover. "Although I might be able to get a hold of my sister so she can meet me at the hospital to take her."

Whitney's voice was soft from the passenger seat. "Lola can stay with me."

"Hold on a sec, Parker." Steven glanced at her from the driver's seat and asked softly, "Are you sure?"

"Of course."

"Parker, I should be there in forty minutes."

Dr. Preston thanked him, and he ended the call.

"I can call Hope..." he offered.

She shook her head. "Lola's no problem, and frankly, even if she was... I think you getting to the hospital as soon as you can is more important. But fortunately, she's an angel, and Ralph will be thrilled."

He took his eyes off the road to look directly at her as he said, "Thank you. I really appreciate this."

"I'm happy to do it. You need to get to the hospital and help save people's lives; it's the least I can do."

Maybe it was because she was feeding his ego, but in that second, he liked her even more than he already did. And that was saying a lot because he'd been enamored since he met her, and it'd only been getting stronger every day since.

"I'm not sure when I can pick her up..." he warned. "It probably won't be until tomorrow night."

Whitney squeezed his hand on the gear shift. "Relax. She'll be fine. I'll let my dog walker know about her and to expect her tomorrow. I'm sure Claire won't mind walking an extra dog this one time."

"I can let my dogwalker know your address... Billy's already paid for the month, and I think he actually lives closer to you than me, so he'll be happy. Maybe he can coordinate when your girl comes and just swing by then to walk Lola."

"Claire comes on Mondays at one-fifteen, like clockwork. It's after her last class, so she comes by before going home. I don't think she'll mind walking Lola, too..."

"You're already doing me a big favor. I don't want you to be on your dogwalker's shitlist for springing an extra dog on her. Besides, for what Billy charges me, he can be flexible. At least, he better be."

Steven dictated a message to his dogwalker via voice-to-text, telling him Whitney's address and what time he needed to be there.

Billy responded swiftly with a thumb's up emoji—nothing else, which was typical for the carefree twenty-something.

He pulled into Whitney's drive and quickly helped unload her bags and the dogs, then planted a quick kiss on her lips at her door.

"I owe you."

"You really don't, but if you want to think so..."

"I do, and I look forward to paying my debt."

He kissed her again, whispered, "Thank you," one more time, then turned to run down her porch steps to his still-running Land Rover.

He pulled onto the main street in her neighborhood, and his phone pinged with a text from Whitney: **I look forward to that, too.**

****

Whitney

Claire didn't seem excited about the prospect of another dogwalker showing up at Whitney's—even if the guy was only there to walk Lola.

Still, Whitney knew she could rely on the young woman to help Billy in and out of her brownstone.

Ralph wasn't the only one happy to have Lola there for the night. Having Steven's pup stay at her house was comforting for Whitney, like a little piece of Steven was there with her.

It also guaranteed she'd see him again. Not that she needed that extra assurance. He'd made it clear that he wanted to keep seeing her—despite her protests to the contrary.

Whitney was glad she'd relented. They'd had a great time—in and out of bed. As long as they kept it light, there'd be no harm in spending more time together.

I mean, a girl has needs, right?

CHAPTER EIGHTEEN

Steven

He'd been on duty for almost twenty hours before he had a chance to send Whitney a text.

Steven: Sorry I didn't text earlier—this is the first break I've gotten. Thank you again for keeping Lola.

She replied right away.

Whitney: You've got to be exhausted. Lola is welcome anytime. She's such a good girl, and Ralph loves her.

Steven: That's good to hear. Billy's text said there was no problem walking her with Claire.

Whitney: LOL Claire didn't exactly share the same sentiment.

Steven: Oh damn. You'll have to tell me about it when I pick you up for dinner.

Whitney: Let's reschedule that. I can't even imagine how tired you are.

Steven: I'm not too tired to see you. How about I bring takeout?

Whitney: I'll pick up takeout from a little Chinese restaurant by my house. Go home and sleep for as long as you need. And don't worry about Lola. She's fine with me. I promise I'll take good care of her.

Steven: I'd rather sleep in your bed.

He'd written it to be flirty, but he never expected her to respond like she did.

Whitney: I'm going to be at the office for a while, but I can unlock the door from my phone. Make yourself at home. I'll try not to wake you.

Steven: I want you to wake me, otherwise I'll be wide awake at 2 a.m. and starving.

Plus, he wanted to hold her. Maybe fuck her.

Whitney: Okay. I'll wake you up when I get home. After I pick up takeout, it will be closer to 7:30. Let me know what you want.

Steven: Thanks, baby. General Tso's chicken and white rice.

That meant if he left the hospital soon, he'd have time to let the dogs out and get a few hours' sleep before she got home.

He grabbed a quick shower in the doctor's locker room and put on the change of clothes he kept in his locker. He rang her doorbell and waved into the camera, then heard the door unlocking, as if someone were home.

Technology is creepy, he thought as he walked in her front door. The dogs were happy to see him—even Ralph seemed to remember who he was. Either that or he was just following Lola's lead. Either way, he wagged his tail enthusiastically and came when Steven called him back inside after letting them out in the brownstone's little backyard.

Whitney's place was bright and inviting, with a lot of designer touches. Steven had a case of crown-molding envy as he lay on her couch and stared up at the ceiling.

Next thing he knew, he felt a hand on his stomach, and Whitney's voice softly saying, "Baby, why didn't you sleep in my bed?"

It took him a second to remember where he was, and the smell of food made him realize he was hungry. But all of that took a backseat to the fact that she'd called him *baby*.

Or had he just imagined it?

****

Whitney

Steven was groggy when he opened his eyes, but he smiled when he saw her.

"Hi, beautiful. You're home," he murmured as he sat up and pulled her into his lap.

She brushed the hair on the back of his neck with her fingers. "Why didn't you sleep in my bed, silly? It's so much more comfortable than this couch. You said you wanted to sleep in it, remember?"

"I thought the *with you* was implied."

She smiled and shook her head. "I told you I would be late. Promise me that next time, you won't sleep on the couch."

He squeezed her middle. "I like the idea of there being a next time."

So did she, but she wasn't going to admit that—even to herself.

"I brought dinner," she said as she got off his lap and pulled containers from the large brown bag and set them on the coffee table.

"It smells great. I'm starving."

"Are you able to eat when you're working?"

"Usually there's a lull, and I have time to grab a bite in the cafeteria, but not last night. Fortunately, the nurses took care of me and shared their emergency stash of energy bars."

She bet there were more than a few nurses who'd like to take care of him in other ways. The fact that idea made her jealous surprised her.

"I'm glad you didn't starve, but you should consider having your own stash."

"I do, but I'm bad about dipping into it even when it's not an emergency, then I forget to restock it."

Whitney laughed as she dumped some white rice into the orange chicken container.

"You need to add that to your weekly grocery list."

"Who has time to grocery shop on a weekly basis?"

"Ever heard of delivery? You set up a standard weekly order, then you just go in and add to it if you want. But, at the very least. you get the basics every week."

"Maybe with Hope there, I'll think about it. My schedule is so crazy, I worry that the groceries would sit on my doorstep for hours at a time. But I think she'll have a more regular schedule."

"What do you do with Lola now when you can't get home?"

"Well, I have Billy come every day, and my neighbor is helpful."

"Oh, Billy," she said with a smirk. "He and Claire did not hit it off."

"I'm surprised. He usually charms the ladies. I get the feeling he gets away with a lot because of his good looks and charisma. Obviously, that doesn't work on me, but fortunately for him, Lola loves him, and I'm not particularly concerned with how tight he keeps his schedule. As long as he shows up every day—which he does, I don't care about the time."

"Claire is a stickler with time, and he was a half hour late. Let's just say, there was an exchange of words."

"Oh boy. Sorry about that."

"Honestly, I thought it was comical when Claire told me the story. He really got under her skin today."

He set his empty takeout container on her coffee table and wrapped his arms around her middle, while nuzzling her neck. "Maybe they're attracted to each other."

"I kind of got that vibe, too. *The lady doth protest too much, me thinks.*"

Whitney felt his chuckle vibrate through his chest. "Did you explain it's better if she just gives in and goes with it?"

"No, I didn't say anything. Besides, if I had, I would have told her to never surrender."

"But, baby," he murmured as he slid onto the floor between her legs and pushed her skirt up her thighs. "Surrendering is so satisfying."

Whitney closed her eyes with a moan. She couldn't argue with that.

CHAPTER NINETEEN

Steven

He woke up in the middle of the night with Whitney's round bottom snuggled against his hard cock and decided he could get used to this.

She'd been so great, taking Lola and then letting him crash at her place. Even though his condo wasn't that much farther from the hospital than her brownstone, he was happy when she told him to sleep in her bed, even though he'd fallen asleep on her couch. He got to see his dog—and her.

When she'd suggested he stay over, he didn't hesitate to take her up on it. They'd crashed out by nine thirty; dinner and orgasms after a long day of working made that easy.

Steven gently brushed his fingers through her hair as he thought about their time together so far. And how he greedily wanted more.

His crazy schedule had made relationships difficult in the past. No one had understood the sacrifices he had to make for his career. And he hadn't met anyone worth the effort in favor of his job. But he wanted to try with Whitney. It seemed like if anyone would understand what it took to get ahead, it'd be her.

Except she made him not want to work at all. Forget going to the hospital, he'd much rather be hidden away from the world with her by his side. He'd be happy being a beach bum with a little place on the ocean, with Lola, Whitney, and Ralph.

Fortunately for his career path, his sense of duty to his patients would never allow that. Not for long anyway. Although he'd have no problem scheduling time off to take her and the dogs to the Cape for long weekends. Maybe some tropical getaways, too, like Zach did.

As long as I can talk her out of having a schedule once we get there, he thought with a grin as he pulled her closer to him. They'd need flexibility for all the dirty things he wanted to do to her.

Or maybe they'd just need to include it in the schedule.

Thoughts of making love to her on tropical beaches lulled him back to a peaceful sleep. His last coherent thought was, he needed to ask Zach who his travel agent was.

****

Whitney

A foreign noise pulled her from a dead slumber.

"Go back to sleep, baby," Steven's voice, husky from sleep, whispered in her ear.

It was still dark outside, but the absence of his warmth next to her kept from doing as he instructed. She heard him getting dressed.

"Is everything okay?"

"I just got called back to the hospital."

She glanced at the clock on her nightstand. It read 3:36.

"I'm glad we went to bed early."

"Me, too." He sat on the bed next to her and tucked her hair behind her ear. "I hate to ask, but is it okay if Lola stays until I can pick her up later? I can have Billy walk her again—and I'll make sure he's on time this time."

She turned away so not to breathe on him.

"Claire usually comes at noon on Tuesdays. But now that I know he's trustworthy, it's no problem if he doesn't make it then. Just have him text me, and I'll unlock the door remotely."

"Thanks. And now I owe you double."

He made her smile, even half-asleep. "Like I said before, you really don't, but if you want to think you do, I'll take it."

"I was thinking we should do a long weekend to somewhere in the Caribbean, soon."

"Steven, we've barely even known each other a week..."

"So?"

"So, it's a little early to be planning trips together."

He kissed her hair. "We'll talk about it tonight at dinner. Are you working late again?"

"No, I should be home by six." She was too tired to recognize that she should protest having dinner again with him.

"I'll be by then." He kissed her cheek this time. "Make sure you eat breakfast."

"Mmm hmm," she mumbled with her eyes closed.

Her doorbell rang ten minutes before she was set to leave for work. The same delivery driver from last week stood on her doorstep with another brown paper bag and a cup of coffee.

"Steven says it's the most important meal of the day," the young man said as he handed her the breakfast, then turned and ran down the steps to his waiting car.

She smiled when she closed the door, looking down at Lola, who had been supervising the transaction, along with Ralph.

"Your dad is pretty great," she told the waiting pup, who seemed to thump her tail in agreement.

Oh, this was bad.

CHAPTER TWENTY

Steven

Whitney: It's like déjà vu all over again. Thank you for breakfast.

Steven: I'd rather have made it myself and served it to you in bed, but that was an acceptable alternative.

Whitney: Well, it was very thoughtful, and unnecessary, btw. I usually just grab a granola bar on my way out the door.

Steven: Thank you for proving my point that it was completely necessary.

She sent him an eyeroll emoji, and he sent her back a kissing face. Their text exchange was enough to keep a smile on his face until lunchtime, when he dared text her again.

Steven: Did Billy show up on time?

Whitney: I'm not sure. He hasn't contacted me to let him in, so maybe? Either that, or he hasn't arrived yet.

Steven: I should be getting off by three, so I can make dinner tonight.

Whitney: At my house or yours?

Steven: Either one.

He thought about it for a second and decided it was time to bite the bullet and let Hope meet her.

Steven: Actually, let's do my place. I can introduce you to Hope.

Then he'd tell his younger sibling to get lost for a while after dinner.

Whitney: Okay, text me your address, and I'll bring Lola home after I get out of work.

Steven: Ralph is welcome, too.

Whitney: I think those two need a break from each other.

Steven: Why? Are they misbehaving?

Whitney: No, quite the contrary. They're both as good as gold. I just worry they're going to get too attached.

Steven: No such thing, baby girl.

He could practically see her pursed lips while she muttered, "Hmph."

He'd make a believer out of her yet.

Steven: See you tonight.

****

Whitney

He opened the door to find her holding two dog leashes while trying to balance a cheesecake she'd picked up at her favorite bakery on the way home.

"I thought…" he started, looking at the dogs.

"Ralph almost lost his mind when I leashed Lola up but not him," she explained as she handed him the dessert. "I figured I either brought him, or came home to a destroyed brownstone."

Steven moved to the side to let her and the dogs through.

"It's good that you brought him then."

He set the pink bakery box on the entry table and knelt to unhook Lola's lead and rub her ears, telling her how happy he was to see her in a high-pitched voice. He then unhooked Ralph's lead and scratched his ear affectionately, too, before standing up straight.

"Go show Ralph your toys," he told his pup like she was his kid.

Whitney laughed when the two raced away, as if they were going to do just that.

"Those two..." She shook her head.

"Are lucky they found each other," he said with a wink as he reached for her.

"Something like that." She refused to take the bait he'd lobbed in like a softball. Instead, she turned her face up to be kissed.

"Hi, beautiful," he murmured before planting his mouth on hers.

His lips were soft as he kissed her tenderly. She let out a deep sigh and felt herself relax in his arms. It should be alarming how easily he made her do that.

"Hi," she whispered as she attempted to twirl the short hair at the back of his head. "Something smells good."

"I hope you're hungry."

"Starving. I was thankful I had a good breakfast because I had to eat lunch at my desk."

"Hey, Steve," a woman's voice called. "I shut your burner off—oh." A beautiful blonde woman with long, toned legs stood in the doorway to what Whitney assumed was the kitchen, wearing yoga pants and a tank top. "Hi, I'm Hope—sister and roomie." She offered her hand with a warm smile. "You must be Whitney. I've heard a lot about you."

Whitney glanced sideways at Steven, wondering what he'd told his sister about her. Hope must have caught the side eye because she added, "All good things."

"It's great to meet you. How are you liking Boston?"

"Well, it's been interesting so far."

Steven grumbled, "I told you—just let me talk to Parker."

Hope turned to him, her hand on her hip. "I don't need my big brother to fight my battles for me. I can handle Evan Lacroix."

"The point is you shouldn't have to."

"Please. Just let me deal with it."

"Fine," Steven said with a sigh. "But he's fair game if he acts like an ass in my ER."

Hope rolled her eyes. "I doubt he'll be anything but professional in *your* ER." She used air quotes around *your*.

"Unless he's a patient. The rules don't apply when you're a patient—you know that."

"If he's a patient, he better go to Mercy General."

They walked into the kitchen, and Hope gasped theatrically. "Are you saying you'd let your personal feelings keep you from providing Evan Lacroix with the best care possible, Dr. Ericson?"

Steven pulled plates from the cupboard. "No, I'd give him the best care, but my bedside manner might be lacking."

Whitney was dying to know what Evan Lacroix did to get on Steven's bad side.

"I think you're all talk, big brother," Hope said with an eyeroll as she distributed the silverware.

Steven changed the subject. "Sweetness, do you want a glass of wine?"

"Yes, please. What can I do to help?"

"Not a thing. We've got it under control," he said, pouring her a glass of wine.

Hope set a large salad bowl on the table, while he pulled a casserole dish from the oven. The siblings laughed and teased each other as they prepped dinner, and Whitney felt like she was witnessing a slice of what it had been like for them growing up.

"Were you two close as kids?"

"Oh, no. He and my older sister Ava were, but they're less than eighteen months apart."

"Hope didn't come along until I was nine," he supplied.

"So, he was off to college by the time I was in third grade. But he was always a great big brother." Hope looked at him with adoration. "Grace and I knew we could always go to him if we needed help."

"Grace?" Whitney asked. "Oh, she's your younger sister—the psychiatrist, right?"

"Yeah. She was so stressed when she was applying to med school—Steve was great. He took a week off work and helped her with her applications. She got into every school she applied to."

"Aw, what an amazing brother," Whitney said, rubbing his arm.

Steven made a face and shook his head. "I didn't do anything other than hold her hand."

"She got a B in her stats class, and you would have thought the world was coming to an end," Hope said, pouring water into the glasses on the table.

Steven laughed at the memory. "Her test scores were so high, there was no way she wasn't getting into wherever she applied. But she wouldn't listen, so it was just easier to come home and walk her through everything and calm her down."

"She still talks about how you saved the day."

"It wasn't a big deal," he said dismissively.

"It was to her. You came through for her."

Whitney wasn't surprised. He was proving over and over that he was someone who could be counted on.

But she would never put that to the test.

CHAPTER TWENTY-ONE

Whitney

Dinner with Steven and Hope was fun. The two had her laughing the entire meal. There was obvious love between the siblings. How lucky for them to have grown up in such a nurturing household.

Whitney wondered how differently her life would have turned out if she would have had people looking out for her who weren't on the government's payroll. She was grateful to the teachers who exhibited kindness and made sure she had food in her backpack on Fridays, so she didn't go hungry over the weekend. They were the light in her otherwise chaotic childhood. The social workers did the best they could once they were finally called by a concerned neighbor when her mother was passed out in the street. But the innocence of childhood had been long gone by the time CPS knocked on her door at the age of thirteen.

Watching Steven and Hope interact with one another and talk about their childhoods, it was easy to see why Steven couldn't understand why Whitney was the way she was. Therapy had helped with the chip on her shoulder, but she would always be jaded and guarded.

She worried that she'd be a terrible mother because she never had a proper role model. Her therapist assured her she'd be fine if the time ever came.

Whitney wasn't so sure and had considering having her tubes tied to guarantee she wouldn't have children and wreak havoc on innocent lives. But she'd yet to schedule an appointment to explore it further.

Maybe she should. There was no way she'd be able to give her offspring the type of childhood the Ericsons had. Something every kid deserved. She wouldn't know how.

Sitting with her dinner companions, Whitney laughed until her sides hurt as they talked about what it was like growing up with Richard and Frannie Ericson as their parents. Frankly, it sounded like heaven.

Hope teased Steven about how excited he'd been to get an NSYNC letterman jacket and concert tickets for Christmas one year.

Steven sang, "Bye, bye, bye," to his sister, complete with the hand choreography from the music videos.

Hope wasn't the least bit fazed and completely ignored what he implied. Instead, she asked, "What about you, Whitney? What was your best Christmas present as a kid?"

Steven took a breath through his nose and looked at Whitney with questioning eyes—as if looking for a sign from her that she wanted him to change the subject. She'd shared with him what some of her childhood had been like, and she knew he was only trying to protect her. Still, she could answer the question.

"Probably a baby doll I got when I was in second grade."

She remembered it was second grade because Mrs. Lewis, her teacher, had been the one to give it to her, along with food that she could easily hide, and a delicious chocolate bar she'd never tried before.

Mrs. Lewis had handed her the bag before she left her classroom to get on the bus for the long Christmas break, putting her hand on her shoulder and telling her, "Everything in here is for *you*. You only share if you want to."

Whitney hadn't wanted to. She made that chocolate bar last an entire week, eating just one square after she ate her only meal of the day—that was also found in the bag Mrs. Lewis had given her.

Mrs. Lewis had been one of her shining lights. Whitney invited her to her law school graduation, where the older woman openly cried and apologized that she didn't do more.

"You did more than you could possibly know," she'd assured her former teacher.

Whitney smiled at Hope. "I actually still have her tucked away in a box in my closet. She's one of my most treasured possessions."

Steven reached under the table and squeezed her hand, as if to say he knew there was more to her story.

"I thought you were going out tonight with people from the hospital. Shouldn't you get ready?"

"Really subtle, big brother," Hope said, rolling her eyes as she got up. She cleared her and Whitney's plate but left

Steven's. He smirked at her attempt to slight him and called out, "Don't worry—I'll take care of my dishes."

Hope sighed theatrically as she set the plates down in the sink and came back for his place setting.

"Only because you won't take my rent money," she said before breaking into a grin and kissing the top of his head.

"Come on," Steven offered Whitney his hand with a wink, then said loudly for his sister's benefit, "Let's go make out in the living room."

"Ew. Can't you at least wait until I leave?"

He wrapped his arms around Whitney's middle as they walked out of the kitchen, murmuring in her ear, "Nope."

****

Steven

It physically hurt when he closed his front door after walking Whitney and Ralph to her car. He'd asked her to stay while they were naked in his bed, but she'd given him a sad smile and said she had an early meeting in the morning.

"So, just leave from here," he moaned as he kissed her neck. "Ralph can stay."

"I don't have any clothes."

"Just wear what you wore here."

That caused her to laugh. "I think Alan Crawford would fire me on the spot if I showed up to the office in jeans."

"Good, then I can have you all to myself."

"Oh, please." She ran her fingers through his hair while he kept kissing her. "With how much you work?"

That caused him to lift his head and look at her. "Fair enough. Go work with Zach, but do it part time. Or better yet, start your own firm instead so you can be completely flexible with your hours."

"And work around your schedule, I assume?"

"Duh."

She shook her head. "Maybe someday."

"Why not now?"

"In about four more years. I need to have a business plan in place and a year's salary saved first."

"My little planner. Have you given any thought to what Zach said—"

She cut him off. "I'm happy where I am."

Steven didn't understand how that was possible, but she'd made it clear it wasn't up for discussion.

"Well, four years will fly by."

"Yep. But it means I have to go home tonight."

"Why didn't you bring clothes for tomorrow with you?" he whined as she eased out of bed and started getting dressed. "You need to bring at least two work outfits and two casual outfits to leave here."

Her only response was a smile as she pulled her shirt over her head.

"I'll do the same." Steven didn't care that she hadn't extended the same invitation. He did, though, stop short of inviting himself back to her brownstone. However, he would have taken her up on it in a heartbeat if she would have offered.

He took comfort in her slow walk to the front door and Ralph's blatant disobedience as he lay next to Lola when Whitney called him.

"Ralph!" she called again—firmer this time.

The Labrador mix whined, then slunk to the front door, clearly conflicted at leaving his girlfriend.

I know the feeling, pal.

Except Steven couldn't even call Whitney his girlfriend yet.

"God, he's making me feel bad," she lamented as she clipped the leash on.

He slipped an arm around her waist. "So, stay."

"I can't. I already told you I have an early meeting tomorrow that my boss will be at."

"I should have cooked dinner at your house," he groused.

That elicited a laugh from her, and she put her hand on his shoulder to stand on her tiptoes and kiss his cheek. "Next time."

He gripped her hips tighter. "Tomorrow?"

He knew that made him sound desperate. He didn't care—he was.

She dropped to flat feet. "Aren't you sick of me yet?"

Steven kept his eyes locked on hers. "Nope. Not even a little."

She returned his stare for a beat. "You will be." Then a small smile crept across her face like she hadn't just predicted their relationship imploding. "But since it hasn't happened yet... I'll be home earlier than usual tomorrow, since I'm going in early, so I can make dinner. What time are you scheduled to leave the hospital tomorrow?"

"Five."

"I'll have dinner ready by six. Bring Lola, of course."

His heart beat faster, and he wanted to do a fist pump, but he played it cool. Well, as cool as he could after practically begging to spend more time with her.

He dropped a kiss to her forehead. "I'll bring her and dessert."

They held hands as they walked to her car, and he helped get Ralph situated, then kissed her again.

With a sigh, she pulled away from his embrace and slid in the driver's seat.

"Text me when you get home," he told her before closing the door.

And now here he was—acting like a lovesick teenager waiting for her text before going to bed.

Times certainly had changed. He couldn't even remember the woman's name that he'd slept with seven months ago at a conference in Hawaii. He'd been thankful to find her gone when he woke up the next morning. They only exchanged a nod when they ran into each other again at the luncheon later that day, and that had been fine by him.

He only slept with women he met outside the hospital after making the mistake of hooking up with a nurse from the ICU who'd thought it meant more to him than it did. He'd been screwing nurses and other doctors regularly, and they'd all seemed to share the understanding that it was a casual, one-time thing. Scratching a mutual itch.

Then came the Addison Hall incident, and he immediately quit dipping his pen in the company ink. His career was far too important to be derailed by some crazy nurse who tried to stir up drama—all because he hadn't called the next day. He didn't need to get laid that badly.

And now here he was, thinking about running away to be a beach bum with Whitney.

He had it bad.

But as he lay staring at his ceiling, that he now noticed was lacking in the crown molding department, he wondered if she was right. Would the shine eventually wear off?

From where he was standing—or rather, lying, it didn't seem possible. If anything, she'd only become more enchanting.

CHAPTER TWENTY-TWO

Whitney

She heard the ping of a text message as she lugged the grocery bags up her brownstone steps but didn't look at the message until she'd set everything on the counter and let Ralph out. What she read, made her face fall.

Steven: Not sure how late I'm going to be. Raincheck on you cooking dinner?

Whitney: No problem. Everything okay?

Steven: Bad accident on I-695. Helicopters are en route now. I should have a better ETA when they get here. I still want to see you tonight, and I can still bring dessert.

She was disappointed—she'd researched recipes for Swedish meatballs and was going to try to impress him with a dish from his motherland. But she understood this was the nature of his job.

Whitney: What kind of dessert?

Steven: Whatever you want, baby. He included a winking emoji.

Whitney: I like you. And cheesecake.

Steven: At the same time?

Whitney: I hadn't thought of that, but the idea has possibilities.

He sent her back emojis of a smiling devil face, an eggplant, and a slice of cake. **See you later.**

****

Steven

He didn't make it to Whitney's house that night.

Or the next.

He had been working nonstop, and when he wasn't working, he was sleeping. He was grateful Hope was now staying with him to help with Lola.

Friday afternoon, he sent Whitney a text.

Steven: Can you take Monday off? I want to go down the Cape tomorrow. I think the only way I'm going to avoid working 18-hour days is if I'm out of town.

Whitney: I can't. I have court.

Steven: Can you go tomorrow?

The three little dots appeared, then disappeared, several times, as if she was editing her reply. Finally...

Whitney: I can, but I'll have to do some work while I'm there.

Steven: I don't care. I'll lie with my head in your lap while you work. I just want to be next to you. Fuck, I've missed your face.

Whitney: I've missed yours, too.

Steven: Do you want to have dinner tonight?

Again, with the three dots starting and stopping and starting again.

Whitney: I'm sorry. I made plans to go to happy hour with my coworkers. I just assumed you'd be working again.

He couldn't fault her, but he desperately wanted to see her.

Steven: Okay. I'll pick you up in the morning. Eight too early?

Whitney: Eight is fine, but do you want to come to happy hour tonight?

Fuck no, he didn't want to spend time in a bar with people he didn't know and compete for her attention. But he wanted to be the one taking her home afterwards, so...

Steven: Baby, you say when and where, and I'll be there.

CHAPTER TWENTY-THREE

Whitney

She didn't know what possessed her to invite Steven to happy hour with her colleagues. Frankly, she didn't know what had possessed *her* to say yes to the happy hour invitation.

That wasn't true. She hadn't been looking forward to another night of staring at her phone, wishing he'd text while she did anything she could to occupy her mind. She wasn't a look-at-her-phone-obsessively-wishing-a-man-would-call type of woman. At least, she never had been, and she didn't like that she was becoming one. So, when Laura, the lead paralegal, asked her to come to happy hour—like she always did on Fridays—Whitney shocked them both by agreeing.

"Yes!" Laura had said with a shake of her fist. Whitney pulled her shoulders back in surprise at the woman's excitement, so Laura explained, "It's just you hardly ever go. You work too hard not to loosen up every now and then."

Drinks with coworkers that she had nothing in common with other than work, so that was all they were going to talk about, didn't constitute as letting loose in Whitney's book.

Letting loose for Whitney involved a certain blond-haired doctor, preferably naked.

Laura interrupted her thoughts. "Everyone usually gets there around five, but we send someone early to make sure we have enough tables for the group."

"Tables—plural? How many people go?"

Maybe this was something she should have been going to more often. The last time she went, there'd been six people: two paralegals, the front receptionist, Whitney, and two other lawyers.

"Depends on the week. Usually twenty or so."

That many? How did I not know?

Probably because she'd been busy keeping her head down and working her ass off. And, again, had no interest in socializing with anyone from the firm outside of work. Not exactly the best strategy for her future networking. She'd always just assumed the offices were empty by five on Friday because it was the start of the weekend.

"How long do people stay?"

Laura shrugged. "It varies. Some people leave by six. The single people usually leave a lot later."

"I probably won't get there until after six," Whitney warned.

"You'll have to pay full price, then. Happy hour ends at six."

She smiled. "That's okay." She could swing the extra two bucks for her glass of white wine.

Best of all, she wouldn't think of Steven.

When he unexpectedly asked her to dinner, she had been filled with regret for accepting Laura's invitation. Whitney had no desire to go to happy hour now but felt like it'd be bad form to back out once she'd gotten a better offer.

But she *really* wanted to see Steven.

And apparently, he felt the same because he accepted her invite to happy hour with no hesitation.

Except, shit.

What would she introduce him as? He wasn't her boyfriend... was he?

No. No. No. She didn't want a boyfriend—especially not Dr. Steven Ericson. He'd wreck her and her plans.

The old saying her favorite law professor used to spout popped into her head. *If it looks like a duck, swims like a duck, and quacks like a duck, then it probably is a duck.*

Whitney was so ducked.

****

Steven

It took a second for his eyes to adjust when he walked into the dark bar, the smell of colognes and perfumes mingled with greasy food filled the air. He looked around for a few seconds until his eyes fell on her, and he couldn't help but smile. She wore a grey suit like the one she'd had on when he'd first met her, except the jacket was now hung over the back of her chair, so her cleavage teased through her white silk blouse. Her chestnut hair was in a messy bun on top of her head like she tended to do at the end of the day, and her fucking glossy, red lips just begged to be kissed.

There's my girl.

He stopped short. They'd only known each other two weeks, yet he already wanted her to be his girl. He also knew that Whitney, on the other hand, was not on board.

She's not your girl, he reminded himself.

But as he started toward her again, Steven noticed the man in a suit that she had been talking to put his hand on her arm, and his hackles went up.

It sure as fuck felt like she was his girl. And he was going to stake his claim, whether she was on board or not.

Wrapping his arm around her waist from behind, his lips moved against her ear as he whispered, "Hi, baby."

Her body that had gone rigid when he first touched her, relaxed against him. She turned to him with a smile. "Hi."

The other man hadn't moved, so Steven dipped down to plant a chaste, but possessive, kiss on her lips. "I fucking missed you."

She stared at him wide eyed, and he couldn't look away. A man could get lost in that sapphire gaze.

He'd been on a mission, to make sure the man in the suit knew she was taken, and now it seemed like no one else was even in the bar with them.

"I missed you, too."

He leaned down and kissed her again, less chaste this time, and he felt her hand slide around his neck while the other held onto his shoulder for support.

Or restraint.

She broke the kiss and looked up at him with a dazed smile. Steven knew the feeling.

A red-headed waitress in a white tank top and dark, painted-on jeans interrupted with, "What can I get you?"

He glanced at the near-empty wine glass in front of Whitney. "Do you want another one?"

"Um, sure. One more." Lifting the glass to her lips, she drained the contents, then set it on the server's tray with a smile.

"I'll have a scotch and soda. Glenlivet, if you have it."

"Last time I checked we did," she said as she scribbled on a notepad. Without another word, the server disappeared, and Steven turned his attention back to Whitney.

The man who she'd been talking to when Steven first walked in was still standing there, so he stuck out his hand. "Steven Ericson."

"Greg Stark," the man said as he shook his hand. "I work with Whitney."

Steven looked at her sideways with a grin. "I'm dating her."

"I kind of figured that out. I didn't realize she was seeing someone."

She slipped her hand in Steve's and squeezed while replying, "Now Greg, you know I like to keep my private life private."

"Yeah, I know." Greg turned to Steven. "So, what do you do, Steven?"

"I'm the head of Boston General's ER."

That usually brought the dick measuring to an end. He'd come to learn that men, especially men with high-powered jobs, liked to compare careers and judge if a man was a worthy competitor.

ER doctor, or *head of ER*, normally made him a formidable opponent.

Greg must have thought so, because he turned to Whitney—his body poised like he was ready to walk away. "Let me know if you want my help. Like I said, I'm happy to lend a hand."

"I'm going to look at it over this weekend, and I'll let you know on Monday."

He left, and the waitress appeared with their drinks, and he pulled out his wallet to pay. Good grief, was he ever going to have just a second alone with his girl?

There he went with that *his girl* shit again. But dammit, he wanted her to be his—all of her.

He lifted his glass. "To a weekend away. Just the two of us."

She clinked his glass, but before taking a sip, added, "Well, Ralph and Lola, too."

"Of course, Ralph and Lola."

"I think Ralph has been missing Lola."

Steven eyed her for a minute. "I know how he feels."

She tucked her hair behind her ear and changed the subject. "How was work?"

"Swamped. How about you?"

"Busy, but I wouldn't classify it as *swamped*. I've also been busy with the gala. I saw the hospital board bought a table, as did you."

"Did you think I wouldn't?"

"No. I know you're true to your word. Thank you. The foundation is important to me."

Her observation made him feel good. He liked that she knew she could count on him—it seemed like an important step in getting the *boyfriend* label. He was also glad to be supporting something important to her.

"I'm always true to my word."

She looked down shyly and traced the base of her wine glass with her finger. "So I'm finding out."

There was an air of vulnerability about her tonight, and he wanted to take her home and make love to her. Let her know she was safe with him.

He looked around at their surroundings. "How long do you have to stay?"

"We can leave anytime. Let's just finish our drinks and go."

He leaned in and whispered, "Good. I need to show you how much I've missed you."

A slow smile formed on her lips as she caught his meaning, and she took a big gulp of wine, followed by another.

"Have you eaten?"

"Nope." She swirled the wine in her glass. "And I'm a grown woman who is purposefully getting tipsy, knowing I'm going home and having hot sex with you, so please, no lecture on how I need to eat something."

"I wouldn't dream of it. I'm all for hot, tipsy sex."

"Good."

She finished the last of her wine, and Steven took another swig from his glass before setting it down and standing.

"We can wait until you're done," she said, gesturing to his half-full glass.

He stood at her side and snaked a hand around her waist. "Maybe *you* can sweetness, but I can't."

She giggled and slid off her barstool, leaning into him.

"My place?"

He nodded. "Your place."

"It'd probably be bad manners if I left without saying goodbye, huh?"

"Do it fast, baby."

She gripped his biceps and steered him toward a dark-blonde woman in her late-twenties holding court at the next table.

Whitney waited until there was a pause in the conversation and announced, "Thanks for the invitation, Laura. We're going now."

Laura smiled and said, "I'm glad you could make it," as she looked Steven up and down. "I don't think I met your date."

Whitney looked up at him and smiled. "This is Steven Ericson. Steven, this is Laura Zimmerman. She's the lead paralegal at my firm."

Whitney still had her arms looped through his, so he offered a smile and head nod instead of his right hand, and said, "Nice to meet you."

"You too. How long have you been dating our Whitney?"

He blurted out, "A while now," before she could answer. Turning her toward the front, he said, "But we have a reservation, so we have to be going. Have a nice night."

He felt the entire table watch them walk away.

"We have a reservation?" Steven looked down and found her pouting. "I thought we were going back to my place?"

"That's our reservation, sweetness."

Her face lit up. "Ohhhh. I like that."

****

Whitney

His voice was deep and husky when he murmured, "Good, baby. Let's get you home," as they walked out the bar door.

"And get naked?" she giggled, feeling the effects of the three glasses of wine on an empty stomach.

"I like the sound of that."

"I like being naked with you—a lot."

"Me too, sweetness." He kissed her softly, then pulled away before it got too heated. "Did you drive here?"

She nodded and reached into her purse for her keys. "Here you go." Then a thought occurred to her, and she surveyed the parking lot for his Land Rover or Porsche. "Oh, shoot. Did you drive here, too?"

"Nope. I took a cab."

"Well, that's convenient for me, then."

"Me too." He turned the key over in his palm and examined the emblem. "Where'd you park?"

She pointed to her black Beemer under a light in the middle of the lot, and he grinned. "Nice ride."

"It's no Porsche, but I like it."

He opened her car door for her and said, "It suits you," as she slid into the passenger seat.

When he got in the driver's seat, she asked, "What's that supposed to mean?"

Leaning over the console, he whispered, "It's sexy and elegant. And surprises you when you hit the gas." He drew her bottom lip between his teeth.

She closed her eyes and sucked on his top lip in response, then pulled away abruptly after processing his comment.

"Wait, a good surprise or a bad surprise? Because, my car is pretty quick."

He chuckled and tucked her hair behind her ear. "Good surprise, baby. Very good."

"Okay, just checking." Whitney leaned closer to him again. "Where were we?"

Steven winked and reached for his seatbelt, clicking it into place before pushing the button to start the engine.

"We were going back to your place and getting naked."

She fastened her seatbelt, too, then leaned her head on the headrest and smiled with a sigh. "Oh, that's right. I like being naked with you—have I mentioned that?"

"You did, baby. But it's worth repeating."

CHAPTER TWENTY-FOUR

Steven

She was fucking adorable, not to mention brave, when she was tipsy.

"Have you ever had road head?"

He nearly choked at her question and started coughing.

"Is that what I think it means?"

"Have you had your cock sucked while you drove?"

"Um... no? I think I'd crash."

But now his dick was hard thinking about it, and she reached over and stroked the bulge in his slacks. "Wanna try it?"

Gee, did he want this sexy goddess to suck his cock... hmm... decisions, decisions.

"Are you sure, sweetness? I can't imagine it'd be very comfortable for—"

Her seatbelt was already off, and she was on her knees in the passenger seat with her ass up as she leaned over the console and unbuttoned his pants before he could finish his thought.

She pushed his underwear down so his cock was free.

"Fuuuuck, baby," he moaned when she took him in her mouth without hesitation.

He felt her smile as she slurped up and down his shaft, then plunged her mouth to take him deep in her throat.

"Fuck!"

She'd reduced him to one-syllable cuss words.

His tip bobbed in her throat, and she pulled off slowly, stroking his slippery shaft with her hand as she did.

Steven looked down to find her studying his dick in the dashboard light while jerking him with her hand.

"Have I told you that you have a really nice cock?"

He smiled, amused by her alcohol-induced observations.

"You haven't."

He could feel the precum leaking from his tip as she continued stroking him while she examined him.

"It is. It's veiny, but not too veiny. And thick, but not too thick. And it's the perfect length for hitting all the right spots."

"It curves to the left, though," he said with a grin, even though part of him wanted to pull over and close his eyes with a long groan while she kept caressing him.

"I noticed that." She continued stroking him reverently. "But, I think it gives it character."

He swallowed hard, trying to focus on the road and not get them in a wreck with his pants undone. "My cock has character... good to know."

She slipped her lips around the tip and ran her tongue under it, and Steven gripped the steering wheel harder.

Approaching the stoplight before her street, he breathed a sigh of relief. He stroked her hair with his right hand and murmured, "You know what else it has?"

With his dick still between her lips, she looked up at him. "Hmm?"

"Abilities... Let me show you them."

****

Whitney

She'd enjoyed teasing Steven; it made her feel powerful. Probably the same reason she liked sucking his cock—there was something about being in charge of his pleasure that turned her on.

But it also helped her realize that she could give Steven the reins—in the bedroom, and that wouldn't make her weak. When he had been at her mercy, she knew he was still strong and capable.

They made it into the house, and littered the stairs leading to her room with their clothes. So, by the time they made it to her bed, they were both topless, wearing only underwear.

"You are so fucking beautiful," he whispered harshly as he hovered over her and stared into her eyes.

She never knew how to respond to that.

Thank you?

So are you?

Guess my yoga classes are paying off?

Instead of a verbal response, she cupped his face and pulled his mouth back to hers.

Steven let out a low groan and moved his hand up her side until he reached her boob. He kneaded gently, then broke the kiss and dipped his head down to suck on her right nipple while shifting his weight so he could use his other hand to massage the left one.

His tongue swirled around the puckered peak before he sucked it between his lips. Whitney arched her back and held his head, trying to bring him closer. She could feel the wetness pooling between her thighs.

He switched breasts, and again, she bowed off the bed when he initially sucked.

She'd never had a lover pay this much attention to her boobs before, so she'd never known how much she liked it.

"God, that feels good," she cooed, while her pussy started to throb for attention.

With her nipple gently between his teeth, he looked up at her with a cocky grin. He released it briefly and murmured, "Oh, sweetness, we're just getting started."

"I don't want to wait. Please. I need to feel you inside me—now."

He reached between her legs and pulled her panties to the side. Running one finger slowly down her slit, then back up again, he asked, "You need to feel me here?" He traced his tongue around her areola before she could respond.

Whitney wove her fingers in his hair and moaned. "Yes, please..."

Rubbing her clit, he teased, "Not here?"

"Well, there is nice, too, but... Oh!"

He'd pushed one finger inside her, his thumb now circled her nub while he resumed sucking on her nipples.

It felt amazing, and she relished the sensation but soon realized it wasn't enough.

"I need your cock, baby. Please fuck me."

He released her nipple with a pop. "As you wish."

Of course, he likes The Princess Bride. That was her favorite movie of all time.

He slid her panties down her thighs, and she pushed them off the rest of the way while he tugged his boxer briefs down to his ankles and kicked them to the floor.

Whitney quickly forgot about movie lines, right along with her own name, when she felt his cock enter her.

They moaned in unison as he pressed his entire length in.

"Fuuuuck, you feel good, sweetness" Steven whispered as he moved, then leaned down and kissed her.

She lifted her hips to meet his thrusts and murmured against his lips, "So do you."

Their eyes met as his cock moved slowly in and out of her pussy, and for the first time ever, she understood what it meant to make love.

And it scared the bejesus out of her.

Closing her eyes tight, she commanded, "Faster."

He didn't comply, just continued at his leisurely pace, and she opened her eyes to find him watching her as he moved.

"It's okay, baby. I've got you. I promise."

Whitney was at war with herself. She knew Steven was a good man, and yet, that made him more dangerous.

"Only for tonight." She said it out loud, but it was like she was bargaining with herself to let him in her heart—just for tonight.

"Just tonight," he assured her as he sat back and massaged her clit while he continued to fuck her.

Whitney allowed herself to get lost in what he was doing to her. It was like nothing else existed but the two of them. When he had her at the edge, his deep voice commanded, "Come for me, baby."

She happily plummeted over the cliff, calling his name as she fell. He dropped to his forearms and pumped his cock hard and fast, burrowing his face in her neck as he started to moan. She felt his spurts of cum inside her and wrapped her arms around his neck, holding him close.

He picked his face up and stared at her before kissing her tenderly. And in that moment, she knew they both knew that everything had changed. They'd lied—it wasn't just for tonight.

A wave of panic swept over her, and once again, he immediately knew. Wrapping her in his embrace, he rolled off to her side. "I've got you, sweetness."

No! No, no, no. I don't want you to take care of me!

She didn't say that; instead, she concentrated on her breathing, while he stroked her hair until she finally relaxed. Her last thought before slipping into slumber was, *things will be back to normal in the morning.*

****

Steven

He knew he needed to fix what happened between them, or she was going to bolt.

His dad was right; he'd know it when he found her. Except he'd never imagined once he did, she'd not want to be found.

Whitney Hayes was unlike any woman he'd ever met. He knew she felt what was happening between them, only instead of embracing it like Steven was, she seemed to want to run far away from it.

He knew she was scared—but of what, he wasn't exactly sure. What he did know was he needed to approach this slowly, ease her into the relationship, or he would lose her.

It was the middle of the night, and he didn't realize she was awake until she reached out in the darkness to stroke his cock. He'd only been semi-hard, but her soft fingers quickly remedied that. When she had him stiff as stone, she purred, "I want you to fuck me—hard."

Oh sweetness, challenge accepted.

CHAPTER TWENTY-FIVE

Whitney

They were awake surprisingly early for how little they'd slept the night before. Things had felt like they'd returned to normal after he'd pulled her hair while fucking her doggy style and smacked her ass a few times.

It'd been exactly what she needed.

"Good morning," he murmured with a kiss to her temple.

She burrowed in closer to him. "I know we need to get going, but let me just lie here in my Steven cocoon for a few more minutes."

"We can lie here as long as you want, baby."

He ran his fingers up and down her back, while she closed her eyes and breathed in his scent.

There were no expectations; whatever had happened between them last night had passed. Maybe they hadn't lied after all—it had just been for last night.

In that moment, she felt content—and relieved things weren't weird between them. She'd been worried last night that their weekend at the Cape would be ruined by complicated feelings.

Ralph's whine to be let out broke the silence.

He slid out from the covers, then tucked them around her. "I've got him. You sleep."

She sat up. The cocoon was gone with him out of bed.

"No, I need to get up and get in the shower." She called as she walked toward the bathroom, "I don't have much for breakfast. I'm sorry."

"We can stop and eat once we get out of the city. There's a great diner in Quincy that has a patio that's dog friendly."

"That sounds great."

Ralph let out a bark, letting them know he needed to go out—*now*.

Steven moved toward the door. "Okay, okay, Ralph. Let's go, buddy."

When she appeared in the kitchen less than twenty-five minutes later, Ralph's travel bag was on the counter, and his leash was next to it.

"He's been fed, and I packed his bowl, food, treats, and a toy that I've seen him and Lola play with. I think he's ready to go. What about you?"

"My bag is by the door." She loved that he'd taken the initiative to get Ralph's stuff around. "Thank you for packing his bag."

"It was no problem."

She returned the favor for Lola when they got to his condo, and he disappeared to grab a shower and pack a bag.

The dogs yelped excitedly at seeing each other, and Hope came in the kitchen wearing only a t-shirt that was several sizes too big for her.

"Good morning. I'm sorry if they woke you—they're happy to see each other."

Hope glanced around nervously as she poured a cup of coffee that must have been on a timer.

"Hi. No, I was—I was awake. Um, are you guys still headed to the Cape?"

"Yeah, we just stopped to pick up Lola and a bag for Steve."

"So, are you leaving soon?"

"I think once he gets out of the shower. Did you need him?"

"No!" she quickly exclaimed. "I mean, I'm going back to bed, so, no." Hope shuffled toward the door. "Okay, well, tell Steve goodbye for me. Have a great time—I'll see you when you get back." She paused. "You're coming back tomorrow night, right?"

"Yeah, unfortunately I have to work on Monday."

"So, not during the day or anything."

Whitney cocked her head. "We aren't planning on it."

She nodded her head, "Good, good. You both deserve some time away, even if it's just overnight." She took a sip of her coffee and, without waiting for Whitney to respond, said, "Well, have fun," over her shoulder as she made her way back to her bedroom.

"Thanks," but the door was already closed.

Steve's hair was wet when he walked in the kitchen.

"Did I hear Hope?"

"Yeah."

"Oh, good. I needed to ask her if the maintenance people showed up to fix her toilet."

"Well, she made it a point to let me know she was going back to bed and to tell you goodbye for her."

"But she was just out here five minutes ago. You don't think she already fell back to sleep, do you?"

Whitney shrugged. "I don't know; she seemed half-awake."

"Hmm..." He tiptoed to her door and knocked lightly. "Hope?"

No answer. He tried turning the doorknob, but it was locked.

"I guess I'll talk to her tomorrow night. Ready to get going?"

"I am."

She couldn't wait. It was like she was playing pretend when they went to his beach house, and she could be somebody else, just for the weekend.

They were pulling out of his parking space when he did a doubletake to look at a fancy, shiny black car backed into a far corner space.

"Everything okay?"

"I'm not sure."

He circled the lot and stopped in front of the Mercedes.

"That's a nice Benz," she commented.

"Yeah, it is. I'm just wondering what it's doing in the parking lot of my condominium complex."

"Do you know the owner?"

"I think so. It looks like Evan Lacroix's car. He works at the hospital with me, but we don't get along very well."

"Maybe he knows somebody who lives in your complex."

He furrowed his brows and put the SUV in drive, slowly pulling away. "Yeah, maybe."

CHAPTER TWENTY-SIX

Steven

He was looking forward to getting out of town. The Cape seemed to be the one place where Whitney completely let her guard down with him.

Even her shoulders looked more relaxed as she looked over at him from the passenger seat with a soft smile. He grabbed her hand and kissed her knuckles.

"I'm glad you could get away to come with me."

"I'm sorry it's only for the night. I probably should have just driven separately, so you could've stayed longer."

"I'd much rather spend my drive with you."

"But you have a whole day that you could still be at your beach house."

He squeezed her hand he was still holding. "There'll be plenty of days where we both can be there. How much time can you get off for the Fourth?"

He'd said it like it was the most natural thing in the world for them to spend the holiday together, but he was holding his breath, waiting to see how she'd respond. Would she scoff or make an excuse?

She didn't hesitate with her reply, and he gave an internal fist pump. "I can get Friday and Monday, for sure. Maybe even the Thursday before."

"Terrific. Is there anybody you want to invite? I think we're going to have a full house—at least Friday and Saturday night, but we can always make room for more." Again, he was hesitant telling her about the house being full, thinking that might turn her off from coming. But he also wanted her to have full disclosure, so he tried to keep his tone even, like it was no big deal.

"Oh? Who's coming?"

"Well, there's Hope, although she's waiting to see if her friend Yvette, who's coming from San Diego, wants to go or if she'd rather stay in Boston. Zach and probably his flavor of the week. Zach's brother, James—an anesthesiologist that I work with. I'm not sure if he's bringing someone. Aiden Matthews, he's a cardiologist who just went through a nasty divorce—pretty sure he's sworn off women forever and won't bring anyone."

She grimaced. "Ouch."

"Yeah. It was bad—it got ugly from what little he's told me. I also invited my boss, Parker Preston—the chief of staff, and Liam McDonnell—the hospital CEO, but I'm sure neither one will come. Those two work more than I do. I don't think either has a life outside the hospital."

"That's kind of sad."

"They're big boys. They can make their own decisions."

"That's true, I guess."

"So, is there anyone you want to invite?"

"There's a woman on the ARF committee with me. She'd be fun. Dakota Douglas."

"Feel free to invite her. What about your friend, Gwen?" The more people expecting Whitney, the better. Less chance of her canceling.

"No, she's going to Michigan to spend a few weeks at her family's cottage on the lake and won't get back until the weekend before the fundraiser."

"A cottage on the lake? Nice. Michigan is beautiful this time of year."

"Yeah, one of the benefits of being a teacher."

"Is she married?"

"Single as a pringle." He felt his eyebrows go up, so she added, "Her words—not mine."

"What about anyone from work?"

"I have no interest in hanging out with work people outside the office."

He laughed. "I gathered that, based on how many people seemed surprised you were at happy hour last night."

"Some people can let their hair down around their colleagues... I'm not one of them."

"Why not?"

"Well, for one, I don't trust any of them as far as I could throw them. How could I relax, knowing they're just dying for me to make a faux pas they can use against me later? And two, attorneys aren't that fun to begin with."

"I don't know, Zach is fun."

"There's an exception to every rule."

"You're fun."

"No, I'm really not. If you weren't blinded by my magical vagina, you'd realize that. But you will—eventually."

"Although, I will admit your vagina is fucking spectacular and magical, we will have to agree to disagree that I'm blinded by it, Counselor."

"Hmph," was her only reply.

"No *hmph*. It's true."

He decided to drop it. As he exited the highway for the breakfast diner, he asked with a grin, "Do you like omelets?"

"As a matter of fact, I do."

"Good, 'cuz you're about to have the best one of your life."

****

Whitney

She watched Steven interact with the diner hostess, then Lola and Ralph, and now the waitress. He was never *not* charming—even the dogs stared at him like he was a god. But the difference between him and the players she'd dated in the past was that she wasn't worried about him getting the waitress's phone number while she was in the bathroom. Even as he made women swoon with his disarming smile and friendly banter, his arm was either around Whitney or caressing her hand across the table. He never left any doubt who he was with.

He made it easy to spend time with him.

Too easy.

She had been planning on applying the brakes, but fortunately, his job had taken care of that for her. The problem was, she'd missed him and had looked forward to every call and text from him. And their night away from the city.

Don't get used to this.

But it was hard not to. And now she was making plans to spend the Fourth of July at the Cape.

Maybe she could just go with the flow and not worry about labeling things.

Yeah—that might work.

He reached across the table and touched her hand with his pinky. "I'm glad you were able to get away tonight. This week sucked... I hardly got to see you."

"Thanks again for coming to happy hour last night and all the way downtown to take me to lunch on Wednesday. That was a nice break in my day."

"Next time, I want to watch you in court. You're sexy as fuck when you're cross-examining someone."

"Really? You think so? I was so nervous—knowing you were in the gallery watching."

"I never would have known. You were incredible to see in action."

She cocked her head. "Why were you in the courtroom that day?"

"You left Rousso's before I could get your number. There was no way I was leaving downtown without talking to you."

She smiled at his admission and responded with her own. "I almost didn't come into the restaurant that day. I'd seen Zach walk in ahead of me, so I kept going and ended up at Founders, the restaurant next door. But they had a wait, so I came back."

He squeezed her hand. "Then the hostess seated you right next to us. It was serendipity."

Whitney had considered the same thing. What if Founders hadn't had a wait? What would she be doing right now?

Not sitting across from a gorgeous man on their way to the beach with their dogs—that's for sure.

CHAPTER TWENTY-SEVEN

Steven

They held hands as they walked along the beach Sunday morning before breakfast. The dogs were chasing each other in the surf and seemed to be as happy to be together again as Steven felt being there with Whitney.

He knew he was in love with her. How could he not be? She was brilliant, beautiful, and his dick was hard twenty-four/seven when he was around her. Hell, even when he wasn't around her, but just thinking about her.

But she was wounded. Anytime he felt her allowing herself to get close to him, she'd pull back. He knew he'd have to proceed with caution. Prove to her that he'd always have her back, and she could trust him. In the meantime, that meant keeping his feelings to himself as best he could.

Still... It was hard not to blurt it out when he watched her in the morning sun, with no makeup, laughing at the dogs as they chased each other through the water along the beach.

Steve took a deep breath and took in the moment of being there with her.

She must have felt him watching because she turned to look at him. Her laugh morphed into a soft smile as she returned his gaze.

Words weren't necessary—their exchanged look spoke volumes. He knew she felt the same about him. The tricky part would be getting her to acknowledge it without running from her feelings.

CHAPTER TWENTY-EIGHT

Whitney

"He better be in the bathroom," Gwen declared when she sat down at the restaurant table where Whitney was waiting. She had left work early for a change, following the crowd out for the long holiday weekend, and had been able to secure a table before it got too busy.

"No, I'm sorry. He got called into work."

Her friend pursed her lips. "Well, that sucks."

"I know. It's the nature of the job, I guess. And since he's going to be unavailable this weekend, I think he felt like he should be there tonight."

"Do you think you'll still head out tonight, then?"

"That's the plan, but I've learned to be flexible. It'd be nice to get there tonight, since everyone else is getting there tomorrow, but if not, we'll just leave early in the morning."

"Do you know anyone who's coming—other than Dakota?"

"Just Zach and Steven's sister, Hope."

"So, this is kind of a big deal—meeting each other's friends!"

"It's not a big deal. It's the holiday weekend, and he has a house on the ocean. I think half the people going have never met each other."

Gwen eyed her like she wasn't buying it. "I'm kind of put out that I don't get to be your first friend to meet him, now."

"Aw, I'm sorry. I wish you were coming, but I was relieved when Dakota said yes. At least I'm guaranteed to know someone I can talk to."

The waitress appeared and took Gwen's drink order, then asked, "Do you know what you want for dinner?"

"We haven't even looked at the menu—sorry!"

"No problem. I'll get that drink order in for you."

They opened their menus, and Gwen commented without looking up from the food selections, "So, it sounds like it's getting serious."

"No," Whitney replied.

Gwen looked at her across the table with one eyebrow raised. "Sounds like it is. Are either of you dating other people?"

That made Whitney pause. She wasn't dating anyone else—but that wasn't necessarily a big deal since she hardly dated before meeting Steven. It hadn't even occurred to her that he might be seeing someone else. The idea didn't sit well with her.

"I don't think so. I mean, I'm not, and I don't know when he'd have time."

Gwen flipped the page of her menu. "I hate to break it to you, sweetie, but you have a boyfriend."

"Nope."

Her friend shrugged. "If you say so," then muttered under her breath, "But you really do."

"No, I don't!"

"Okay! Okay!" Gwen threw her hands up in the universal, *I surrender* position, then dropped them down as she asked, "But what's wrong with having him as your boyfriend? He sounds like he's been great, so far."

Whitney let out a long sigh. "He is. Really. But he's out of my league..."

Gwen interrupted, "Yeah, I'm going to call bullshit on that."

"He's rich, and comes from this great, accomplished family—"

"Um, not sure if you've noticed, but you're kind of accomplished, too. Harvard Law? Heard of it?"

"I got in because Alan Crawford saw me as a project."

"Who the fuck cares? You held your own the whole three years. Summa cum laude sound familiar?"

"Yes, but—"

"No buts, bitch. I wish you would start accepting how amazing you are. And for fuck's sake, quit that damn law firm."

"I owe Alan."

"You don't owe Alan dick, anymore. You've paid him back and then some. Anyway, back to the reasons why the good doctor can't be your boyfriend."

"I'm sure he's going to want kids someday..."

"So?"

"So, I don't think I do."

"You aren't your parents, Whit."

"I think by the time I could be ready, it'll be too late."

"According to my mother, if you wait until the time is right, you'll be waiting forever."

"Anyway...." Whitney needed to deflect. Her friend's interrogation was cutting a little too close to home. "What about you? You're the one who became a teacher because you love kids."

"I know. But unless I want to shell out thousands of dollars to be artificially inseminated, it's not happening anytime soon. Is it possible for your hymen to grow back if your vagina isn't getting any action?"

"Not even by yourself?"

"Meh," Gwen replied, reaching for the basket of bread the server had brought earlier while Whitney waited. "It's not the same."

"That's true..." A small smile escaped Whitney's lips as she thought about her and Steven's sexy times together.

"Based on that smile on your face, we obviously don't have to worry about your hymen growing back."

"No... I'm pretty safe in that department."

"I'd hate you if I didn't love you so much. Sexy doctor with a beach house giving you lots of sex. Oh, you poor thing. Please tell me you have to at least fake your orgasms."

"Nope, not a problem there either."

"Actually, I'm glad about that. I wouldn't want that for you. Life's too short to fake orgasms."

Whitney raised her glass in a toast. "Amen to that."

****

Steven

He walked in the restaurant with a bouquet of flowers he'd bought from the street vendor outside. *Better late than never, right?*

The hostess suggested he look around the restaurant when he described the woman he was looking for, and he spotted her the minute he walked into the dining room.

She was laughing with her friend and seemed relaxed as she sipped a glass of wine. He wondered how many glasses it'd taken to get her that unwound. It usually took getting her out of the city for Steven to see her shoulders that loose.

He approached the table with a sheepish smile. "Any chance you haven't had dessert yet?" he asked as he stood there with the flowers in his hand.

"Hi! We were just thinking about ordering some," Whitney greeted him warmly. Based on her enthusiasm, he'd bet she'd had at least three glasses. "I thought you had to work late?"

"I did, but I wanted to meet Gwen, so the second things died down, I made a run for it." He shifted the bouquet to his left hand and held his right one out to the cute woman across from Whitney. "Steve Ericson."

She took his offered hand with a knowing grin, like she knew secrets about him. "Gwen Gowen. Nice to meet you. I've heard a lot about you."

"All good things," Whitney blurted out.

The corner of his mouth turned up, and he nodded slowly as he glanced over at her.

"These are for you. I'm sorry I was late."

Her eyes widened as she took the red roses wrapped in green tissue paper and scooted over in the booth to make room for him. "You got me flowers?" she asked breathlessly. "Thank you so much."

"I didn't know what your favorite is, so I went with classic red roses," he said as he sat next to her. "I hope you don't think I'm cliché."

She hadn't stopped smiling since Steve approached the table.

"No, these are perfect. Thank you."

"For future reference—what is your favorite?"

Whitney cocked her head as she pondered his question, finally answering, "I don't know. I've never gotten flowers before, but these are beautiful."

"Never?"

"No."

He bent down with a grin and said softly, "So, I'm like, your first?"

Whitney reached behind his neck and drew his face closer. "You're my first."

He leaned in for a soft kiss, when—

"Hi!" Gwen snapped her fingers over her head. "Best friend... sitting right here."

Steve sat up straight, throwing his arm around Whitney's shoulders. "I'm sorry, best friend. I just haven't seen my girl all week." He turned to Whitney. "You look fucking hot, by the way."

That elicited a giggle from her, while Gwen sat with her mouth slightly agape as she watched them. Shaking her head, she shifted in her seat and picked up her wine glass, muttering, "You two are ridiculously adorable."

He hoped she meant that in a good way.

"I'm sorry you aren't able to come to the Cape with us this weekend."

"Me, too. Do you have any brothers in town?"

That made him laugh out loud. "Three sisters, sorry. But I have plenty of good-looking single friends."

She nodded her head as she set her glass down. "We'll talk."

CHAPTER TWENTY-NINE

Whitney

He was so damn handsome, it took her breath away. Whitney was a little tipsy and had been happy to see him.

She'd shared a bottle of wine with her best friend at dinner and had just received flowers for the first time in her life, so she was feeling rather frisky as she exited his Land Rover at her house. Lola, who they'd picked up on the way, jumped out behind her, and Whitney grabbed the pup's leash, then pressed her tits against Steven's chest. She whispered, "Thanks for popping my floral cherry."

His grin morphed into a wide smile, and he held her hips tight as he murmured in her ear, "I'll be extra gentle when I pop your anal cherry, too."

She reached down to cup his balls over his pants and squeezed slightly while whispering back, "Who says I'm an anal virgin?" before spinning on the ball of her foot and walking toward her front door with an extra sway in her hips, even with Lola in tow.

"Wait... what?"

Whitney only laughed, both at Steve's response and at Ralph going apeshit at the front window after seeing Lola. She opened the door before Ralph broke it down. Her dog was out of his mind to see his girlfriend, and the two exchanged excited whine-barking before racing through the house.

"So..." He slumped his shoulder against the doorjamb with a wicked gleam in his eye. "Are we doing butt stuff tonight?"

She shrugged like it was no big deal, but it was a huge deal. She had just been yanking his chain for being so cocky, thinking he knew her anal virginity status. But he'd been exactly right.

"Probably not tonight. I kind of wanted to suck your cock and then ride it."

His Adam's apple bobbed up and down like he was swallowing hard. Good. Her intention had been to fluster him a little.

It was fleeting, and he quickly regained his composure with a nod. "Yeah, that could work." Wrapping his arm around her waist, he pulled her against him and uttered, "And what kind of assholes have you dated that I'm the first to give you flowers?"

"You don't even want to know."

"You're probably right. But you realize I'm going to get you flowers all the time now."

"That's not necessary. As it is, I feel bad because we're leaving, and I won't be able to enjoy them."

"I thought you could take them with you. If you just wrap the stems in wet paper towels, they'll be fine until we can put them in water."

She stared at him. "How do you—"

He shrugged. "Cotillion classes, remember?"

"They teach *that* in cotillion classes?"

"Probably not," he confessed with a laugh. "But I've transported a lot of flowers for my mom to her events over the years and noticed a thing or two."

"Well, I learned something new today."

Whitney pulled three sheets of paper towels from the roll and wet them under the faucet before wrapping them around the stems. She looked up at him with a smile. "I'm ready when you are."

"Let's get going, then. You have a cock to ride tonight."

She couldn't wait.

CHAPTER THIRTY

Steven

Something startled him awake, and it took him a second to comprehend what it was: the doorbell, mixed with dogs barking from the laundry room.

Shit, what time is it? They'd stayed up doing dirty things, culminating with Whitney riding his cock. Then she woke him up in the middle of the night with her lips wrapped around it.

"Sweetness..." he'd whispered when he realized what was happening.

She slurped off him; he could see her beautiful face in the moonlight when she murmured with a grin, "I told you I wanted to suck your cock."

They finally went back to sleep just before the sun came up, and now he was trying to get his bearings and figure out how late they'd slept.

The clock on the nightstand read 10:07.

Aw, damn.

Then he grinned, remembering why they'd overslept. *Totally worth it.*

"Baby, we've got to get up," he whispered as he nudged her softly.

She grumbled in response and burrowed closer to him.

The doorbell rang again, followed by loud knocking.

"Come on, sweetness. Someone's already here."

She sat up like a shot. "Oh my god, What time is it?"

"It's ten o'clock," he said as he pulled on a pair of shorts. "I'll go see who it is. Take your time."

He heard the shower start before he even closed the bedroom door, and the doorbell rang again.

"Jesus, I'm coming. Hold your damn horses!" he shouted as he walked toward the door.

He threw open the door to find Zach standing on the front step with a shit-eating grin. On one side of him was a stunning, tan blonde who was twenty-three if she was a day, and on the other was his brother, James.

"'Bout time, fucker. I thought I was going to have to crawl through an open window."

"You would've been out of luck, then. The alarm company makes sure this place is locked up tight."

Steven held his fist out to bump his friend, then did the same with James.

"Sorry to wake you up," the younger Rudolf brother said. "I thought I saw you leave the hospital early last night."

"I did. But then we went out to dinner and had to pick up the dogs, so we still got here late."

"This is my friend, Barbie Anderson," Zach said.

Of course her name was fucking Barbie.

Steven offered the blonde on Zach's arm his hand. "Steve Ericson."

She giggled—fucking giggled—before shaking his hand like a limp dishrag. Her voice sounded like a little girl's when she replied, "Nice to meet you."

Steve tried to keep his face neutral as he looked at Zach—telepathically conveying, "Seriously, dude?" Hadn't Zach just been talking about finding a woman with substance?

Zach subtly lifted one shoulder, as if to convey, "What can I say?"

It took everything for Steve not to roll his eyes as he stepped back to allow them to pass. She was hot, he'd give her that. But he also knew he wouldn't see her again after this weekend.

"I hope we're the first ones here," Zach said, a duffel bag in one hand as he walked inside and looked around. "I wanted to make sure to claim the best guest room."

"You know where it's at."

Zach and Barbie escaped down the hall.

"I'll be happy with a pillow and a hammock," James quipped as he surveyed the back patio through the sliding glass door.

"That's probably a good thing because we're expecting a full house."

"Oh yeah? Any single ladies?"

James was a good guy and a great doctor. Steven would be okay with his little sister dating him.

"Actually, yeah. My sister, for one."

"Hope? I met her the other day. She seems great; Parker has been on Cloud Nine since she started. But I thought she was dating Evan Lacroix?"

"*What?*" Steve fought to contain his snarl. Evan was their colleague, and more importantly, worked for Steve. He needed to keep his words in check. "No, I can promise you she's not dating Evan."

James tilted his head. "Oh? I guess I heard wrong."

"You definitely heard wrong. They've been butting heads since her first day."

"I guess the gossips got it wrong," James said with a polite smile. "Wouldn't be the first time."

"And I'm sure it won't be the last."

"Hellllllo?" Hope's voice called from the entry. Lola must have recognized it because her warning bark she'd given when the doorbell rang earlier, turned into an excited one. And Ralph quickly joined in.

"Speak of the devil," Steven said with a laugh, then yelled louder, "In the living room!" as he made his way to the laundry room. He was glad he'd let the dogs out in the middle of the night, otherwise he'd probably have a mess to clean up.

He stepped back as he pushed the door open, and the dogs bounded out and headed straight toward Hope.

"You just saw me last night!" his sister scolded while kneeling to greet the happy pups. She tried holding Lola's face at bay to avoid being licked, but then Ralph got in a slurp.

Steven grabbed their leashes from the hook in the laundry room. "All right, you two, let's go outside!"

"I can take them," James offered.

Yvette, Hope's friend from San Diego, chimed in, "We'll help."

"Thanks," Steven replied. "I'll put your bags in my office. You guys will have to sleep on the pullout. Zach already laid claim to the guest room, and we're putting Whitney's friend in the smaller guest room."

"I'm sleeping in the hammock," James said with a smirk.

"Oh, we can sleep on the patio loungers," Hope said. "Don't worry about us—give your office to someone else."

"You sure? You got here first."

"Positive. I'll have plenty of weekends to come visit."

He handed her the leashes and kissed her forehead. "I hope so. Have I mentioned how glad I am that you moved here?"

She beamed up at him. "I am, too. Thanks for helping make it happen."

The doorbell rang again, so he left the dogs in their hands and went to answer it just as Whitney appeared, wearing a pair of jean shorts that showed off her toned legs and a fitted t-shirt, the color of the Stanford cardinal—his alma mater. Her hair was damp and piled high on her head. She wasn't wearing an ounce of makeup, and she was fucking stunning.

Her bare feet somehow made it feel like she belonged there—which she did.

"I think that's Dakota. She just texted, wanting to make sure she was in the right place."

He opened the door, and Whitney stepped out to exclaim, "Dakota! You found it!"

A stunning woman who appeared to be in her mid-thirties stood on his front step. In her black yoga pants and tan linen top with spaghetti straps, it was obvious she kept in shape. Her jet-black hair was pulled back with a paisley headband in earth tones, and she wore dangling earrings with aqua-blue stones that matched a larger stone in her brown nylon choker. Her makeup was muted, and she gave off a hippie chick vibe when she smiled warmly and grabbed Whitney's hands and said, "Hello, Whitney. Thanks for having me. You look relaxed. Ocean air is good for you." She then glanced at Steven. "Or maybe it's all the great sex you're having."

"Dakota!" Whitney gasped as a blush crept across her cheeks. He'd never seen Whitney blush before. Just like everything about her, it was adorable.

"Oh! Has it not been great?"

Steven cocked his head with raised brows and a smirk while he waited for Whitney's response.

She glanced at him with a small smile. "It's been beyond great."

Dakota patted Steven's cheek with a manicured hand, her many bracelets jingling as she did. "It's important to connect with her mind, body, and soul. Remember that."

"Yes, ma'am."

The woman stared at him for a moment with kind eyes, then back at Whitney. "You're going to have beautiful babies."

Whitney's wheeze of surprise at Dakota's observation turned into a fit of coughing with Steven patting her soundly on the back until she stopped.

Her face was red, and her eyes were watery, but it seemed like she had the need to correct her friend. "I'm not having kids. Ever."

Her revelation took him aback. He'd always envisioned himself with a wife and houseful of kids someday—in spite of what his college girlfriend had said about his ability to be a good father and provider. Would being with Whitney mean that dream wouldn't be realized?

Dakota tilted her head with knitted eyebrows and looked thoughtfully at Whitney for a moment, then reached for her hand with a smile. "Everyone forges their own path. Whatever you decide, it will be for the best."

He felt a sense of panic at her words. *No, lady. That's not what you should be telling her. You're supposed to tell her that she'd be a great mother, and I'd be a terrific father.*

Instead of acknowledging their discussion, he changed the subject altogether. Taking the handle of her small rolling suitcase, he said, "Let me show you where your room is."

****

Whitney

Although she hadn't envisioned discussing children with Steven, it was probably good that it was out in the open.

He'd realize now that they really were just a fling.

Yet, the thought of him with someone else made her feel nauseous.

Dakota had squeezed her hand again before Whitney left her in the guest room to get situated. Whitney loved how calm she always felt being around the woman. Dakota wasn't that much older than her, but she had an old soul and had a tendency to have that peaceful effect on both people and animals.

Unfortunately, the calm wore off the minute she closed the guest room door. She could tell by Steven's ramrod-straight posture and the way he wouldn't look at her when they walked onto the patio where all his guests had gathered, he was upset. That bothered her, except she wasn't sure how to smooth things over.

The dogs bounded up with a ball and dropped it at Steven's feet. His jaw was set when he picked it up and tossed it to the sand, following the dogs toward the water. She wasn't sure if she should follow, partly because she wasn't sure if she'd be welcome, and partly because she knew he'd want to talk, and she didn't know what she'd say.

Fortunately, Hope noticed her and squealed, "Whitney! There you are!" Steven's younger sister grabbed her arm and tugged her to where another cute woman about their age was standing next to what could only be Zach's younger brother— he looked just like him. Next to mini-Zach was an older man with greying temples. He was handsome, but there was something in his eyes that told Whitney he was unhappy. Aiden, she presumed.

"This is my friend from San Diego, Yvette Sinclair. We've been friends since middle school! She decided to come see why I've been gushing about Boston. I'm hoping she'll love it, so I can convince her to move here with me. I know she'd be so much happier here than in California."

"What do you do?" Whitney asked, shaking the strawberry blonde's hand. Even though the other woman was dressed casually in khaki shorts and a polo, she still put off a vibe of being classy and put together.

"I'm a hotel manager."

"But she wants to open her own bed and breakfast someday," Hope chimed in. "And, um, hel-lo? New England is famous for them!"

"Well, not all of us have a coveted prosthetic patent and are rolling in the dough."

"I told you, I'd love to invest in your B and B."

Yvette shook her head. "And I've told you—money and friends don't mix."

"And I've told you, that's what contracts are for."

Yvette silently mouthed, "No."

Whitney respected Yvette's reluctance to take her friend up on the offer to invest in her bed and breakfast but agreed with Hope—that's what contracts were for.

Hope gave Yvette the stink eye and said, "We'll talk about this later," then continued with introductions. "Whitney, I don't know if you've met James Rudolf and Aiden Matthews. They work with Steven at Boston General. Guys, this is Steven's girlfriend, Whitney Hayes."

She opened her mouth to correct Hope, then stopped. She wasn't technically his *girlfriend*, but she had to concede that they were dating—at least they had been up until ten minutes ago. Now, she wasn't sure what he was thinking. Still, at this point, whether they were boyfriend and girlfriend or just dating was semantics and saying anything to the contrary would make her look petty. Instead, she asked the men, "Do you work in the ER, too?"

James shook his head. "I'm an anesthesiologist."

Aiden added, "I work in cardiology. What about you? What do you do?"

"She's an attorney that I'm trying to bring on board with my firm." Zach appeared with a leggy blonde in a bikini and see-through coverup clinging to his side. "But for some reason, she's not interested in doubling her salary."

"Pretty presumptuous of you to assume to know how much I make."

"I don't know how much you make," Zach admitted. "But I know my boss would double it—whatever it was."

James's eyebrows were raised as he murmured, "Damn."

That seemed to be the group's consensus, based on the nodding heads and murmurs.

"I doubt they would offer to double my salary—especially if they found out I'm not interested in making partner."

"You're not interested in making partner?" Hope asked. When Whitney shook her head, she followed up with, "Why not?" She seemed to be genuinely interested in Whitney's reason.

"Sure, the money would be great, but I want to hang my own shingle someday and take the cases that I think are worthwhile, not just because they pay the bills."

A deep, quiet voice murmured, "You can do both, you know." Steven was suddenly at her side, his hand coming to the small of her back in a possessive manner. The gesture made her want to lean into him. Even though it had only been a short period, she didn't like the idea of him being upset with her.

"Seriously, Whitney—just come talk to the partners. What would it hurt? I can set something up for next week."

"I'll think about it."

She said it to appease Zach and change the subject. Could she leave Crawford, Holden, and Crane to work for a competing firm? She owed her education and career to Alan Crawford and Arthur Crane. It felt like it was one thing to go out on her own, but to take a job with the competition was something else entirely.

"You should seriously consider it," Steven said in her ear. "What's the worst that could happen?"

Maybe he was right. She should at least take the meeting. If nothing else, she could use McNamara, Wallace, and Stone's offer to negotiate a raise.

She nodded, his lips brushing against her ear as she did. Suddenly, she couldn't care less about any meeting or raise. She wanted nothing more than to turn and burrow herself against his chest with his arms wrapped around her.

He gave her a polite smile and dropped his hand from her back as he took a step to the right, away from her. It was such a small gesture, but she felt it as if he'd slapped her.

"I'll think it over. I'll be right back," she managed to murmur before spinning on the ball of her foot and heading toward the bathroom.

She closed the door just as the first tear fell.

CHAPTER THIRTY-ONE

Steven

Whitney walked out of the house and looked up at him with a timid smile.

"Are the dogs worn out yet?"

He chuckled. "Not even close. There are too many potential ball throwers in their midst."

As if to emphasize his point, they looked over to see Ralph drop his ball at Hope's feet, then stare at it intently as he waited for her to pick it up and throw it for him.

James sat in the next lounger over, scratching Lola's ears while she, too, focused on the ball next to Hope's sandal.

When Hope didn't lean down to get the ball right away, Ralph picked it up and dropped it again—directly on her foot this time.

"Okay, okay, Ralph," Hope said with a laugh as she stood up with the ball and walked toward the edge of the patio. "Let's go play on the beach."

Lola galloped after them, and Yvette and James followed. Zach and Barbie had already left to lay in the sun by the water, while Aiden volunteered to help Dakota make lunch for everyone. That left just him and Whitney alone on the patio.

He desperately wanted to ask her if she was serious about not wanting kids—and if so, why. But he was afraid of what her answer would be. Right now, he could still hope.

Opening that can of worms had the potential to dash that. Still, the elephant was in the room.

"Should we see if Dakota and Aiden need help with lunch?"

"Nah," he said, shaking his head. "They were just making salad and sandwiches; I'm sure they've got it."

They stood there, for the first time since they met, in awkward silence.

Finally, she suggested, "So, how about a beer?"

That sounded like a damn fine idea.

He'd just opened a bottle and taken a sip when everyone came back, at the same time Dakota and Aiden brought out platters of sandwiches and a big bowl of salad. Whitney dashed inside to get plates and silverware, and they all ate on the patio. The company took the pressure off he and Whitney trying to navigate around each other.

Noticing Whitney and Steven's half-empty beers, Zach helped himself to the outdoor refrigerator, with the rest of the group following.

"Can we have a bonfire tonight?" Hope asked.

"I was planning on it," Steven replied.

"Good, because I invited your neighbor Zoe, and her boyfriend."

"Zoe has a boyfriend?"

"Well, to be honest, he kind of looked like a boy toy."

"Yeah, that's more like it."

Zoe was a divorcee whose cutthroat lawyer found the assets her rich husband had been hiding. As punishment for trying to be a sneaky bastard, the judge awarded her enough money and property that she never had to work again. As a result, she'd sworn off relationships but had no problem taking lovers. Especially if they were younger than her.

"Younger men are just less complicated," she'd explained to Steven one afternoon on the beach while her weekend companion was trying to catch a wave.

She was a great neighbor, so as far as Steve was concerned, to each their own.

"We also ran into Evan Lacroix," James said with a sly grin.

"Oh yeah," Hope said casually. "I guess he's here with his sister and some friends. I invited them, too. I hope that's okay?"

Steven wasn't buying her feigned nonchalance. "I thought you didn't like Evan?"

She shrugged, running her fingers along the condensation of her beer bottle and refusing to look at him. "We work at the same hospital. I might as well be polite and try to make the best of it."

Steve raised an eyebrow, but she still refused to look at him. Something definitely was amiss.

He noticed Dakota and Whitney walk off to the kitchen and decided he had other things to worry about right now than his sister's love life.

****

Whitney

"You doing okay?" Dakota asked as she handed her a water.

"I don't know. I think I upset Steven with my 'no kids' declaration, and now things are weird between us."

"He seemed surprised."

"He comes from a great family—of course he's going to want kids someday. All the more reason that we can't be more than a summer fling."

"I think you have more than just summer fling feelings for him," Dakota replied with a quiet authority. "May I ask why you don't want children?"

"I don't think I'd be a good mother. I never had a role model. What if I screwed up my kid?"

"You never had a role model, yet look how great you turned out. A juris doctorate from Harvard, a successful career, a boyfriend who adores you... I think you'd be a wonderful mother because you'd want to be."

She winced. "That's just it, Dakota. The universe never lets me have it all. For every good thing, there's always a bad that soon follows."

Dakota took her hands in hers and looked directly in her eyes. "That's not true, Whitney. The universe wants you to have it all, you just have to learn to accept the gifts it gives you."

Whitney shook her head vehemently and pulled her hands away. "What gifts? Whenever my life is going too well, the universe pulls the rug out from under me. Every time. It definitely does not want me to have it all. If anything, it wants to remind me that I *can't* have it all."

She learned at an early age to dread when good things happened because that always meant something bad was waiting just around the corner.

If they had food in the refrigerator, it meant her mom would disappear a few days later. When she found out she was accepted into Boston University on full scholarship, her grandma had a heart attack the following week. When she got her internship with Crawford, Holden, and Crane, she got evicted from her apartment the next day.

After Alan helped her get a spot at Harvard, she thought she was finally going places. She started going out and was active in a few clubs, and that's where she met Derek Farnsworth. He'd been charming and spent lots of money trying to impress her. Being the poor girl she was, it'd worked. Then, the Wednesday before the weekend she was supposed to meet his parents, he found out she was on full scholarship and dumped her. "My parents would never approve," he'd said before walking away and never looking back. Word must have gotten out she was a charity case because the invitations to go out on the weekends soon dried up. It was probably a good thing because she was able to concentrate on her studies again with no distractions.

Good things always came at a price. As it was, she knew she was pushing her luck being happy with Steven.

Dakota reached for her hands again and held tight this time as she stared into her eyes.

"Listen to me, sweet girl. If you don't think the universe is giving you gifts, then demand them. Don't accept that you are only allowed so many good things, or that your good and bad must be equal. You are entitled to *everything* you want if you're willing to not accept anything less."

In that moment, looking into the eyes of this woman who seemed to be so in touch with her spirituality, Whitney believed she was right. Whether or not she'd feel that way after this weekend when she was back to her own devices, was debatable. But right then, she was a believer.

She nodded her head subtly to signal her acceptance.

"So, knowing you can have everything you want, you need to ask yourself, what do you want?"

Steven's face flashed in her mind. She wanted a future with him. She wanted to feel safe in his embrace again.

And she envisioned her name on a sign outside a building. Her own firm. She allowed herself to feel the pride of what that would be like that.

An image of a little blonde girl playing in the sitting room of her imagined big office, emulating Whitney on the phone, popped into her head.

"I want it all," Whitney whispered. "The successful career, the guy I'm in love with, the family... all of it."

"So go get it."

"It's not that easy."

"Yes, it is. You just need to decide you're worthy. And I'm here to tell you that you are."

For the first time that she could remember, Whitney felt worthy.

"I'm so glad you came this weekend," she blurted out before wrapping her arms around Dakota's shoulders and hugging her tightly.

"Me, too." Dakota hugged her back. "Me, too."

CHAPTER THIRTY-TWO

Steven

While he was grateful for the houseful of people helping make things less awkward between him and Whitney, part of him wanted to be alone with her so they could talk. The sooner they cleared the air, the sooner things could get back to normal.

Her revelation earlier had taken him aback, but now that he'd had time to process it, he decided there was no use getting upset about it right now. It was obviously too soon to be worrying about having kids, and while it gave him pause that she didn't think she wanted children ever, it wasn't a dealbreaker for him. Although, if he were honest, the idea of not ever having children made him sad, and part of him was hoping she wasn't as set in her decision as she'd sounded.

And Steven at least wanted to hear the reasons she felt the way she did.

He was surprised when she walked into the master bedroom while he was changing into jeans and a sweatshirt for the bonfire.

"Hey," she said softly as she sat down on the foot of the bed.

"Hey."

She twisted her hands in her lap. "I think everyone's having a great time, so far, don't you?"

"I haven't heard any complaints."

"The guys all grabbed some firewood from your stack on the patio. They've all headed to the beach to start the bon fire."

"I figured as much. You're going to want to bring a sweatshirt. Even with a fire, it gets chilly at night."

"That's why I came in here. Well, and I was hoping to find you."

"Oh?" He cocked his head. "It seems like you've been avoiding me all evening."

Whitney glanced at the floor and said softly, "Maybe I was."

Steven sat next to her but resisted reaching for her like he wanted to. "Wanna tell me why?"

"It feels like you've been upset with me ever since I told Dakota I didn't want to have kids."

He jutted his bottom lip out and shook his head. "Not mad. Surprised. Maybe a little confused."

She tilted her head. "Why confused?"

"I know we've just started dating, but hearing you say that made me sad."

"Because...?"

"Well, it's obviously way too early to be thinking about having kids together, but I could see myself someday with you and..." he broke off before completing the thought.

"And now," her voice was barely above a whisper. "You can't see yourself with me."

"No! I still see myself with you. I just have to get used to the idea of what that will look like, and what it won't include."

"That's kind of what I wanted to talk to you about. It's not that I don't want children *someday*, not anytime soon, but the idea scares me—for a lot of reasons. You know I didn't have the best childhood, and I'm sure that has played a big part in why it scares me. I'd always convinced myself that it wasn't going to happen for me. But now..."

His heart skipped a beat. "Now?"

"I don't know. Maybe... someday... I could see it happening?"

He felt his face light up from ear to ear and wrapped an arm around her waist.

"Yeah?"

She looked up at him, her eyes tender. "Yeah."

He dropped his forehead to hers and closed his eyes. "What made you change your mind?"

"Something Dakota said."

He raised his eyebrows, silently willing her to continue.

"That I'm allowed to have it all and be happy."

"I'll agree with that. You make me so fucking happy, I can't even put into words how happy."

"Really? Why?"

"Yes, really. The first time I saw you, I thought you were the most beautiful woman I'd ever laid eyes on. Then I got to know you—the real you. The one who lets me see her vulnerable side. I know not many get to see that side of you.

Not only are you a force to be reckoned with, but you're brilliant, and kind, and witty. You keep me on my toes." The corner of his mouth turned up. "And you give the best blow jobs."

She slapped his stomach playfully. "Oh my god."

"What?" he asked, protecting his center. "It's true. And Dakota's right—we will have beautiful babies someday."

"Maybe someday. Not anytime soon."

"Agreed, although we definitely need to keep practicing. You know what they say—practice makes perfect."

He lifted the hem of her shirt, but she stopped him, asking, "Shouldn't we get outside with our guests?"

He continued pulling the fabric over her head. "Nope," then kissed from her neck to the top of her breasts peeking out of her bra.

****

Whitney

Any thoughts of protests on her part were quickly quashed as his tongue darted under the lace cups and swirled around her stiff nipple.

She let out a soft moan as she ran her fingers through his thick hair.

Steven reached around and unclasped her bra. The straps falling to her elbows as her boobs became fully exposed. He leaned her onto the bed and tossed the garment aside before feasting on her breasts.

"So fucking beautiful," he murmured as he pushed her mounds together in his hands.

With Steve, she *felt* beautiful. Adored, even, and, dare she say, loved?

Woah, woah, woah. Slow your roll, missy. She was just getting used to the idea of accepting they were dating, there was no need to be throwing the L word around.

Hell, they hadn't even said they were exclusive.

Wait, were they exclusive? She assumed they were— they'd been having unprotected sex for fuck's sake, but her grandpa always said, 'when you assume, you make an ass out of u and me.'

No time like the present to clarify.

"Are you dating anyone else?"

He slowly lifted his head from her chest with a scowl.

"What? No! Of course not. Why? Are you?"

"No. I was just double checking we're on the same page."

He used both hands to pinch her nipples softly while he looked in her eyes.

"I don't want anyone but you, sweetness. I guess I thought the no-condom thing made it a given."

"I just wanted to be sure."

"Just you, baby."

"Good. It's just you, too."

He gave her a smug smile. "I know. There's no other man who could satisfy you like I can."

"You do have a magic tongue..." she concurred, then reached down to stroke him over his jeans as she pushed her boobs against his chest. "And your dick's not too bad either."

The loud knocking on the bedroom made her jump and let out small gasp.

"Dude! Are you in there?" It was Zach's voice.

"I'm going to kill him," Steven grumbled as she pulled away. Instinctively, she crossed her arms over her bare chest while she looked for her bra and shirt.

"Yeah, I'm in here. What do you want?"

The doorknob rattled, making her scurry to the bathroom with her clothes in her hand, even though she'd locked the bedroom door behind her when she came in.

"Can I come in?"

"Um, kind of busy at the moment."

"Well, hurry up. I need to talk to you."

He pointed a finger at her before she closed the bathroom door. "We'll finish this later."

She wasn't sure if that was a warning or a promise. Maybe both.

CHAPTER THIRTY-THREE

Steven

"*This* is what couldn't wait?" he asked Zach incredulously while reaching into his refrigerator for a beer. *I got cockblocked for* this?

Zach sat at the kitchen island. "Well, yeah. I didn't know I was interrupting something."

Steven sighed. "As far as I know, she lives here year-round, but I just bought this place, remember? But I always see her next door when I'm here, and she hasn't mentioned anything about leaving for the winter."

His friend took a long pull from his beer while he contemplated the information Steven just provided.

"And the offer to come stay whenever I want is still on the table? Even if you're not here?"

"Yeah, of course." With a grin he added, "But I want my tab to reflect it."

"No problem," Zach said absentmindedly, obviously lost in thought as he took another drink.

"Okay, Mr. Deep-In-Thought, I'm going down to the fire."

"I'll be there in a second."

Steven didn't have the heart to tell Zach that he didn't seem like his neighbor, Zoe's type. Then again, she didn't exactly seem like his type either, yet here he was, asking about her. Although they were both alike in their penchant for romances with younger, good-looking companions they had little in common with, so they had short expiration dates.

Zach and Zoe were grown, single adults; what they did or didn't do wasn't any of his business. The only person Steven was concerned with was standing by the fire with a smile on her face as she talked to Hope and Yvette.

He was glad she'd sought him out to clarify her position about kids *someday*. All afternoon, he'd had flashbacks of his college girlfriend Marie telling him she'd gotten an abortion because there was no way she was having a child with *him*.

As a freshman, it'd been a lot to digest. Not only that his girlfriend had been pregnant and not told him until she no longer was, but her reasons she'd made the choice she did without even talking to him.

"I just couldn't see myself tied for the rest of myself to someone whose goal in life is to work with fish."

He'd almost argued that dolphins were mammals, not fish, but even his nineteen-year-old self recognized that wasn't the point.

"You're a nice guy, Steven. But I really want to end up with someone with more ambition. Someone who could support his family."

He hadn't been upset about the breakup. Marie wasn't his idea of forever either, if he were being honest.

Still... he'd almost been a dad. Even then, it'd made him sad that he'd missed out. He often played the 'what if' game and decided there would never be a question if he could support a family if he were ever in that position again. He changed his major and never looked back.

He was also a lot more diligent about always using new condoms—not ones that had been in his wallet for over a year. Or, at least he had been. He'd had no problem going bareback with Whitney when she offered it. He'd never done that before, not even if a woman said she was on the pill and willing. But everything with Whitney was different.

It was ironic that the reason he'd changed his major was to support a family someday, but his chosen profession had made finding the time do that almost impossible. He realized that was bullshit when he'd started dating Whitney. He'd just never met someone worth finding the time for.

He might have started falling a little in love with her the day they met, but as she looked over at him with a smile as he approached the sand where she stood, there was no doubt now, he was a goner.

"Hey," he said as he wrapped one arm around her and tugged on her t-shirt. "Do you think this will keep you warm enough?"

"It's July third, Steve," Hope sassed.

"It gets chilly on the ocean, smarty pants. You should know that."

"Actually, the Atlantic Coast is warmer than the Pacific by about sixteen degrees."

"I'm not talking about actually going in the water."

His little sister opened her mouth to argue, but Whitney interrupted, "If I get cold, I'll go in and grab a jacket." She then leaned in to whisper, "And maybe you can help me look for it."

She winked when he looked down at her, and he couldn't help but feel a corner of his mouth turn up.

"I'll keep you warm, sweetness."

"You two are so stinkin' adorable," Hope crooned.

"Aren't they, though?" Dakota chimed in as she and Aiden joined the group, plastic wine glasses in hand. The two of them had been spending a lot of time together since being in charge of making lunch for everyone, although they hadn't been outwardly affectionate toward each other.

Good for Aiden. Dakota might be perfect for helping him heal from his nasty divorce, even if it was just as a good friend. She seemed like she had a natural ability to help people wade through their bullshit. Steven would be forever grateful to her for talking to Whitney this afternoon.

"Hey, everyone!"

He had to bite back his growl when Evan Lacroix appeared. His visibly pregnant sister, Olivia, was right behind him, and she gave a smile and wave.

"Hi, guys!" James said from his chair next to the fire. "Glad you could make it!" He then leapt to his feet and put his hand on Olivia's shoulder and elbow. "You need to sit down, little mama," he told her as he helped the pregnant woman to an empty chair by the fire.

Also at the fire was Zoe and a much younger pretty boy who Steven assumed was her weekend romance. Next to him was Barbie. Zach still hadn't come down from the house.

Barbie and Zoe's boy toy seemed to be hitting it off almost too well. Surprisingly, Zoe didn't seem the least bit upset. Steven would be willing to fight anyone who had cozied up to Whitney like this guy had to Barbie. Maybe that's why Zach was staying away—although Steven knew damn well Zach didn't care about Barbie the way he cared about Whitney.

As if on cue, his friend appeared with two beers in his hand. Zach glanced at Barbie, who was oblivious to anyone but Ken—the name Steven had donned Zoe's 'guest,' since he didn't know his real name. Instead of sitting in the chair next to his date, he brought a chair over and put it between Zoe and James. Before sitting down, he held up the extra beer can, liquid condensing down the outside, as if offering it to Zoe, and she smiled warmly at him when she took it.

"No, I'm good, thanks," James said sarcastically. Steve knew he wasn't as annoyed as he made out to be at being snubbed.

Yvette must have heard him as she was reaching into the cooler because she approached with a smirk. "Your beer, sir," and presented it to him like a model showcasing it on the Home Shopping Network.

"Thanks! Why don't you pull up a chair?" James said to her with a flirtatious grin, then grumbled an aside, "At least someone around here is considerate."

Zach, already deep in conversation with Zoe, didn't give a shit about the snide comment.

With Yvette chatting with James and Olivia, that left his sister, Dakota, Aiden, and... Evan.

God, that guy was a dick. Fortunately, he was a great trauma doctor. Or maybe that was unfortunate since that meant Steven had no reason to fire his ass.

At that moment, Whitney hugged him tighter and pulled him a foot away, whispering, "Behave. She's a grown adult."

Steve actually hadn't been thinking about his suspicions that there was something going on with Hope and Dr. Dick, but now he was.

He must have been scowling, because she caressed between his eyebrows until he felt his face relax. "Hey. You're supposed to be having fun."

"I know, it's just I can't stand..."

She interrupted him with a smirk. "The idea of everyone not enjoying themselves? Me neither, but it seems like they're having a good time. Let's keep it that way."

He gave a solemn nod. "Point taken, Counselor."

He still didn't like it though. Lucky for him, Whitney's tits pressed against his chest made him forget about it.

CHAPTER THIRTY-FOUR

Whitney

Over the next week, she and Steven fell into a comfortable routine. He wasn't technically living at her brownstone, but he was there more than he was at his condo. And Lola and Ralph were like two peas in a pod being together all the time.

Too bad the same couldn't be said for their dogwalkers, but Whitney decided not to devote any energy to worrying about it—something that was hard for her Type A personality to do. But as Steve pointed out—they were young adults; this was a good life lesson about learning to work with others you disagreed with.

"Like you and Evan?" she'd teased.

"Yeah," he grumbled in response. "Something like that."

Whitney was happy, too. She felt more content than she could ever remember and was consciously trying to embrace the idea of having it all, like Dakota had told her that the universe wanted for her.

Still, there was always the niggling of doubt in the back of her mind that she'd never been able to have it all. That things were too good to be true and not push it. So, she decided to cancel her meeting with Jim McNamara, the partner at Zach's firm.

Steven asked her about it while making dinner that night, and she knew Zach had called him to tattle on her.

"I'm swamped with work and didn't see the point of taking time out of my day when I know I'm not leaving my job," she replied as she went about setting the table.

"But what harm would have taking the meeting done? At worst, you'd have leverage to ask for a raise."

Whitney shrugged. She knew her fears wouldn't make sense to Steven—especially after her declaration over the Fourth that she could, in fact, have it all. She just wasn't willing to risk what she had with him for the chance at a better job.

"You're probably right," she conceded. She felt safe admitting she may have messed up now that she ruined her chance.

"Zach says he can still get you a lunch meeting on Monday."

Fuck.

When she didn't reply, he cocked his head and looked at her from where he stood in his *Kiss the Chef* apron, stirring the spaghetti sauce on the stove. "What's going on? Is there something you're not telling me?"

"Like what?"

"I don't know. I'm just trying to figure out why you won't just meet with them and see what they have to say."

She let out a long breath. He was right, it wouldn't hurt to see what they said. She wouldn't be tempting fate simply by having lunch, would she?

"Let me look at my calendar for Monday."

****

Steven

His phone buzzed in his scrubs' pocket while he walked between patients. He knew Whitney should be done with her lunch with Jim McNamara by now, but instead of Whitney's name on the screen, it was Zach's.

Zach: Dude, you need to talk to your girl. McNamara offered to double her salary and her paid time off, AND give her a fucking corner office with two paralegals and an assistant, and she told him SHE HAD TO THINK ABOUT IT. WTF is there to think about?

While secretly he agreed with Zach's assessment, he wouldn't throw Whitney under the bus by saying so.

Steven: I'm sure she does have to think about it. She's very analytical. She'll want to make sure she's not missing something.

Zach: Like what? We have the same health care coverage, along with a comparable 401K. She'd get way better cases here. Her commute would be the same. I just don't understand what her hesitation is.

Steven didn't either, but he knew better than to push her too hard.

Steven: I'm sure she just needs to weigh the pros and cons.

Zach: What are the cons, dude?

Steven: Well, she doesn't want to be partner. She wants to eventually go out on her own. Maybe she worries if she makes the move, she'll be pressured to get on the partner track, or she'll become too dependent on the money she's making and won't be able to leave.

Okay, so maybe he did understand what she was thinking better than he originally thought.

Zach: Such a terrible problem to have—making too much money.

Steven: She has goals and a plan, asshole.

Zach: And doubling her salary wouldn't help her reach her goals that much faster?

Okay, his friend had a point there.

Steven: I'll see her tonight and talk to her. No promises though. I'm not going to push her. I know better.

Zach: This is an incredible offer, Steve. But it's not going to be on the table long. I wouldn't steer you or her wrong on this.

Steven: I know you wouldn't. Thanks.

That wasn't bullshit. He knew Zach had Whitney's best interest at heart—if for no other reason than because his friend knew Whitney was important to Steven.

A thought hit him—was it because of Steven that she didn't want to make the move? Was she worried about them breaking up, then she'd have to work with Zach regularly?

It was a plausible reason, and he didn't know why he hadn't thought of it before.

Plausible or not—it was a shitty one. Why would she think they were going to break up? He could see their future together, and it included babies, and grandkids, and growing old together, with his ring on her finger.

They were not fucking breaking up. And she needed to take this job.

He knew, however, it would be more complicated than him just telling her it was a great offer, and she should take it. This would take some finesse.

CHAPTER THIRTY-FIVE

Whitney

And that offer was why she didn't want to take the meeting with Jim McNamara.

Now what the hell was she supposed to do?

Zach had joined them for lunch, and part of her had been grateful to have a friendly face there. She and Zach had talked a lot over the Fourth of July weekend, laughing about all the lawsuits waiting to happen while the roadside stand fireworks were going off. It was evident how much he cared for Steven by the admiration in his voice whenever he talked about his former roommate. That made her like him even more.

Everyone should have a friend who had your back like that. Thank God, she had Gwen.

But when Jim talked numbers openly in front of Zach, that had made her uncomfortable. Obviously, the younger man was being groomed for bigger and better things at McNamara, Wallace, and Stone. When she hadn't jumped at the chance to sign her name on the dotted line, Zach looked at her like she was crazy.

And maybe she was. But she knew it was just too good to be true, and the universe would want something in return. She liked her life the way it was. She wasn't willing to sacrifice anything for this great job opportunity.

Whitney had tried calling Gwen, but her BFF was on a pontoon boat in the middle of a Michigan lake, so her reception kept cutting in and out.

She hovered over Steven's name but exited out of his contact before hitting the button. She had a feeling Zach was already on top of filling him in. Besides, she wouldn't even know how to explain her hesitation to him in a way that he'd understand.

She'd even considered calling Dakota, but when she scrolled through her phonebook on the walk back to her office, she stopped. What would she even say? Dakota had already given her a pep talk, which Whitney had told her she bought into but was now obviously ignoring. Would Whitney's 'problem' exasperate her? Because, in one corner of her mind, it was frustrating herself. Like, *get your shit together, you're being ridiculous* level annoying.

But there was that little voice, reminding her the universe would balance out her good fortune. Better to just stay in her lane.

Double my salary though. And double my paid time off.

How could she walk away from that?

It made her sick, but she wasn't sure if she could. What would she have to sacrifice for it? Her stomach reeled at the thought.

She should have trusted her intuition and never have taken the lunch.

****

Steven

The dogs greeted him at the door when he walked into her brownstone. She'd given him the code to her lock, telling him to just come in whenever he came over—which was becoming more and more frequent. So much that Lola stayed there during the day now instead of at his condo.

He followed the smell of something cooking into the kitchen where he found her standing at the stove, already changed out of her work clothes and in a pair of grey yoga pants and the Stanford t-shirt he'd bought her online.

"Something smells good. What're you making?" he asked as he kissed her cheek and wrapped an arm around her waist to peer over her shoulder.

"Just something I saw online. It sounded delicious. It's got chicken, peppers, zucchini, broccoli, butternut squash, portabella mushrooms—"

"I thought you didn't like mushrooms. You turned your nose up at them when they served them on your steak on our first date."

"I can't believe you remember that. I was as surprised as you when I was buying them. But the way the YouTuber described the flavor caught my attention, and when I was watching the video, they just looked good, so I thought I'd give it a shot. It turns out I do like them after all. I guess my taste buds are changing as I get older."

He gave her a thoughtful look. "Well, it looks great. Let me go wash up, and I'll set the table."

When he returned, she was in the middle of putting their plates on the table.

"I said I would do that."

"I know, but dinner's almost ready, and I had a few minutes. It's not a big deal. It's just the two of us."

He pulled silverware from the drawer, then placed them around the plates while she grabbed glasses from the cupboard.

"How'd the dogs do today?"

"I think fine. I came home early, so they were happy to see me and get let outside not long after their walk."

"You came home early?"

"Yeah. I had a lot of things to think about."

"Oh? What about?" Steven was dying to ask her about her lunch meeting but decided to let her steer the conversation.

She was moving the contents from the skillet onto a serving platter when she shot him a look. "Please. You know damn well what about. Don't even act like Zach didn't call you the minute he walked out of the restaurant. I'm pretty sure I saw him dialing as he waited for a cab."

"He didn't call me."

She raised an eyebrow at him, obviously not buying it.

Steve confessed with a grin. "He might have texted though..."

Setting the platter down on the table with a thud, she exclaimed, "I knew it! What did he tell you?"

He sat and put a napkin in his lap while she did the same.

"He was just surprised you weren't more enthusiastic about the offer."

Whitney was quiet while scooping the contents onto his plate, then hers. Finally, she said quietly, "It was a really nice offer."

"Buuuut?"

"But I don't know if I want to take it."

While he wanted to jump to his feet and ask, "Are you insane? Of course you want to take it! What's the problem?" he forced himself to take a drink of water before he spoke next.

"How come?"

"It's hard to explain. Change is hard for me as it is, and too much change... I'm just not sure I'm at a place where I want to make a move."

"It's a lot of money though," he reminded her. "And Zach says much better cases."

"I know! I *know* it's the smart move. I *know* I'd be an idiot to pass up this opportunity. But I don't know if I'm ready!"

"You'll never be one-hundred percent ready. Sometimes you just have to take a leap of faith."

"I can only leap so many times in such a short period."

He knew she was talking about being with him.

"Your last leap turned out pretty good, didn't it? Why wouldn't this one, too?"

She let out a big sigh. "It did. It's just—I—" She sighed again and slumped her shoulders. "Can we just drop it for now? I don't want to talk about it anymore tonight."

He didn't want to drop it but knew pushing her would be counterproductive.

"Sure." He reached for her hand. "I'm on your side, you know. I can be a great sounding board—I don't have to say anything, I can just listen and only offer my advice if asked. All I want is to help you figure this out."

The line between her eyebrows softened, and she squeezed his hand. "I know. Thank you for not taking this personally. I'm so stressed about what I should do. I just need some time to process everything on my own first before I can talk about it."

"Fair enough."

He tugged on her hand until she stood, and then he pulled her onto his lap, where he brushed her hair off her shoulder so he could murmur in her ear, "I know the perfect cure to help you relax..."

With a small smile, she twisted so she was straddling him with her arms around his neck.

"Oh, you do?"

"Yes," he said solemnly, fighting back his own smile. "I'm a doctor. I know these things."

"Okay." She moved her hips in small circles over his growing cock. "What should I do first?"

Steven groped her tits over her tight t-shirt.

"Well, I'd have to examine you before I could make a final recommendation. Maybe we should go upstairs, so I can do a thorough assessment while you're lying down."

"Whatever you think is best. You are the professional."

The corner of his mouth lifted as he patted her bottom and helped her off him. "You'll need to be naked, too."

She nodded as they walked up the stairs. "Of course. I suppose you'll have to be naked, too?"

"It will help with my examination, yes."

"Makes sense," she replied once they reached the top of the staircase.

He fondled her tits as he walked behind her down the short hall. "You might need an injection."

"I think you might be right. I've heard they can help."

"Let me help you with your shirt," he murmured as he shut the door with the back of his heel and reached for the hem of her tee.

She lifted her hands over her head, and he pulled the garment off in one motion The tops of her breasts spilled out from her lacy black bra, her flat stomach exposed above her tight yoga pants.

"Fuck, you're beautiful."

"Do you say that to all your patients, Doctor Ericson?"

"Just the ones I fuck." He paused when she smirked. "Wait—that came out wrong." Now he was flustered. "Just one. You. Only you."

He picked her up and tossed her on the bed, then tugged on her pants.

"And I suppose I'm the only one you help undress?"

"You would be correct." He tossed her leggings on the ground and spread her legs wide as he climbed between them. "But you get special assistance, Ms. Hayes, since I'm about to devour your pussy."

He didn't know if her gasp was because of his words or because he'd dove headfirst between her thighs, but there was no doubt her low moan was because he was dragging his tongue down her slit.

He felt her hands in his hair as she bucked her hips up and pressed against his mouth, murmuring, "Ohhhh, yes."

"You taste delicious, baby."

His tongue explored her folds before circling her clit, while he slid two fingers inside her wet pussy. His mouth and hands worked in tandem: one finger fucking her while the other polished her clit. He lifted his head to whisper the dirty words he knew turned her on.

"Your pretty pussy is so wet, sweetness."

"You make my cock so fucking hard."

Her breaths became shallower, and he felt her body tighten around his fingers.

"Are you going to come for me?"

She let out a low moan, then chanted, "Yes, yes, yes!" before her legs shook. She bowed up off the bed while crying out his name.

"That's right, baby. Say my name as you come for me," he growled.

She was still quivering when he stripped his clothes off and slid his cock inside her. Her pussy welcomed him by pulsing around his shaft.

"Fuuuuck, Whit. You feel good."

"God, so do you," she moaned as she clung to his back.

Resting his weight on his forearms, he burrowed his face into her neck, while thrusting in and out of her heat.

He loved how responsive she was, lifting her hips to meet his, while digging her nails into his back and whimpering softly, "Yes, Steven. Oh god, just like that!"

Her moans spurred him to pick up the pace and slip his hand between them to stroke her clit.

"Come again for me, dirty girl. Come on my cock."

Thankfully, she did exactly what he told her, because his control was slipping. The second he felt her pussy shudder around his dick, he thrust once before he spilled his seed deep inside her.

"Goddamn, woman, you are fucking incredible," he panted as his arms came tight around her.

They lay still for several seconds, wrapped in each other's arms, while their breathing evened out. It was a moment of bliss, and he wanted to commit to memory how perfect she felt underneath him.

His dick began to go soft, and he pulled out and rolled to the side, then sat up, preparing to get a washcloth to clean her. But not before he took a minute to admire his cum leaking out of her, using his fingers to separate her pussy lips.

"Damn, that's sexy."

"You're a weirdo," she said with a laugh.

"Bullshit. I'm a man, and it's fucking primal that I think that's hot."

She stared at him with wide eyes.

"Wow. I kind of like the Neanderthal side of you."

Steven winked before standing. "Good. You might want to get used to it." He leaned down and kissed her forehead, whispering, "Take the damn job, woman," before he went in search of a washcloth to clean her.

He smiled when he heard her mutter, "Oh, my."

CHAPTER THIRTY-SIX

Whitney

Gwen walked into the restaurant Friday evening, looking tan and rested, and smiled brightly when she noticed Whitney already at a table.

She stood and gave her friend a long hug. "How was your flight?"

Gwen shrugged as they broke apart. "Uneventful."

"I guess that's good, right? I'm so glad you're back. I have *a lot* to tell you."

"I told you I'd be back in time to help with the gala. I know how much it means to you." Gwen pulled out her chair and gave Whitney a scrutinous inspection from head to toe. "What's wrong?"

"I, uh, quit my job today," Whitney gulped as she sat back down.

Gwen gasped as she plopped in her seat and covered Whitney's hand with hers and squeezed. "You're kidding! That's great! Are you going out on your own?"

"No, I got a job with McNamara, Stone, and Wallace. But with what they're paying me, I should be able to hang my own shingle a lot sooner than I'd planned."

"This is so exciting, Whitney. I'm glad you're getting the fuck out of there. They have never valued you. I never understood why they pushed for you to go to Harvard only to hire you and treat you like your degree is from Rocco's School of Law and Refrigerator Repair."

The waitress appeared and took their drink order, then Whitney responded, "Having a Harvard grad on staff looked good on their website. I'm not sure why I was the designated patsy either. Maybe it was better to have one attorney with a shitty record, while the others were stellar."

"Yeah, it also meant they could pay you accordingly. I bet they thought no other firm would want to steal you if your wins weren't above average."

"They were probably right, except Steven's friend, Zach works at McNamara, and I guess he vouched for me. They offered me a job on the spot when we went to lunch."

"I'm so fucking happy for you. New job, new man... Congratulations!"

Whitney gave her a nervous smile.

"Why aren't you thrilled? This is a huge deal, and you look like you're going to be sick."

"Because I feel like I'm going to be sick. I've been nauseous since they offered me the job. I thought after I told Alan, I'd feel relieved, but I don't. What if—"

"Stop. Whatever you're about to say, just stop. What if your new firm recognizes how fucking awesome you are and you *thrive* there?"

"But then—"

"Your new man falls head over heels in love with you and wants to marry you? Then I guess you'll live happily fucking ever after, won't you? We'll live next door to each other and raise our kids together and watch our grandkids grow up. And it'll be great, Whit."

She opened her mouth to argue, but Gwen squeezed her hand again, effectively silencing her. "Just let yourself be happy. You deserve it."

Whitney was still skeptical but decided to shut up about her doubts. She didn't want to sound like an ungrateful twat.

The server appeared with their drinks and asked if they were ready to order.

"We haven't even looked at the menu, sorry."

"Take your time. I'll check back in a while."

"So," Gwen said in a hushed, conspiratorial tone. "What did Alan Crawford say when you gave him your notice?"

"He seemed surprised, then offered me a ten percent raise. I think he thought it was a tactic on my part to get a pay increase from him."

"It's bullshit that you'd have to resort to something like that since they wouldn't have offered you one otherwise. Even though you fucking deserved one."

She felt herself smile. "I *did* deserve one, didn't I?"

"Sounds like they're going to appreciate you at your new firm."

"It feels like it. Did I mention they doubled my PTO, too?"

"Damn! You're going to have as much time off as me!"

"Ha ha, not quite teacher time off. But I'll have more, so maybe we can do a girls' trip when you're on your fall or spring break."

"I am so happy for you."

Whitney let herself feel happy, too.

"Anyway, Alan didn't want to accept my two weeks when he realized I was serious. So, he told me to pack my stuff and then had security escort me from the building."

"Oh. My. God. Are you serious? What a dick."

"It's standard procedure, which is why I stayed late the last few nights, tidying up loose ends. I knew that's what would happen. Which is fine, because now I can help more with the gala next week since I won't be working and can slowly get moved into my new office the following week, then hit the ground running on my official start date."

Gwen beamed at her across the table. "I'm just so proud of you for taking the leap."

"Steven said the same thing."

"Well, he seems great. I like him."

Whitney rolled her eyes. "So you've said. A few times now."

"How's that going?"

So good it scared the crap out of her.

"So far, so good. Our dogs are in love, and we've managed to find a good routine with our schedules. Enough about me! I want to hear all about your vacation! You look fantastic. The Michigan sunshine and fresh air definitely agreed with you."

The waitress appeared, and they both just shook their heads at her. A small smirk escaped her friend's lips. "I might have had a little romance myself."

"Shut the front door! Who? Where? When? How? Tell me everything!"

"It's not a big deal. We had a lot of fun for the few weeks I was there, but we both knew it couldn't go anywhere. His job's there and mine's here, and neither of us is interested in moving."

"So, tell me about him!"

"We actually used to hang out as kids—but let me tell you, he is *all* grown up now. I ran into him at a bonfire my first night there, and we realized who the other was and ended up talking all night. Then we ran into each other again the next day at the breakfast diner in town, and he asked me to dinner, and the rest, they say, is history."

"I love it! What does he do?"

"He's the local sheriff, so we had to try to be discreet."

Whitney scrunched up her nose. "Why? A single guy can't date just because he's in law enforcement?" After a beat, a thought occurred to her, "Oh my god. He is single, right? Tell me you weren't messing around with a married man!"

"What? Of course I wasn't messing around with a married man. I mean, I guess he's *technically* still married, but he's supposed to sign divorce papers next month. She's moved out and is dating someone else. We actually ran into them at the movies."

"Ouch. I bet that was awkward."

"Only for a minute."

"But you're not going to try to do the long-distance thing?"

"No. That just gets too complicated."

"So, you're not going to see him again?"

Another small smile formed on Gwen's lips. "I mean, it's possible I could run into him when I visit my family at Thanksgiving and Christmas. And he might possibly spend Labor Day weekend in Boston seeing the sights."

"Yeah, seeing the sights all right. You mean your bedroom. Wait. You're going for Thanksgiving *and* Christmas? You've never done that. Never. Not once since I've known you."

"Well, my grandparents are getting old," she said defensively as she picked up her menu to peruse it. "And my parents are no spring chickens either."

Whitney scowled at her with her unopened menu in her hand. "Nice try."

"It's not serious."

"Yeah, that's what I tried telling you about Steven. You didn't believe me, either."

"It *can't* be serious, then; how's that? It's just not practical. We live a thousand miles apart. There was no rational reason you and Steven couldn't get serious, other than your own hang ups. Which, I'm super proud of you for working through and letting yourself be happy."

Whitney shook her head. "I don't know. I'm just waiting for the other shoe to drop, like it always does."

"Nope. Not this time."

The waitress came back, and they finally were ready to order. Gwen ordered the filet mignon.

"Bleu cheese or mushrooms with that?" the young girl asked to upsell. Whitney respected that. Always upsell.

"Mushrooms."

"Mashed potatoes okay?"

"Yes."

The server looked over at Whitney and gave her a patient smile as she waited for Whitney's order.

"I'm easy. I will have the exact same thing as her," she said, handing over her menu.

Gwen cocked her head and opened her mouth to say something, but Whitney smiled and said, "So does the sheriff have a name?"

"Of course. But I'm not telling you."

"Why?"

"You'll stalk him."

"So?"

Gwen smiled and tried changing the subject, asking, "So, how can I help you next week with the gala?"

"It's not that hard to do a Google search and figure out you know."

"Go ahead, I can't stop you. But I don't have to make it easy for you. *Now*, how can I help with the gala?"

They talked about all the errands Whitney needed to run for the foundation and which ones Gwen would help her with. It was important that the event made a lot of money so they could continue being a no-kill shelter.

Before she knew it, their server was opening a stand and bending at the knees to drop the tray holding their food.

"Wow, that was fast."

Gwen's plate was placed in front of her, followed by Whitney's identical order.

Her friend looked across the table and remarked, "*You're* having mushrooms?"

The server paused, waiting for Whitney to confirm her order was correct.

"Yes." The younger girl walked away, and Whitney continued, "I don't know. I saw them on a cooking show and decided to give them another try. Turns out I like them. Weird, huh? To have a sudden change in palate like that."

Gwen's brows furrowed as she cut her steak. "Something like that happened to the teacher across the hall from me. She hated dill pickles, then one night at dinner, her husband was having a hamburger with pickles, and she could *smell* them across the table and had a sudden craving for them. That's how she knew she was pregnant."

Wait, pregnant?

What. The Fuck.

And here Whitney was craving mushrooms—a food she used to hate.

She dropped her silverware, her hands shaking, and leaned down to rummage through her purse.

"What are you looking for?"

"My phone. It's got my period tracker on it."

"Your peri—Are you late?"

She pulled out her phone and blew out a breath as she opened the app. "I don't know. I haven't been paying attention."

Her heart dropped when the week in pink flashed on the screen. "I should have started six days ago."

Gwen popped a piece of steak into her mouth and chewed thoughtfully before responding. "There's a lot of reasons you could be late. You've been under a lot of stress with the job change and the upcoming gala. We'll go get a test after dinner."

"I don't know if I can wait that long."

"We're going to finish dinner," Gwen said sternly, taking another bite.

"Fine. But I'm getting a to-go box. I've lost my appetite."

CHAPTER THIRTY-SEVEN

Whitney
Two pink lines.

It was a good thing she was already sitting on the closed-lid toilet, or she might have fallen when she peered at the stick she'd just peed on five minutes earlier.

"Are you okay?" Gwen whispered as she rubbed circles on Whitney's back.

She opened her mouth, ready to blurt out, "No!" but stopped. *Was* she okay?

There was no sense of panic or impending doom. The timing wasn't exactly ideal for a baby, given that she was starting a new job in two weeks, but it was doable. She made a decent salary, so she wouldn't be destitute and pregnant.

The bigger question was, could she be a good mom?

She'd allowed herself to picture it, after Dakota practically gave her permission over the holiday weekend, but that had just been daydreaming. Now the real thing was here, and the self-doubt started to creep in.

"I think so," Whitney whispered.

"What are you going to do?"

"I guess—" She swallowed hard. "I guess I'm having a baby."

Gwen squealed. "I'm going to be an auntie!"

Whitney tried to muster up a smile at her friend's excitement but couldn't.

"What about Steven? How do you think he's going to react?"

"I don't know. He's alluded that he wants kids *someday*, but I don't think he meant *today*."

"Yeah, well, you didn't get pregnant by yourself."

"True. But if he decides he's not ready, I guess..." She took a deep breath, then let it out. The mama bear instinct she was feeling was a surprise. "I guess I'll do it by myself."

"You'll always have me. Remember that. No matter what, you're not doing this alone."

She let out a mirthless laugh. "I was just saying over the Fourth that I didn't want kids—ever. What a difference a few weeks makes."

A thought occurred to her. Dakota was kind of hippie-ish and always struck Whitney as abnormally intuitive. Did Dakota know she was pregnant the holiday weekend? Had she been pregnant then?

She would have to ask her when she saw her at the gala Friday night.

"You're going to be a great mom." Gwen pulled her in for a hug. "This is a good thing, Whit. Don't overthink it, okay? I know a lot is changing—but change can be good."

That'd never been Whitney's experience, but she'd have to trust it would work out. What choice did she have?

****

Steven

Friday night shifts were always busy. The good thing about that was it meant the night flew by. He'd barely had time to scarf down a cafeteria sandwich that he'd sent one of the residents to get before he worked on another patient.

His phone buzzed while they waited for an ambulance to arrive with a heart attack patient.

Whitney: Were you still planning on coming here tonight after work?

Steven: That's my plan. Although I'm not sure what time it's going to be. Hopefully, no later than midnight. Is that okay?

Whitney: Yes. I'll wait up. We need to talk.

His first instinct was dread. Nothing good was ever waiting on the other end of 'we need to talk.' But then he remembered Alan Crawford had her escorted from the building earlier, so it was probably about that.

Steven: Everything okay?

Whitney: Um. Maybe? I'll wait up for you, and we'll talk more about it when you get here.

He didn't have a good feeling about this.

CHAPTER THIRTY-EIGHT

Steven

Whitney was in her pajamas, lying on her couch under a blanket, watching TV when he came through the door a little before midnight. The dogs, nestled at the other end of the couch on her blanket, looked up and offered a few thumps of their tails when they noticed his appearance, but they didn't get down to greet him.

Her cryptic texts had put him on edge and the minute Dr. Connelly walked in for her shift, he briefed her on the current ER patients. Ten minutes later, he was in the locker room, changing out of his scrubs. It was fair to say he didn't drive the speed limit to her brownstone.

She looked tiny under the blanket, and there was an air of vulnerability about her. His caveman liked it when she was vulnerable—he liked the idea of being the one to protect her.

He sat on the edge of the cushion and pushed her hair behind her ear. "Hey, sweetness. Thanks for staying up."

With a sad smile, she replied, "I don't think I'd have been able to sleep even if I tried."

"What's going on?"

Without a word, she pulled her hand out from under the thick comforter and handed him something.

It took him a second to register what he was looking at.

A pregnancy test. And it was positive.

Steven tried to keep his face neutral as he swallowed hard while he digested what was going on. He knew she was probably freaking out. He only had one shot at his reaction.

Cupping her behind her head, he brought his lips gently to hers.

"I'm fucking thrilled. Please tell me you think this is a good thing."

He didn't know if he could handle her not wanting to go through with the pregnancy. This was his second chance— and this time, he was ready. Emotionally and financially.

Tears welled up in her eyes, and she whispered, "I didn't know how you'd react. We very specifically said we weren't ready just a few weeks ago."

"Things change, baby. I'm fucking over the moon."

"Are you sure?" she squeaked.

"Positive. What about you? How do you feel about this?"

The floodgates opened, and tears streamed down her face as she sobbed. "I'm scared. I can't believe I'm going to have a baby."

Well, that was promising. There was no talk of her wanting to terminate the pregnancy.

Steven gathered her up in his arms and sat on the couch, rocking her gently. "You're going to be a great mom, sweetness. I know it. And Dakota's right, we're going to have beautiful babies."

The dogs had taken notice of her crying, and Ralph let out a low whine.

Steve reached over and patted the dog's head. "She's okay, buddy. Just a little emotional."

"And overwhelmed." She'd stopped crying but stayed snuggled against his chest. "And scared. And happy, too. How can I have so many feelings at once?"

He kissed the top of her head and chuckled. "Well, baby, I think those are probably normal emotions with an unexpected pregnancy."

"Are you scared?"

"Nope. I'm excited as fuck. I'm going to be a kickass dad. *We're* going to be kickass parents."

He wanted to talk right then about getting married but decided against it. Her head was already spinning. There was a lot he would have to ease her into. Even before tonight, he'd started easing her into living with him—he just hadn't verbalized it. But Lola stayed here all the time, which meant he did too. Whitney was a smart girl, he knew she'd noticed, but she'd seemed to have been on board.

Maybe it was because it hadn't been said out loud so it wasn't official.

Unfortunately, they no longer had that luxury. Shit was about to get official, and there was a lot they would have to discuss. Fortunately, they had some time.

"You must be exhausted. It was a busy day for you."

"I'm pretty wrung out, emotionally."

He stood with her still in his arms. "Let's get you to bed. We've got a busy day tomorrow."

"A busy day? Doing what?"

"We were going to the Cape, remember?"

"Oh, yeah."

When she'd called to tell him about Alan not accepting her notice, he'd told her, "Good. That means we can stay at the Cape until Monday afternoon."

At the time, she'd been on board. Now, judging by her lack of enthusiasm, he wasn't so sure.

"We don't have to go."

"I want to go. I just have a lot of things to do for the gala, and I wanted to get started Monday morning."

"How about we leave in the morning and come back Sunday night? That will give us two days there."

He wanted her to relax and take it easy. That was easier to manage if she was away from everything.

"Can Gwen come?"

"Of course."

"Good, since I already invited her."

"I thought you'd forgotten we were going?"

"I invited her before... everything happened."

Despite her protests that she could walk, he didn't let her go until he reached the bed. There, he yanked the covers back then set her down as gently as he could. His baby was in there. He needed to be careful.

Stripping down to his boxers, he turned out the light and crawled next to her, putting his arm around her, and rested his hand on her belly.

"I love you, Whitney."

"You're just saying that because I'm your baby mama."

Steven rolled her onto her back and pinned her wrists over her head with one hand while hovering over her body as he stared down at her.

"I'm saying it because it's true. I think I fell in love with you on our first date, and I've just been falling deeper ever since."

Tears sprang up in her eyes again. "I love you, too. This baby just has complicated things."

"No. This baby has made things clearer."

He captured her lips with his while still holding her wrists in his grasp. She sighed into his mouth as he felt her relax in complete surrender.

"That's my girl," he murmured as he let go of her wrists and pulled the pink satin pajama top over her head. He knew it technically had buttons, but he couldn't wait the time it would take to unfasten them. He needed to feel her bare skin.

He pulled his shirt off and reached for her, then paused. Here before him was this woman he was in love with, who was going to have his baby.

Steven must have been staring because she glanced down at herself as she asked, "What?"

"Nothing." He shook his head and pulled her into his arms. "You're beautiful, is all. I can't believe I'm the lucky son of a bitch who knocked you up."

"I don't know how it happened. I'm religious about taking my birth control."

He knew that was true. She even had a daily alarm on her phone to remind her. Whenever it went off, she'd stop whatever she was doing and take it. The only time she hadn't was when he was in the middle of licking her pussy. He'd lifted her head and said, "I'll remind you," before resuming work on her clit until she came. And he had reminded her later.

"It just means it was meant to be."

He caressed her flat stomach, then slipped his hand underneath the waistband of her silky pajama bottoms.

"You're not wearing any underwear," he murmured in her ear as he spread her juices through her folds and onto her clit. "And you're already wet for me. Such a naughty good girl."

"I like being naughty with you."

"Yeah?" He sat up on his knees and tugged her bottoms off. "Do you like being my little slut?"

She visibly swallowed hard, while lifting her hips subtly. "I love it."

He spread her legs wide and ran one finger up and down her slit. "I know you do."

Spreading her further to accommodate his wide shoulders, he lay down between her thighs. "I'm going to be dirty as fuck with you until you come all over my tongue, then I'm going to revere your beautiful body as I make love to you."

She let out a little gasp as he circled her swollen knot with his tongue.

"Your slutty pussy tastes so good, sweetness. I could eat you all night long."

Except if he did his job right, he'd only be eating it for six minutes before he was balls deep inside her quivering cunt. He loved fucking her after she'd just come. Her pussy gripping his dick and milking it was the best feeling in the world.

Sliding one finger inside her wet heat, he fucked her in rhythm with his tongue working her clit.

She bucked her hips up, and he held her in place with his forearm, while his fingers pulled her apart, and his other hand continued finger fucking her.

"God, you have such a pretty pussy, baby."

He flicked his tongue along her pearl, then paused to admire her some more, while continuing his dirty talk. "It tastes so sweet. It's like sugar on my tongue."

Her hips pressed against his forearm, and he held her firm.

"Do you want to come, baby?"

"Yessssss."

Fucking her faster, he sucked on her clit, flicking his tongue as he did.

"Oh my god, Steven. That feels so fucking good."

Her pussy gripped his finger tight, and he knew she was ready to explode.

He pressed a second finger inside and shook his head as he lapped at her sensitive spot.

"Yes, yes, yesssss!" she chanted right before she convulsed around him.

Watching her come undone was so fucking sexy, his cock was leaking.

When she stopped thrashing, Steven wasted no time sliding his dick inside her and thrusting hard. He could usually pull another orgasm from her when her pussy was in such a heightened state.

"Fuuuuuck, Whit," he moaned as he pushed his cock in deep.

She dug her nails into his back. "Fuck me, baby. Fuck your little slut."

Holy shit. Talk about turning the tables. Her dirty mouth was hot as hell.

Between how good her freshly orgasmed pussy felt and her sexy aggression, he wasn't going to last long.

He reached down and toyed with her clit as he pumped in and out of her.

"Such a dirty girl."

She grabbed her tits as she arched off the bed, looking like a goddamn porn star, while she came again around his cock. That was all it took for Steven to follow. Grabbing her hips, he thrust in deep as he spurt rope after rope of cum inside her.

After he'd emptied himself completely, he dropped to his forearms, enveloping her under him.

"My beautiful baby mama," he cooed. "You are a dirty girl, and I fucking love it."

"So much for making love," she teased.

"Fuck, baby. I know. I'm sorry."

"God, don't be. That was awesome—and exactly what I needed, I think. We can cuddle tonight and try again this weekend."

He liked the sound of that.

CHAPTER THIRTY-NINE

Whitney

Gwen arrived promptly at eight the next morning, and the three of them, along with Lola and Ralph, piled in the Land Rover to head to the coast. But not before stopping for breakfast in Quincy at the diner with the dog friendly patio.

Of course the waitress remembered Steven.

"She remembered the dogs, not me," he replied when Whitney rolled her eyes once the woman walked away.

"Pretty sure she remembered the handsome blond with the sexy chest and arm muscles, who happened to have two dogs with him. You could have brought two French poodles with you this time, and she wouldn't have known the difference."

He pulled her close to him on the patio bench and nuzzled her neck. "Well, too bad for her that I'm already taken."

"And you wonder how you ended up pregnant," Gwen muttered.

Steve laughed. "Oh, I *know* how she got pregnant..."

Whitney rolled her eyes again. "Yes, he's a doctor, so apparently, he's an expert about how babies are made."

He laughed, then his face sobered. "Speaking of doctors. You need to get in to see your OB/GYN as soon as possible."

"It's already on my list of people to call on Monday."
Whitney let out a big sigh. "I don't know if I should tell
McNamara before I even start."

"No!" Gwen and Steven cried in unison.

"Don't you think that's the right thing to do?"

"Fuck no," Steven growled.

"No," Gwen said, shaking her head.

"No? Why not?"

"Well, because we're not telling anyone but your doctor
until you're past your first trimester. And second, he doesn't
need to know unless being pregnant somehow affects how
you do your job. You know that."

She did know that, but still felt guilty not telling him
before starting.

"Wait. Why not until I'm past my first trimester?"

"Because you're at the greatest risk for losing the baby
until you hit your thirteenth week. One in eight pregnancies
end in miscarriage."

She felt her eyes widen. "Really? I had no idea."

Gwen cocked her head from across the table. "You really
didn't know that?"

Whitney felt herself getting defensive, and grumbled,
"Well, considering I wasn't planning on having kids until a
few weeks ago, why would I?"

"I guess I just thought it was common knowledge."

"Maybe common knowledge for people who pay
attention to that kind of thing. But I never had any interest."

"I remember," Gwen said with a small smile. "Then you go and meet Mr. Wonderful here..." She gestured toward Steven with her head. "And everything changes."

Whitney had to admit, he was pretty wonderful.

"I guess. It was just something Dakota said that made me look at it from a different perspective, and I realized maybe it was in the cards for me." She patted her belly. "I didn't realize how quickly that would happen, but..."

Steven covered her hand with his and kissed her chastely on the lips. "It's gonna be great. You'll see."

"So, are you two going to get married?"

"Yes."

"No."

Steven's *yes* was far more emphatic than her *no*.

Whitney shrugged. "We haven't discussed it. Like you pointed out—there's a lot that could still go wrong. We've got time to figure it out."

"Well, not too much time," Gwen countered. "If you don't want to be showing when you walk down the aisle."

"We don't have to get married before the baby comes."

"The fuck we don't," Steven snarled. "I don't care if you're as big as a house—you're marrying me before that baby gets here."

Goddamn, she wanted to jump his bones when he got bossy like that. Was it the pregnancy hormones making her think him being a caveman was so hot?

Still, she patted his hand and gave a polite smile. "We'll see."

****

Steven

We'll see, my ass. This wasn't up for debate.

"You might as well start shopping for a dress," he warned.

Whitney shifted on the bench next to him, scowling.

"Is this your idea of a marriage proposal? Because it sucks."

Aw, fuck.

He dropped his head. "You're right. I'm sorry. I'll make it up to you, I promise."

The corner of her mouth turned up, even as she tried to keep a stern look by crossing her arms in front of her. "It better be good, too. I want to be surprised."

"I promise."

"Candles, flowers... the whole nine yards."

"Telling me how to do it won't make it much of a surprise then," he said with a smirk.

"Yeah, that's true. Okay. Never mind about the candles and flowers."

The fact that she was telling him how she wanted to be proposed to bode well for how she would respond when he did ask. Which was going to be soon.

There was no question, he was putting a ring on it and changing her last name before his baby was born.

CHAPTER FORTY

Whitney

The second Steven opened the back of the Land Rover to get their bags, the dogs jumped over the third row they were seated in and took off to run around the house like they were greyhounds chasing a mechanical rabbit.

"I thought they were strapped in?" he asked.

Gwen looked sheepish when she said, "I might've unbuckled them as we drove up the driveway. I didn't realize they'd take off like that."

The dogs streaked by, having completed one lap, and Whitney reached for her bag. "Don't worry about it. They don't go far."

"No, I'll go get them," Gwen said and took off in a jog after them, their leashes in hand.

Steven stared at Whitney. "What do you think you're doing?"

She frowned in confusion. "They'll be fine, Steve. You know the farthest they go is to Zoe's, and she'll tell them to go home."

He gestured to her hand on her duffel bag. "No. I mean with your bag."

Was this a trick question? "Taking it into the house?"

"You lift that bag up one inch, and I'm going to spank your ass. You can't be lifting things anymore."

There was the sexy caveman who made her toes curl.

"Bare bottomed?"

He raised one eyebrow at her. "Be careful, little girl."

She crossed her arms at her chest and rested her weight on one hip. "So, I'm to understand carrying an overnight bag is off limits, but having my ass spanked would be fine?"

He hoisted all three of their bags in one hand and closed the rear door. "My house, my rules," he said unapologetically, then with his free hand, grabbed her ass as they walked toward the house.

"Your rules are preposterous. And you're going to make a great dad because that's totally something a dad would say. *To their child.* Which, I'm sure you've noticed, I am not."

"No, but you're carrying my child, so, no more lifting."

"I'm fairly certain you're being over-the-top ridiculous. I'm barely pregnant."

"Don't care," he grumbled as he punched in the code to unlock the door.

"Is this how the next eight months are going to go?"

"I'll probably get worse. Especially once you start showing."

She looked up at the ceiling and let out a dramatic sigh before uttering, "Oh my god. You are a Neanderthal."

But a tiny part of her—the part where no one had ever taken care of her, not even when she was a child—loved his protectiveness. Even if it bordered on absurd.

He dropped a kiss on her forehead. "I already told you, get used to it."

Could she though? It wasn't like her to just give up control and allow herself to be vulnerable.

Hell, she'd been doing a lot of things out of character lately. Maybe letting Steven take care of her could be part of Whitney 2.0. The new and improved version of herself. The one who trusts that everything will work out for her. That the universe has her back, and she can be a successful attorney and mother, and have a healthy relationship.

Maybe.

CHAPTER FORTY-ONE

Whitney

The weekend came to an end way too fast, like it always did. The only difference this time was when she went to bed Sunday night, she wasn't dreading Monday like she did when she worked for Crawford, Holden, and Crane. She had a lot to do over the next few days to make sure the gala's silent auction went off without a hitch, including picking up last-minute donations that hadn't already been delivered. And some of it would involve lifting—nothing too heavy, but more than what Steven was 'allowing' her to do, which was basically zilch.

She'd googled it at the Cape Saturday night while they were sitting on the patio, and what she'd found said not to do *heavy* lifting. Her overnight bag had hardly qualified as heavy.

"You're a doctor—you should know you're being paranoid."

"I prefer to think of it as cautious."

"If I were your patient, would you tell me I couldn't lift anything? I see expectant mothers who also have toddlers carry their two-year-olds around all the time."

"First of all, we already established that you're special. I don't fuck my patients, and they aren't carrying my child. You are. Second, I'm not around after they leave my ER to help them and make sure they don't have to lift anything. I am

274

with you. So, what I would tell one of my patients and what I'm going to tell the woman I'm in love with, who's having my baby, are not going to be the same." He got up and kissed her cheek. "Do you want anything from the kitchen?"

"Maybe something snacky and a soda."

He frowned. "I'll make some popcorn. You've already had two sodas today. How about some water with the berry flavor enhancer you like?"

"Okay," she grumbled reluctantly. He was right, but still...

"How about you, Gwen?"

"I will have another beer, thanks."

"You know, if I can't drink, I don't think you guys should be able to either."

"Fair enough," he replied immediately. *Wow, that was easy.*

Not so with Gwen. "Sorry, but if I'm not getting the benefits of *how* you got pregnant, I'm not giving up anything just to be in solidarity with you."

Steven smirked, then headed toward the kitchen.

Whitney looked at Gwen. "I thought... The sexy sheriff..."

"Lives a thousand miles away. And things didn't get that far."

"Oh. Is that a good thing?"

"I think given our current situation, it makes it less messy." Gwen gestured toward the house. "Is he always this bossy?"

"He's kind of gone overboard right now. I think he'll mellow out once he gets used to the idea."

"How are *you* adjusting to the idea?"

"I'm... scared. Nervous. You know how I like my plans and being in control. This was very much *not* in the plan, and I feel like I have no control."

"Give it some time. You'll get your footing."

"Yeah, and then by the time I do, the baby will be here, and things will change *again*."

"At least you've got a great support system. Steve seems completely on board, and you've got me. I'm sure your mom will be thrilled, along with your grandparents."

While Whitney's mom had tried to make amends, Whitney still kept her guard up around her. And, true, her grandparents would be over the moon, but both sets were happily retired and living in Arizona. It wasn't like they could offer her much assistance. Steven was all in, of that she had no doubt, but he had a demanding job. She was sure if she was in a bind, she could call Hope, or maybe even Dakota.

Gwen was right, Whitney wasn't doing this alone, but she was still apprehensive. She'd barely gotten used to loving Steven and trusting the universe would let her be happy with him. A baby ratcheted the stakes a thousandfold.

She and Steven stayed at her brownstone Sunday night when they got back into town. And, even though neither had to be up early for work the next morning, her internal clock woke her anyway, only to find him staring at her while he lay next to her.

"Good morning," he said, kissing her forehead. "How'd you sleep?"

"I always sleep better when you're here."

"Yeah, me too. What do you want for breakfast?"

She knew better than to tell him she'd just grab a coffee. Not with his *breakfast is the most important meal of the day* mantra. Especially not now.

"Pancakes and eggs."

"How are you feeling? Any nausea?"

"Honestly. I don't feel any different. I'm not tired, I haven't been sick to my stomach, nothing. If it weren't for my period being late, I wouldn't have even thought to take a pregnancy test."

"Make sure you call your doctor for an appointment. We can get an early ultrasound and make sure everything's on track."

"It's on my list of things to do today, in between errands. What about you? What do you have going on?"

"I thought I'd get a few things done around here—unless you need me to go with you."

She tilted her head. "I appreciate that, but Gwen's going to help me. You've got stuff to do? Like what?"

"Just some honey-dos."

"But I haven't asked you to do anything."

"Yeah, well, you should have. The hall light's burnt out, the hinge on the backdoor is loose, the kitchen faucet is dripping…"

"Baby, you're a *doctor*. You have better things to do with your time than be my handyman. I can hire someone to do that stuff."

"Bullshit. I'm perfectly capable of taking care of these things for you."

God, she loved this man. It frightened her how much. And they were going to have a family. She shuddered, feeling overwhelmed that this was *her* life.

"Thank you. I appreciate it, but honestly, you don't ha—
"

"Whitney," he growled her name as if a warning not to finish her thought. "Dammit, woman. Would you just let me take care of you?"

"Okay," she squeaked.

His face softened, as if he realized he was being too stern.

"How do you want your eggs?"

CHAPTER FORTY-TWO

Steven

He looked at the Fitbit on his arm to check the time. He'd been at the hospital since three in the morning and hoped to leave by three this afternoon, so he could get to the jewelers. Barring any trauma patients coming in within the next hour, he'd be able to get out on time.

His mother had promised him his grandma's beautiful engagement ring, but he didn't want to wait for it to be shipped to Boston before proposing—hopefully, this weekend, if all went according to plan. He was just going to buy something simple for now and avoid asking for the ring from his mom until later. There'd be too many questions. He could wait until they were telling people about the baby before requesting it.

Hope had filled their family in on the fact that he had a girlfriend, and he'd respectfully answered his mom and sisters' questions. Ava, the oldest Ericson daughter, had the most. Which was understandable since he and Ava had been best friends growing up, and she wanted to make sure Whitney was good enough for him. He'd done the same with her husband, Travis.

Steven hadn't liked Travis in the beginning, but the way the grumpy attorney doted on his wife and their kids quickly won him over.

Travis had his own firm. Well, it was a fucking monstrosity of a money-making machine now, with dozens of lawyers working there, but perhaps he could give Whitney some tips when she decided to branch out on her own.

Maybe with the baby and his salary, she'd want to do it soon. He'd been looking at buying one of the old mansions downtown that the textile barons built. Steve thought they could convert a wing for her firm and then live in the rest.

That's if she even still wanted to branch out on her own. Maybe she'd love working at Zach's firm and decide to stay.

Or maybe she'd want to take time off and raise his babies.

He didn't care, as long as she was in his bed every night.

"Dr. Ericson?" a nurse interrupted his daydream. "Dr. Heatherton is requesting you in exam room three."

Steven frowned. Dr. Lynn Heatherton was the OB/GYN on call in the ER today. Usually, Steven never saw pregnant patients or people having heart attacks. The intake nurse would bypass him and go straight to the specialist if they were available. He'd only attend as a last resort.

He pulled back the curtain of exam room three, and his heart dropped to his feet. There sat Whitney in a blue hospital gown on the gurney, her face stained with tears, and an IV coming out of her arm. Dr. Heatherton stood at her side, patting her hand in a comforting manner.

Steven swallowed hard and forced himself inside, closing the curtain behind him. In his gut, he knew what he was about to hear and didn't want to.

"Whit?" he asked softly as he approached her. "What's going on, honey? Are you okay? Is the baby—"

He looked over at Lynn, who softly shook her head.

Plunking down on the bed, he pulled her to his chest. "Oh, sweetness. I'm so, so sorry."

Her body shook from her silent sobs, and a tear escaped the corner of his eye. Both for her pain and for his, and for what wasn't meant to be.

He stroked her hair and rocked her softly, barely registering the sound of the curtain opening and closing again. They were alone to grieve together.

She took a deep breath, and her body shuddered in response. "I'd barely had time to get used to the idea," she whispered. "It's not fair."

"It's not, baby. I'm sorry."

He held her for a few more minutes, when she abruptly pulled away from him, her eyes narrowed. "How could you have let me have hope? I knew this would never happen. I knew it! But *you*. *You* did this. *You* made me feel like this was possible. I was okay with my life before you came along. I stayed in my lane and knew what to expect. I knew better. I'm not supposed to be a mother."

"You can still be a mother. These things happen to couples. This doesn't mean we can't try again."

"No! There isn't going to be any *trying again*. This was my wakeup call. I'm not supposed to have kids. And I'm not supposed to be with you."

He felt like she'd just sucker punched him in the gut.

"You don't mean that."

"I do. I'm getting my tubes tied. This will never happen again. You need to find someone else to have your family with, because it's not going to be me."

"Whit. I know you're upset. Let's get you home so you can rest in your own bed."

"Gwen's on her way to get me. I need to be alone tonight."

That was the *last* fucking thing she needed. It was the last fucking *he* needed.

"Babe, don't shut me out. I'm hurting, too."

"I know you are. I know how important this baby was to you. That's why we can't be together anymore. You want a family, and I can't offer that to you."

He reached for her hand. "I want you."

She shook her head as tears streamed down her face. "Please go."

"I'm not going anywhere."

"Go!" she yelled. "Just go! Leave me alone!"

He knew if he stayed, she'd keep yelling and make a scene. Probably not the best thing for his career at Boston General. She wasn't in her right mind.

Then again, neither was he. Although, he must have had a moment of clarity because he stood and with a heavy heart, left the room.

He hadn't taken three steps when Gwen rushed up to him. "I came as fast as I could. Is she okay?"

Steven gave her a sad smile. "She lost the baby, and she wants nothing to do with me. She just kicked me out of her room."

Gwen hugged him. "Oh, Steve. I'm so sorry. I know how excited you were. She'll come around. Just give her a little time."

"I don't think she will, Gwen. She's talking about getting her tubes tied."

"That's just her grief talking. I promise I won't let her do anything rash."

"Take care of her."

She squeezed his forearm. "Do you have somebody who can take care of *you*?"

Johnny Walker and his friend Jack Daniels were probably up for the task.

"I'll call my buddy, Zach." He was always up for a drink. He motioned toward exam room three. "Go. Be with her. Tell her I love her."

Not that he thought it'd do any good right now.

Gwen walked backward toward Whitney's room. "Call Zach. You need to grieve, too."

He needed to get shitfaced so he couldn't feel anything anymore; that's what he needed.

****

Whitney

Steven: Billy is going to bring Lola home after he picks her up for her walk today.

He'd been calling and texting the last two days, asking how she was doing, but she'd ignored him. His latest text seemed like he'd finally given up on her, not that she blamed him. She'd been horrible to him at the hospital. The realization that he had finally thrown in the towel hurt, but she knew it was the right thing. He deserved to be a father someday.

Whitney: Okay. I'll get her things around.

Steven: How are you feeling?

She stared at the screen. *How am I feeling? I lost our miracle baby. I'm ashamed at how I handled my grief in the ER. I'm sad because the universe smacked me down again, and am heartbroken over the life I'd almost had with you. It'd been within my grasp, and it was cruelly taken away. And on top of all that, I feel guilty because I've dumped my silent auction responsibilities on Dakota and Gwen.* But physically, she was better. She'd even gotten out of bed and showered today with the intention of helping with the last-minute gala preparations.

Whitney: I'm feeling better, thank you for asking.

Steven: I could come get Lola myself…

Part of her wanted that so badly. She wanted to see him and apologize and beg his forgiveness. But she'd learned her lesson. Keep her head down and keep to herself. Stay in control. She didn't get hurt that way.

Whitney: No. I think it's better if Billy takes her home.

Ralph was going to be as heartbroken as she was.

Steven: Okay, well maybe I'll see you tomorrow night.

Whitney: You're still planning on going?

Steven: Of course. I bought a table.

She smiled at the memory of their bet, then the tears welled up in her eyes, and she stood as she quickly brushed them away. That was all in the past. She'd just have to make sure she kept too busy tomorrow night to notice him.

It was one night. She could do this. She had to, if for no other reason than to prove to herself that she could and that she'd be okay alone.

CHAPTER FORTY-THREE

Steven

She'd included the clothes he'd left at her brownstone with Lola's things.

Ouch. That had been his Plan B to see her, but she circumvented that.

He'd called and texted, asking her to please let him know she was okay, and had received no reply, other than Gwen's pity texts keeping him apprised of her health status.

Steven: Has she asked about me?

The three dots indicating she was replying started and stopped and started and stopped. Finally, he received a response. **Gwen: I think it's still too soon.**

He'd Hail Mary'd the text about Billy bringing Lola home and was surprised when she'd replied. Although it had been short lived, despite his attempts to engage her.

He'd wait and see how she was around him tomorrow night, but he had a sinking feeling they were really over. The helpless feeling knowing there wasn't a damn thing he could do about it overwhelmed him.

He'd almost punched Zach in the nose when his friend suggested, "Maybe it's for the best." He'd invited the fucker over for drinks and to help cheer him up; that was not his idea of being cheered up.

"What the fuck does that mean?"

His friend shrugged. "You want different things. Eventually, you'd end up bitter and resentful that you never had kids. You've wanted kids since our freshmen year in college, Steve. When that bitch Marie—"

He cut him off. "But I don't think we do want different things. I think she's just scared. The miscarriage really did a number on her."

"Do you think that's true, or just wishful projection on your part?"

"I don't know," Steven said wistfully as he threw back the last of the whiskey in his glass. "Maybe you're right."

Zach, who had been balancing his kitchen chair on the back two legs, set it down on all four with a thud. "Of course I'm not right, you dumbass. But I do think you need to give her some space and let her figure it out on her own that she wants to be with you."

"You're a dick."

"So I've been told by more than one person on more than one occasion. Hey, speaking of my dick... can I bring a date to this shindig tomorrow?"

"Would it matter if I said no?"

"Not really."

"Then, no."

"Great. Portia and I will see you tomorrow."

"Portia?"

"I don't remember. Portia, Lexus... it's one of those car names."

"You don't know her name?"

"I don't think it matters. I'm sure it's not her real name. It's her stage name."

"You're bringing a stripper as your date?"

"Yeah," he replied unapologetically. "She's hot. Although it's going to be expensive as fuck."

Oh, that explained everything.

"I thought you were looking for substance?"

"I am, but in the meantime, a man's got needs. I can see if she's got a friend."

"Fuck no."

Steven didn't want anyone but Whitney. He didn't know what he was going to do if it was really over between them.

And the way Lola had been moping around since she got home, she felt the same way about Ralph.

****

Whitney

"Are you sure you're up for this?" Gwen asked when she walked in Whitney's bedroom and found her sitting at her vanity in nothing but a slip and her bra, no makeup on and her hair still not styled. "Everyone will understand if you're not."

"No. I'm okay. This is important to me." For a few reasons.

"Steven's going to be there, you know."

"I know." She thought about how he'd upped the stakes on helping the foundation if he *won* their bet, because she'd said it was important to her.

"Then you better get ready so we can go."

CHAPTER FORTY-FOUR

Steven

A young woman with a streak of blue in her hair showed him to his table. He searched the crowd of people looking for Whitney, but there was no sign of her chestnut hair.

"Do you know if Whitney Hayes is here yet? She's a volunteer."

"The name is familiar, but I don't know who she is. I'm sorry. I can ask someone else for you."

"No. That's okay." He'd find her himself.

Zach and a busty brunette with blonde highlights, wearing a very low-cut dress were already seated, as was Zach's brother James and a woman who also appeared to have come from the strip club. That was unusual—James normally dated more... demure women. Steven had come with his sister, but she'd excused herself the second they walked in to talk with people from the hospital.

He noticed Parker Preston and Liam McDonald over by the bar and made a mental note to go over and say hi and thank them for coming. Whitney had told him their attendance had had a domino effect for the other bigwigs in Boston to sponsor a table. He was glad he'd been able to help her in at least that way.

It still stung that she hadn't let him comfort her at the hospital. He'd needed that. She wasn't the only one devastated about the miscarriage; then she shut him out of her life completely when he needed to be with her the most—for himself. That day had gone from planning on buying her a ring in the afternoon to finding out she'd lost their baby and being kicked out of her exam room and not hearing from her again. She'd blamed him for 'giving her hope.' Who the fuck *blames* someone for that?

Zach said not to push it and give her time. Gwen had echoed that sentiment. It was becoming harder and harder not to feel bitter though. She just bailed on him with their first crisis. Granted, it was a devastating, life-changing crisis, but he still felt they should have gotten through it together.

"I'm going to go bid on some items," he said, standing from his chair.

"Don't outbid me on that bottle of whiskey," Zach called after him.

That was the first thing he was going to do. He'd had his eye on the fifty-year-old bottle since Whitney mentioned a private donor had offered it. A quick internet search valued it at twelve hundred dollars, so he was planning on bidding thirteen hundred. He wasn't here to find a bargain; he was here to help a good cause raise money.

After putting his bid above Zach's cheap-ass offer of two hundred, he walked around, noting the bed and breakfast stay in Vermont that Whitney had been excited about. "Oh, could you imagine doing a color tour there this fall?" She'd sighed wistfully as she flipped through the brochure.

"Could you do it without a schedule though?" he'd teased.

"Probably not."

Retail value five hundred dollars. He bid six hundred. Maybe he could entice her to go with him.

He felt her presence before he saw her. He didn't know how, but he knew when he looked up, she'd be there. And she was. *Okay, that was freaky.* She was breathtaking in a jade-green gown that brought out the red highlights in her hair that she wore down around her shoulders. Her polite smile was for one of the white-haired guests quizzing her about how long he had to make his bids.

She noticed him watching her, and her smile faltered, but only briefly. But before Steven had the opportunity to approach, she touched the older man's sleeve and excused herself.

His heart sank as he watched her scurry away from him. Maybe it had been a mistake to come here tonight, hoping to talk to her. He needed to let her go and deal with this on her own—even though it went against every fiber of his being, but she obviously wanted nothing more to do with him.

Steven realized he hadn't properly grieved the loss of her or the baby. Perhaps that's exactly what he needed to do so he could start to heal and get his head on straight. His house on the Cape felt like the perfect place to do that, and he was going to head there tonight after the gala.

Word had spread like wildfire at the hospital about Whitney losing the baby and leaving the ER without him. So much for HIPAA. Parker had come to him and told him to take as much as he needed, so that's what he was going to do.

In the meantime, since she'd hightailed it out of the auction area to get away from him, he was going to take his time looking at all the items available and place his bids. He might be hurt at how she'd shut him out, but he still wanted the night to be a success for her.

****

Whitney

My god, why did he have to look so sexy in that goddamn tuxedo? Like the heart-stopping kind of gorgeous. It was just a reminder of how out of her league he really was. If he didn't have at least five women throwing themselves at him by the end of the night, she'd be surprised.

Whitney hadn't had to throw herself at him; he'd pursued her, and he'd been so damn charming in the process, she couldn't help but fall for him.

She had no idea why she'd ran away when she saw him. No, that wasn't true. She knew why, as she brushed back tears. She didn't think she could talk to him without bursting into tears, not to mention she didn't even know *what* to say to him; she was still ashamed of how coldly she'd treated him in the ER, and that she'd all but ghosted him since. He hadn't deserved that.

Someday, he'd find someone who would treat him like he deserved to be treated. The farther away she stayed, the better off he'd be. He'd realize soon enough that she did him a favor.

It didn't mean it didn't hurt like hell. She missed everything about him. Not to mention, Ralph was never going to forgive her. She didn't know if she'd ever forgive herself.

Whitney was hiding in one of the bathroom stalls, drying her eyes, when she heard a group of women walk in. She almost came out and joined them, since there were no more supportive women than those you met in the bathroom.

Before she unlatched the door though, she heard one of the ladies say, "Did you see Steven Ericson? He can wear the shit out of a tux, damn."

No argument here. She waited to open the door, sensing they weren't done on the subject.

"He's still an asshole," grumbled another woman.

"Oh, Addison," a third voice laughed. "You need to let it go. He's hot. I'd even do him knowing he wouldn't call me again."

"I'm not even talking about him not calling me after he whispered sweet nothings in my ear while fucking me."

Whitney's stomach dropped. She knew he hadn't been a monk before he met her, but she still didn't like hearing about it. Or was this more recently?

Addison continued, "His pregnant baby mama came into the ER this week in the middle of having a miscarriage. He went in, got the news, and left, like it was no big deal. He just left her there alone to deal with losing her child all by herself. She had to take a fucking Uber home. Meanwhile, he went back to work like nothing happened. I'm sorry—but he's an asshole. That woman dodged a bullet not having his baby."

No, I didn't. I missed out on a wonderful thing.

"I mean, could you imagine Steven Ericson as a father?"

Yeah, she could.

"That's not what I heard," the first woman replied. "I heard he was really upset and left work and hasn't been back since. For all you know, he's been with her."

"Well, he's here alone tonight, isn't he?"

"That's true," the other women murmured in agreement.

Whitney walked out of the stall, her hands shaking with anger as she washed them.

"She didn't take an Uber home; her friend came and got her. And he left her alone because she yelled at him to go."

Whitney waved her hand under the paper towel dispenser and pulled a sheet off to dry her hands.

"Who are you? How do you know this?"

Whitney tossed the wadded-up paper towel into the garbage and pulled open the door. "I'm the woman you've been gossiping about. And I'm also a lawyer. Don't you all work at the hospital? Isn't that some sort of violation of my privacy?"

All three women gaped at her, not saying a word.

"You might want to check the stalls the next time you discuss patients in public."

She walked out the door with her head held high like the boss bitch she was feeling.

The emotion was short lived when she thought about Steven being the subject of bullshit gossip in his own ER. That couldn't make coming to work easy.

One more thing for her to feel guilty and ashamed about how she treated him that awful day.

She knew she'd need to apologize to him someday—that was if she could ever look at him and not want to cry.

She'd almost had it all. Almost.

Dakota, looking stunning in a red evening gown, approached with a martini glass in her hand but set it down the second she saw Whitney.

"I am so sorry, honey," she said, wrapping her arms around her shoulders. "How are you doing?"

"I'm.... I don't know how I am."

"That's understandable. Has Steven been taking good care of you?"

Whitney looked at the ground. "We kind of broke up."

She glanced up to see Dakota's brows knitted together. "What happened? I mean, if you don't mind me asking."

"I realized I was right all along. No matter what you say about the universe wanting me to be happy, that's not meant for me."

"What do you mean, *it's not meant for you*. What's not?"

"Being happy. Having it all. Losing the baby was obviously the universe putting me back in my lane. Happily ever after is for other people—not me."

Dakota hugged her tighter. "Sweet girl. Have you ever considered the universe was making sure that was what you really wanted? You'd been saying for so long that you weren't going to get involved or have children. Maybe it just wants you to be certain. And based on how easily you've given up, maybe that was a good thing."

"So, what are you saying, Dakota? I didn't want my baby badly enough? That the miscarriage was my fault?"

"Oh no, honey. Not at all. It wasn't your fault. It wasn't anyone's fault. Maybe instead of seeing it as the universe trying to punish you or keep you in check, have you ever thought that maybe it was protecting you? That there's a reason this baby wasn't meant to be? You may never know the reason, but you need to trust there was one. And it wasn't to hurt you."

"But I *am* hurt. I'm devastated. It's a miracle I'm out of bed and functioning."

"Of course, you're hurt. You lost your baby. A baby that you obviously wanted. Maybe that was this baby's purpose— to show you what you really want."

"And I messed everything up," Whitney whispered.

Dakota stroked both of Whitney's arms. "Fortunately, it's fixable. But don't wait too long."

She just needed to figure out what to say.

****

Steven

"You outbid me, didn't you, fucker?" Zach asked as Steven sat back down. Their table was now full, except for Hope's empty chair next to him.

"Yeah, which wasn't hard to do, you cheap bastard."

Aiden had arrived, as had three of the ER nurses Steven had given tickets to as a thank you for picking up extra shifts.

He looked around the table at his friends and colleagues. All these people, minus the stripper twins, he could count on to have his back.

And seriously, what the fuck was James doing with the bimbo? Although, to James' credit, he looked rather uncomfortable and sat quietly, not paying any attention to his date. Still, Hope was not going to be happy. His sister had insinuated that James and Yvette had hooked up over the Fourth, although she had been purposefully vague about where she'd been when that allegedly went down.

Steven knew something was going on with Hope and Evan. The asshole had attempted to be less of his normal dick-self in the ER lately, and he'd even covered some of Steven's shifts this week. But Steven didn't want his suspicions about Evan and his sister confirmed, so he neither investigated it nor asked Hope about it directly. It was better for his fragile mental health if he remained ignorant about it right now.

He looked around the room and saw Hope talking to Parker at the hospital's table. He wasn't surprised to see Evan not far from her, sitting next to Liam McDonald and while he was talking to Liam, he kept stealing glances at Steven's baby sister. Steven recognized a few members of the hospital board and their spouses sitting around the table, along with the president of a big pharmaceutical with his trophy wife.

How the fuck did Lacroix snag a seat at that table?

If Steven were insecure, he'd be worried about Evan stealing his job. As it was, he knew he had nothing to worry about. He was damn good at what he did and dependable as fuck. Well, except for this week.

He casually looked further around the room, trying not to be obvious that he was searching for a glimpse of Whitney. He did spot Gwen in a black cocktail dress, sitting at a table with eight other women. Whitney had told him she had Gwen invite her teacher friends to fill her table, since she would be working the event and hadn't wanted to invite anyone from her work. Maybe she subconsciously knew she was leaving Crawford, Holden, and Stone.

He wished he knew where she was. Was she purposefully still hiding from him or was she working behind the scenes? He hoped she was taking it easy. It'd killed him not being able to personally check on her this week.

A table across the room was filled with more nurses from the hospital. They must have caught wind that there were going to be VIPs here tonight. Addison Hall seemed to be holding court amongst her fellow nurses. Steven didn't get the impression that any of them liked her, but were more scared of her than anything. He wondered what drama she would try to stir up tonight. How he hadn't realized that was her MO before he'd fucked her well over a year ago, he had no idea. But he only had himself to blame for that mistake.

Dakota looked beautiful in a red dress and high heels, walking around with a cocker spaniel on a leash. When she approached their table, Aiden stood and awkwardly hugged her. She smiled brightly at the cardiologist. Far more warmly than the doctor with no game probably deserved.

Finally, he found Whitney again, standing by the women who were ready to take people's money once the silent auction's winners were announced. His heart leapt into his throat at how beautiful she was. To the casual observer, she appeared cool and confident, but he could see the sadness when her polite smile didn't reach her eyes. Steven knew she felt as bereft as he did. The thing he didn't know was if it was only because of the miscarriage or if she was as lost without him as he was her.

Considering she'd wanted nothing to do with him, despite his many attempts to contact her, he guessed her sadness was due to the former.

Zach set a glass of amber liquid on ice in front of him. "Here. You look like you could use this."

****

Whitney

"Madarin Oriental Day Spa—Package Three," Brittany, one of the women who was actually on ARF's payroll, announced as she looked at the silent auction sheet, "goes to—Dana Bradley for two hundred dollars."

A woman with *Julie* on her volunteer name badge quickly typed the results into a spreadsheet on her laptop, while Sandy, another volunteer, clicked away on her keyboard also, asking, "You said two hundred?"

Brittany waited until the women were ready before announcing the next item. "Macallum Reserve—Single Malt Scotch... Steve Ericson for thirteen hundred."

Julie let out a low whistle. "That better be some good booze."

Whitney was glad he'd gotten it. His eyes had lit up when she'd told him about the donation.

"Okay, so wait," Sandy interrupted. "Since Dr. Ericson is actually the one who won that, I don't count it in this total, right?"

"Correct," Brittany replied.

Whitney tilted her head. "What do you mean?"

"Dr. Ericson wanted to beat all the bids he didn't win by a dollar, then donate it back to the highest bidder. So, we're getting paid double plus a dollar for each item he didn't win."

Whitney's hand went to her chest. "He did that?"

"Yeah. He said this was important to someone he loved, and he wanted to make sure the night was a big success."

They were already on their way to shattering previous records. Ticket sales, sponsorships, and silent auction donations had all surpassed anything they'd done in the past. She knew having the hospital bigshots had been a huge contributing factor.

The corners of Whitney's mouth turned up. "That sounds like something he'd do."

"Do you know him?"

"Yeah, I know him."

"Talk about swoon worthy, right? Rich, generous, *and* gorgeous? *Le sigh.*"

"You forgot kind," Whitney said softly. *And sexy. And wonderful.*

"His girlfriend's a lucky woman."

Whitney said nothing as she gave a wistful smile in agreement. Her heart breaking as she thought, "Yeah, I really was."

CHAPTER FORTY-FIVE

Whitney

It came time for the auction winners to get their bills and their spoils. Whitney had volunteered to take Steven's. His total amount due was more than the first car she ever bought brand new. With his invoice, bottle of whiskey, and an envelope containing the details of his stay in Vermont, along with a brochure for the bed and breakfast, she started toward his table, only to find he wasn't in his chair.

"Hey, everyone," she said with a shy smile. "I have Steven's auction winnings."

"You can just leave the bottle of whiskey with me," Zach said with a grin.

"*I'll* take those," Hope said authoritatively as she waved a platinum card. "I have his credit card."

A pang of disappointment hit Whitney that Steve wasn't there, but with a genuine smile, she walked over and handed Hope the items, which she immediately put down and stood to pull Whitney in for a long hug.

"How are you?" Hope whispered as she held her tight.

Whitney felt the tears well up and pulled away to wipe her eyes and smile sadly. "I've been better."

"I'm so sorry, Whit. If there's anything I can do..."

"Did Steven leave?"

"Yeah. He decided to head out to the Cape straight from here."

"Oh." She couldn't hide the disappointment in her voice.

Hope cocked an eyebrow.

"You could deliver these yourself... He's there alone tonight."

Whitney shook her head. "I'm not sure he'd want to see me right now. Besides, I've got Ralph."

"Trust me, he would be thrilled to see you, and I'm happy to pick up Ralph and keep him for the weekend."

Whitney bit her bottom lip as she contemplated showing up at Steven's house on the ocean unannounced. What if he didn't want company? Or worse, already had company?

Zach said softly, "You should go, Whitney."

James agreed, "You two need to talk."

Even Aiden nodded subtly.

"Are you sure you don't mind picking up Ralph?"

Hope laughed. "No. I'd love to. Lola has been moping around all week, so I will definitely be the hero when I bring Ralph home with me tonight."

"I can bring him by if it'd be easier."

Putting her hand firmly on Whitney's arm, Hope said, "I've got it. Tell me the lock code, and I'll get him tonight. Don't think about it anymore, just go. Leave. Right now." Hope picked up the bottle and envelope and handed them back to Whitney. "Do not go home, do not pass go, do not collect two hundred dollars. Get in your car and head to the Cape."

She nodded her head, whispering, "Okay, I'll do it."

Hope leaned over and hugged her shoulders, then kissed her cheek. "He's a good man," she said softly while looking Whitney in the eye.

"I know."

CHAPTER FORTY-SIX

Steven

Losing his jacket the second he walked in the house, he now sat in his favorite patio lounger with his bowtie hanging undone around his collar, and the first three buttons of his shirt open as he stared out at the ocean. A beer bottle dangled from his fingertips while he blew out his breath. He didn't know if he should have left the gala without at least trying to talk to her.

Gwen and Zach said to give her space, but his gut was telling him that had been the wrong thing to do. What if she mistook his giving her space as apathy? He should be fighting for her, not hiding here at the Cape, drowning his sorrows.

He should be outside her damn brownstone with a fucking boombox over his head, while Peter Gabriel blared from it. No, fuck that, he should be pressing her against the wall, her hair in his hand, kissing the hell out of her.

"You dumbass," he muttered under his breath. Glancing at his watch, he wondered if he had time to make it back to Boston before she went to bed.

"I have a special delivery for Dr. Ericson."

His heart leapt into his throat. He knew that sexy voice but was almost afraid to turn around for fear it was only his imagination playing tricks on him.

Slowly, he turned and, as if he'd conjured her up, found her standing on his patio, still wearing her green evening gown and heels.

"What kind of delivery?"

She took a tentative step toward him, swallowed hard, then took another. "A bottle of fifty-year-old whiskey." Another step. "A stay at The Dragonfly Inn in Vermont." Another step. "And... an apology." She froze, not coming any closer.

Steven set his beer bottle on the ground and stood to walk to her. He took the bottle out of her hand, along with the envelope, and set them on the nearby patio table.

"I'm expecting the whiskey and the Vermont stay... but you'll need to elaborate about the apology."

She looked up at him, her eyes rimmed with tears, and whispered, "I'm so sorry, Steven. For everything."

Cupping her face between his hands, he wiped her eyes with his thumbs while staring at her, almost in disbelief that she was actually there in front of him.

"I'm sorry, too."

Whitney shook her head vehemently. "No. You have nothing to be sorry for. I'm the one who—"

He silenced her by putting his mouth on hers. She seemed surprised at first and kept her lips tight. But as he held her face and caressed her lips with his, he felt her entire body relax, and she clung to his shirt as she returned his kiss.

"We don't have to have babies. I don't care about that. I just care about you. I can't lose you, Whitney. I love you."

"I love you, too. I handled everything wrong. I'm sorry. I was so hurt and sad. And scared. I should have turned to you instead of shutting you out."

"I wanted to be there for you, baby. So badly. It killed me that you wouldn't let me hold you."

"I know, and all I can do is apologize and promise to do better. I want to try again. With everything. You and me. Children. When we're ready, and the doctor says I can."

He scanned her eyes. "Are you sure? We don't have to. We—"

She put her fingertips on his lips. "I'm sure. I would be the luckiest woman in the world to have a family with you."

"How about we start with being my wife first?"

"Is that a proposal?"

He smirked, remembering what she'd said about how he better ask her to marry him.

"Pfft. No, of course not. What kind of guy would propose without flowers and a ring?"

"Okay." She wrapped her arms around his neck and pulled his head closer to whisper in his ear, "But if it had been, I would have said yes."

Steven stroked her sides and smiled down at her. He couldn't stop smiling if his life depended on it. "Good to know."

She stifled a yawn, and he pulled her against him. With her heels, she came just under his chin.

"Why don't we go to bed?" He didn't want her overdoing it—which he had a feeling she'd already done today.

He felt her stiffen, and he ran his hand up and down her back. "I don't want to have sex. I know we can't until you've fully recovered. I just need to hold you, sweetness."

"That's not it. I just realized, I don't have any pajamas, or clothes for tomorrow, or even a toothbrush. Or..."

He cocked an eyebrow. "Or?"

"Um... feminine products. I have one in my purse, and that's it."

"Will that tide you over until morning?"

"Yes."

"I have an extra toothbrush you can have and a t-shirt you can sleep in." He gave a small grin. "Although I wouldn't mind if you just slept in your panties. We'll worry about the rest in the morning."

He picked up his thirteen-hundred-dollar bottle of whiskey and the envelope on their way inside. He'd worry about his beer bottle in the morning. Tonight, he just needed to fall asleep with her in his arms.

****

Whitney

He pulled the zipper of her gown down and helped slide it off, reverently caressing her bare skin as he did.

"You can't leave me again," he said in a low voice before kissing her shoulder and unhooking her bra. "My heart wouldn't be able to handle it." He gently palmed her breasts and kissed her neck. "Promise me."

"I promise."

She'd fully intended on groveling at his feet, begging for forgiveness. She'd rehearsed her speech on the drive over, how she'd understand if he needed to take things slow and not make any decisions right away, but if he'd just give her another chance...

He'd made her speech and groveling unnecessary. He'd accepted her apology with a needless one of his own. It almost felt like he'd let her off too easy after what she'd done. She needed to convey to him how genuinely sorry she was.

Turning in his arms, she unbuttoned the remaining buttons of his tux shirt. Damn, he was gorgeous to look at. His defined chest had a small smattering of hair that was a shade darker than his head, and his rippled core was firm under her fingertips.

"I'm sorry, Steven. Truly, truly sorry. You didn't deserve how I reacted."

He brushed her hair behind her ears. "We all react differently to grief."

"I was scared that I'd brought it on myself by being too happy. That there needed to be something to balance out how lucky I was."

"Life isn't an algebra equation, Whit. Both sides don't have to be equal."

"In my head, I know that. But my experiences have proven otherwise, so I'm having a hard time believing it. But I'm trying."

"What made you change your mind?"

"Dakota. Gwen. My heart. The bitchy nurses in the bathroom tonight. Your sister. Zach. Just everything."

He narrowed his eyes and growled, "Bitchy nurses in the bathroom?"

"I'll tell you about it tomorrow. I just need you to know I'm sorry for how terribly I treated you."

"I accept your apology on one condition. From here on out, if there's a problem, we handle it together."

"I promise," she whispered. She'd made a lot of promises tonight, but they weren't empty ones.

He squeezed her butt over her panties. "Get in bed, woman. I want to feel your naked boobs on me."

With a giggle, she scrambled into bed and anxiously waited for him to take his pants off and climb in next to her.

Her phone dinged with an incoming text and seconds later, his did the same. He pulled his phone from his pants' pocket, looked at the text, and smiled, then handed it to her, which she appreciated since her phone was on the floor next to her dress.

On the screen was a picture of Lola sleeping with her head on Ralph's neck, with the caption: **Together at last. I hope this is what you two look like. Or at least something close.**

Steven got in bed next to her, pulled the covers up around her bare boobs, then put his arm around her. "This should answer her question," he chuckled as he stretched his other hand out to snap a selfie. Whitney rested her head on his shoulder and smiled for the photo.

He looked at it and murmured, "It's perfect," before showing her. The couple on the screen looked happy—genuinely happy.

"I love it. Send it to me, too, please."

A second later, her phone dinged again with what she assumed was the photo, quickly followed by another ding.

Steven pulled up the message, so they could read it together.

Hope: Squuuueaaal! I'm so happy for you guys! Don't worry about hurrying back. We're all good here!

He laughed. "I guess we'll need to remember to text Claire and Billy tomorrow about where the dogs will be on Monday."

CHAPTER FORTY-SEVEN

Steven

He hadn't *technically* moved into her brownstone, but when it came time to pack his things for their weekend at the B&B in Vermont to see the beginning of the autumn colors, he pulled things out of a drawer there rather than his condo.

After their walk, Billy and Claire were dropping the dogs off to stay with Hope for the weekend, and he'd called ahead to make sure their room at the inn was filled with flowers. He patted his sport coat to double-check the black velvet box was still in the inside pocket. He hoped she was surprised. The ring had been burning a hole in his desk drawer while he waited for the perfect time to give it to her. The damn leaves couldn't change colors fast enough. The second he saw a hint of orange and yellow, he booked their stay in Vermont at the getaway he'd successfully bid on at the ARF gala.

Whitney had settled in with McNamara, Wallace, & Stone and was kicking ass, at least according to his friend. She didn't talk much about her cases, and he respected that. He didn't tend to talk much about what went on in the ER either. Besides, they had better things to do with their time than talk about their work. Although, their schedules had been keeping them from spending any time awake together, let alone naked. *That* was going to be remedied this weekend.

"Babe?" she called out as she walked in the door. He heard her throw her keys in the bowl on the table by the door like she always did when she got home.

Steven poked his head around the corner of the bedroom doorjamb. "I'm up here! Just finishing packing." He'd seen her suitcase by the door when he got home from the hospital. She must have packed it before she left for the office this morning.

"Don't forget to pack a swimsuit. There's supposed to be hot springs not far from the bed and breakfast."

"We have to wear a swimsuit?"

"Steven Richard Ericson! Yes!"

He grinned when he received the response he expected and went back to packing.

He'd thought about proposing at the hot springs, but then worried that the ring would somehow get dropped in the water and they'd never find it, and she'd see it as a sign from the universe and turn him down.

No, he'd just stick with the traditional, on bended knee scenario, where if the ring fell on the ground, it could easily be picked up. No harm, no foul.

He felt her petite hands wrap around his waist, and her cheek against his back. "Hi. I've missed you."

Steven twisted so he was facing her and held her against his body. "Hi. How was work?"

"It was good. I won my case."

"That's awesome, baby. We need to celebrate."

"We're going out of town for the weekend. That's all the celebration I need."

He winked as he ran his hand down her spine until he reached her ass, where he squeezed. "I don't know... I have a few ideas on how we can celebrate this weekend."

She palmed his semi over his pants. "Did you put it on the schedule?"

He knew she was teasing, but still groused, "I already told you what I think about any damn schedules."

"Aw, you're no fun."

"On the contrary, baby," he said, kissing her neck. "I'll show you how fun no schedules can be."

****

Whitney

Steven had been rubbing off on her because she wasn't even slightly panicked about not having a plan this weekend. She even liked the idea of sleeping as late as they wanted and getting out of bed whenever they felt like it—if they even felt like it—to do whatever it was they wanted to do that day.

Still, it'd been fun to tease him and pretend to make one, only to have him growl when she put it in front of him.

He used a red pen to cross things out and write in naughty things like, "Lick Whitney's pussy" or "Fuck Whitney's ass." She was sure the ass part was meant to make her nervous, since they hadn't ventured into that yet, despite his 'warnings' they were going to. But they hadn't even had time for a quickie lately, let alone anything else.

Their schedules had been hectic the last few weeks, and they'd been like ships passing in the night—or rather, morning, when Steven would be getting home as she was leaving for work. He was usually gone or getting ready to go back to the hospital when she walked in the door at night.

He'd all but moved in, they just hadn't labeled it. She knew he thought she'd freak out if they had, so he'd just been slowly bringing clothes and shoes over and would come to the brownstone right after work without a word. Lola never left, except when Billy came by to walk her. A few months ago, he might've been right—she might have hyperventilated at the term *living together*, but not now. This weekend, she was actually going to suggest he move his dresser from the condo, or buy one, so she could have her drawer space back. They needed to talk about renovations to make the closet bigger, too.

Fortunately, they had the house at the Cape where there was a huge walk-in closet and plenty of drawers.

"I hope this place is as nice as the brochure," she said once were on the road. They'd taken his Porsche, which was parked at her brownstone rather than his condo. Another sign he was living there.

"I went online and read the reviews. They were all great, and the staff was very friendly when I called and made the reservation."

"Good." She looked at him with a naughty grin. "I hope the rooms are well insulated."

Steven ran his hand up her thigh and under her skirt. "Oh? Why's that, sweetness?"

"So, we can watch TV as loud as we want, duh."

He rubbed her pussy over her panties until she let out a soft moan. "Oh, I thought it was because you didn't want the whole place to know my name when you scream it as I make you come."

"Well..." She pretended to ponder what he'd said while subtly spreading her legs for him. "That too, I guess."

"We can save the screaming for the hot springs." He pulled her panties to the side and slid his finger through her wet folds. "Or in the car."

"No. I don't want to come in the car. I want to come with your cock inside me."

He swallowed hard and pulled his hand away, but she put her hand on top of his to hold it in place. "That doesn't mean you have to stop playing..."

With a grin, he resumed playing with her pussy.

Of course, that led to him pulling over and making her beg to come as he ate her pussy right there on the passenger seat with her legs spread wide for anyone to see if they came upon them.

"I don't give a fuck," he snarled when she tried to protest. His magic tongue made her quickly not give a fuck either.

"We were supposed to wait until you were inside me," she pouted as she adjusted her panties and then her dress before they got back on the road.

"Sweetness, I'm going to be inside you more than I'm not this weekend. I promise, I'll make you come with my cock in your cunt more times than you can count."

"So vulgar," she tsked as he put the car back in drive.

"What word would you prefer?"

"Oh, I didn't say I didn't like it. You know it makes my toes curl when you go all dirty alpha male on me."

He grabbed a handful of her hair in his fist. "Good. Get over here and suck my cock."

Without hesitation, Whitney was on her knees and leaning over the center console to undo his pants, moaning as she felt how hard he was.

Steven moved her hands away from his pants. "You know what? On second thought, that's a bad idea. It's been a while, and I think you'd make me come in two minutes, and we'd probably wreck as I did."

"We could pull over," she purred as she rubbed his length over his pants. She was turned on and wanted him in her mouth.

"We need to get to the bed and breakfast before eight, and we're already going to be cutting it close with our last detour."

"I'm sorry."

He quickly glanced at her. "I'm not. That was hot as fuck."

It really was. She loved when he just *had* to eat her pussy and couldn't wait any longer. It made her feel sexy and desirable.

And right now, she wanted to return the sentiment. But, he had a point. He *was* driving. And they did need to check in before eight.

"I'm dropping to my knees and sucking your cock the minute we get to our room, then."

He grinned. "No, you're not."

"Yes, I am."

Steven shrugged. "If you say so."

They made it to the inn with only ten minutes to spare. Lorelai Danes, the owner herself, helped check them in, and she didn't stop smiling the entire time while she kept sneaking glances at them like she knew their plans once they got into the room.

Were they that obvious?

Her grin was sly as she handed Steven the keys. "Enjoy your stay at the Dragonfly Inn. I hope you find your room to your liking. Please let me know if you need anything at all."

Steven gave her an odd smile, then picked up their bags as he followed Whitney up the stairs and to the right, down to the end, just as Lorelai had instructed. She waited patiently for Steven to put the bags down and open the door. He fumbled with the key, and she noticed his hands shook a little. Was he that excited about a blowjob?

Mine are pretty epic, she thought with a smug grin. She loved having that effect on him.

He pushed open the door and gestured for her to go first. Whitney noticed the room smelled nice—like roses, as she felt for the light switch along the wall once she entered the dark room. She heard a click, and the room was illuminated. Steven stood next to the switch, the bags just inside the door.

She looked around and realized the entire room was filled with roses of every color. Red, white, pink, yellow, purple, and hybrids with multi-colored petals. There wasn't a surface that didn't have a vase on it. The bed was even covered in rose petals.

"Wow, they really go all out for their guests," she murmured as she leaned down to smell the dozen red ones closest to her.

Glancing in Steven's direction, she noticed he was a lot closer to her now, kneeling as he murmured, "I've got the ring and flowers this time."

It took her brain a second to catch up to what was happening, and she looked down at him again. This time, she noticed the black box in his hand, and tears filled her eyes.

"Whitney Jane Hayes..." he started. "The first time I laid eyes on you, I knew you were special. It didn't take me long to realize how special. I love you, sweetness, and if you'll have me, I'll spend the rest of my life trying to make you happy."

He opened the box to reveal a stunning cushion-cut diamond that had to be at least three carats, surrounded by smaller round diamonds, in an eternity band setting. "Baby, will you marry me?"

"Yes," she whispered as the tears fell. "I would love to marry you."

Steven slid the ring on her finger, then stood and pulled her into an embrace. His lips found hers for a gentle kiss, before holding her tight against his strong body.

"You did it. You surprised me. The flowers, the ring... I wasn't expecting this," she murmured with her cheek against his chest.

He stroked her hair and kissed her temple. "I thought for sure you knew."

"Not a clue."

"The ring... it's my grandmother's." He held her hand out and looked at the engagement ring on her finger. "If it's not your style, we can get something else. I won't be offended."

Whitney snatched her hand away. "Don't you dare. I love it."

He brushed her hair behind her ears. "Good. I love *you*."

"I love you, too." She stood on her tiptoes and whispered in his ear, "I think you should make love to me now."

Steven looked down at her with a grin. "As you wish."

EPILOGUE

Steven

Whitney had ordered a dresser for him online as they lay in bed yesterday morning before getting up to go on a color tour.

"We're really doing this," she said before clicking 'buy.'

He pulled her closer and kissed her temple. "We've been doing this. Just informally."

"But now we're official..."

"We're official. Which means San Diego for either Christmas or Thanksgiving. Together. And meeting your family, too."

She sighed. "Okay. But I think we should elope. Go somewhere warm, just the two of us on a beach with an officiant."

"I hadn't considered that, but it has possibilities. Although, my mom would probably kill us."

"We could still let her throw us a party."

"She'll like that idea." Steven was glad Whitney understood how important it was that his mom be involved *somehow,* and that she was willing to let Frannie plan a reception for them in California.

On their way to his condo to pick up the dogs and a few more of his clothes, they talked more about their schedules and when they could possibly both get away.

"We'll need two weeks. At least," he told her. "We can do the wedding and honeymoon all at once. Then probably a week in San Diego, down the road."

"*Plus* the holidays? I mean, I'll have the time off but will you?"

Probably not.

"Maybe we should wait a year or so," she said softly.

"Fuck that. It will just have to be a whirlwind in-and-out trip for you to meet them over the holidays. Thanksgiving might be better suited for that. Although, Hope may have ratted me out, and my mother could already be on a plane headed here, so we won't have to make the trip."

They laughed as they walked in his front door, but a tiny part of him was worried that was a possibility. Hope knew he'd planned on asking Whitney to marry him over the weekend, but he didn't think she'd preempt him by telling their family.

The dogs didn't come bounding to the door to greet them, even though they weren't quiet as they walked in.

"That's weird," Whitney murmured, looking around. "Where is everyone?"

"Hope?" Steven called out as he walked further inside into the living room. There his sister lay on the couch looking mindlessly at the TV. Lola sat on the cushion next to her chest, and Ralph lay on her legs. Her eyes were puffy and red, and there were tissues everywhere, along with numerous empty pink pints of Baskin Robbins ice cream.

"Are you sick? What's wrong?"

She looked up at him in surprise, as if she hadn't heard them come in. Then her face scrunched up, and she shook her head as tears started streaming down her face. Lola let out a whine and laid her head on Hope's shoulder, while Ralph pawed at her legs.

"What's wrong?" he asked again, more emphatically this time.

"Nothing!" his little sister cried out as she flopped to her side, with her back away from him. "I'll be fine. Just leave me be. Let me wallow in peace."

"Wallow? What are you wallowing about?"

He took a step toward her, but Whitney tugged on his sleeve and subtly shook her head as she pulled him out of the room.

"I'm no expert, but I think she has all the tell-tale signs of nursing a broken heart."

Steven's eyes narrowed. "Fucking Evan Lacroix. I'm going to kill him."

Wicked Hot Medicine—Hope and Evan's story. Get it here!
https://books2read.com/wickedhotmeds?affiliate=off

WICKED HOT MEDICINE

Vengeance never tasted as sweet as it did on Hope Ericson's skin.

Sleeping with his rival's wife was an opportunity Dr. Evan Lacroix couldn't refuse.

Except, it turned out, she wasn't his wife—she was his sister.

Oh, the irony. It made it that much sweeter.

Unfortunately, when Hope realized his intentions, she didn't appreciate being a pawn in his game, and the sassy spitfire turned the tables on him.

Evan never saw it coming.

And now he needs to decide which is more important—love or revenge.

This isn't a book about enemies *to* lovers. It's about enemies with benefits—until the line between enemy and lover gets blurred.

https://tesssummersauthor.com/wicked-hot-medicine

WICKED HOT BABY DADDY

The player doctor left behind more than a broken heart.

Dr. James Rudolf made Yvette Sinclair believe in fairytales, and he was her Prince Charming. Then out of the blue, he stopped taking her calls. Blocked them would be a more accurate descriptor.

Devastated, Yvette had no idea why the man she thought was *the one* had ghosted her. Even harder, she was three thousand miles away, so she couldn't just show up at his house and demand an explanation. Then her best friend started seeing him around Boston—a different beautiful woman on his arm each time. She felt like such a fool.

She was determined to move on and forget all about the playboy. Until two pink lines made that impossible.

https://tesssummersauthor.com/wicked-hot-baby-daddy

WICKED HOT SILVER FOX

It all started with a dirty photo in his text messages...

Yeah, Dr. Parker Preston's intentions when he gave Alexandra Collins his phone number at the animal rescue gala were more personal than professional. But he'd never expected the sassy beauty with the blue streak in her hair to send him a picture of her perfect, perky boobs as enticement to adopt the dogs she was desperately trying to find a home for.

But dang if they weren't the ideal incentive for him to offer his home to more than just the dogs. In exchange for adopting the older, bonded pair, she'd need to move in with him for a month and get the dogs acclimated. Oh, and she wouldn't be sleeping in the guest room during her stay.

The deal is only for a month though. And she insisted they weren't going to fall in love, something he readily agreed with. They had the rules in place, what could possibly go wrong in four short weeks?

THANK YOU

Thank you for reading *Wicked Hot Doctor!* I hope you loved it! I've been thinking about Steven's story ever since he was introduced as the protective older brother in my debut novel, *Operation Sex Kitten* five years ago. I'm glad I finally was able to get his book written, along with the other Ericson sibling, Hope (*Wicked Hot Medicine*, now available!) I think this is going to be a fun series.

If you enjoyed the book (and even if you didn't), would you mind leaving me a review on Amazon and/or Goodreads (and Bookbub if it's not too much trouble)? Believe it or not, your review does help get my book seen by other readers, which lets me keep writing.

Don't forget to sign up for my newsletter to get free bonus content and be the first to know about cover reveals, contests, excerpts, and more!

https://www.subscribepage.com/TessSummersNewsletter

xoxo,

Tess

ACKNOWLEDGEMENTS

Mr. Summers: Thanks for always being my biggest cheerleader. I appreciate your support more than you'll ever know. Your dick's not bad either.

To the awesome readers who pointed out the errors that were missed in the original version. Thank you. I appreciate your feedback in helping make this book better.

OliviaProDesigns: Thanks for another great cover. Damn, you piss me off during the process, but I always love the end result.

Alyssa Faye and Truly Trendy PR: I appreciate everything you do for me so that I can spend my time writing and not worrying about all the things.

Darla Edison: Talk about hometown love. Thank you for being such a great supporter.

Carrie and Mike Seegmiller: You guys suck at euchre, but you're amazing at TikTok. I love you both so much! Thanks for all your help. Next summer is going to be awesome. Viva la Mexico!

Renee Rose and Misty Malloy: Thanks for being the best sounding board a girl could ask for. You make my soul smile.

My wonderful extended family: Thanks for always showing up. Every time.

Everyone at Tess Summers' Playhouse: You're amazing. Thank you for being such a great group.

Lastly, to my readers: You're why I'm able to be on this wonderful ride. Thank you. I'm humbled that you choose to spend your time reading my books.

Other Works by Tess Summers:

SAN DIEGO SOCIAL SCENE

Operation Sex Kitten: (Ava and Travis)
 https://books2read.com/u/3yzyG6?affiliate=off
The General's Desire: **(Brenna and Ron)**
 https://books2read.com/u/m2Mpek?affiliate=off
Playing Dirty: (Cassie and Luke)
 https://books2read.com/u/3RNEdj?affiliate=off
Cinderella and the Marine: (Cooper and Katie)
 https://books2read.com/u/3LYenM?affiliate=off
The Heiress and the Mechanic: **(Harper and Ben)**
 https://books2read.com/u/bQVEn6?affiliate=off
Burning Her Resolve: (Grace and Ryan)
 https://books2read.com/u/bzoEXz?affiliate=off
This Is It: (Paige and Grant)
 https://books2read.com/ThisIsIt?affiliate=off

AGENTS OF ENSENADA

Ignition: (Kennedy and Dante)

https://books2read.com/u/47leJa?affiliate=off

Inferno: (Kennedy and Dante)

https://books2read.com/u/bpaYGJ?affiliate=off

Combustion: (Reagan and Mason)

https://books2read.com/u/baaME6?affiliate=off

Reignited: (Taren and Jacob)

https://books2read.com/u/3ya2Jl?affiliate=off

Flashpoint: (Sophia and Ramon)

https://books2read.com/TessSummersFlashpoint?affiliate=off

ABOUT THE AUTHOR

Tess Summers is a former businesswoman and teacher who always loved writing but never seemed to have time to sit down and write a short story, let alone a novel. Now battling MS, her life changed dramatically, and she has finally slowed down enough to start writing all the stories she's been wanting to tell, including the fun and sexy ones!

Married over twenty-six years with three grown children, Tess is a former dog foster mom who ended up failing and adopting them instead. She and her husband (and their three dogs) split their time between the desert of Arizona and the lakes of Michigan, so she's always in a climate that's not too hot and not too cold, but just right!

CONTACT ME!

Sign up for my newsletter: BookHip.com/SNGBXD
Email: TessSummersAuthor@yahoo.com
Visit my website: www.TessSummersAuthor.com
Facebook: http://facebook.com/TessSummersAuthor
TikTok: https://www.tiktok.com/@tesssummersauthor
Instagram: https://www.instagram.com/tesssummers/
Amazon: https://amzn.to/2MHHhdK
BookBub https://www.bookbub.com/profile/tess-summers
Goodreads - https://www.goodreads.com/TessSummers

Printed in Great Britain
by Amazon

22227499R00192